SOMETIMES A BAD

Lucasta Collyer is about to resign herself to an arranged marriage. First, however, she wants one night of discovery, on her own terms, with a complete stranger. But Lucy's plan for one night of anonymous passion is destined for trouble. Her fortress heart, once fiercely protected, is suddenly breached. John Carver, a blue-eyed, salty-mouthed, yeoman farmer and self-professed former rogue, has found a way in. He's everything she shouldn't want. He's brazen, arrogant and refuses to obey her orders. Lucy simply can't resist the challenge.

John Carver never bows to the wretched nobility and he won't be the passive plaything of this imperious, icy-tempered young hussy who offers him three sovereigns to take her virginity *sans* touching her with his filthy hands. Clearly she needs a lesson, and he'll gladly teach it.

But this rogue isn't as reformed as he wants everyone to believe and Lucy soon knows that better than anyone.

A Lyrical Press Historical Romance | Lyrical Press Vintage

Once A Rogue

Jayne Fresina

Lyrical Press, Inc.
New Jersey

Lyrical Press, Incorporated

Once A Rogue
ISBN: 9781616504335
Copyright © 2011, Jayne Fresina
Edited by Tiffany Maxwell
Book design by Lyrical Press, Inc.
Cover Art by Renee Rocco
Line: Vintage

Lyrical Press, Incorporated
http://www.lyricalpress.com

All Rights Are Reserved. No part of this book may be used or reproduced in any manner whatsoever without written permission, except in the case of brief quotations embodied in critical articles and reviews. The unauthorized reproduction or distribution of this copyrighted work is illegal. No part of this book may be scanned, uploaded or distributed via the Internet or any other means, electronic or print, without the publisher's permission.

PUBLISHER'S NOTE:

This book is a work of fiction. The names, characters, places, and incidents are products of the writer's imagination or have been used fictitiously and are not to be construed as real. Any resemblance to persons, living or dead, actual events, locale or organizations is entirely coincidental.

The publisher does not have any control over and does not assume any responsibility for author or third-party Web sites or their content.

Published in the United States of America by Lyrical Press, Incorporated

First Lyrical Press, Inc digital publication: November 2011

First Lyrical Press, Inc print publication: February 2013

Dedication

To Jan Jan.

Acknowledgements

Thanks to friends and family for their continued encouragement and support.

Lisa
Best wishes
Jayne Fresina

Chapter 1

May 1588

The first time she saw him, she knew he was the one.

Squinting through a peephole, heartbeat falling like coins from a tumbler's pockets, Lucasta Collyer made the decision that changed her life.

To this man, a complete stranger, she would give her maidenhead.

She watched him for a while. Careful assessment suggested he was ideal for the job: sturdily built, quietly confident, a man of few words. Compared to the other available choices at hand, he looked sober. Participating in none of the games taking place, he sat at one corner of the hearth, mellow-tempered and disinterested, legs stretched out and crossed at the ankle. One might even say he looked bored, until one of the resident old dogs slouched over to inspect him. Then his eyes lightened, his face relaxed in a smile and he leaned down to pet the animal. He wore no doublet, just a shirt with a jerkin over it, loose breeches and lugged boots. A simple peasant, with broad shoulders and a build carved through hard physical labor, he was certainly no one she was ever likely to encounter elsewhere. Their worlds would never meet again after tonight.

"Yes. He'll do." A pulse, reckless and runaway, hummed through her veins, but her voice remained composed. She hoped.

Mistress Comfort, the proprietress of this establishment, needed no assistance from her sharp eyes while efficiently counting the coin in her wrinkled hands. Instead she stared curiously at Lucy. "Are ye quite certain, madam?"

"Yes. The dark-haired man by the fire. Now I'm in haste. Where might I..." Tattered courage momentarily deserted her, shortened her breath so words expired on her tongue. Planning this daring escapade was one thing; actually carrying it out another. "Where might we have privacy?"

She was escorted up a narrow set of stairs and along a dark hallway to one of the small bedchambers. Mistress Comfort asked no further questions. The weight of her coin purse would silence any. Sometimes it was useful to have a wealthy father, although until now, as the somewhat inconvenient, least favored child, Lucy had never felt much benefit.

"This is my best chamber, madam," the old proprietress assured her. "It is on the quieter side of the house," she added.

Eager for some fresh air, Lucy hurried around the bed to open the window. It was a chilly evening with a hint of rain, but she would rather be cool than too hot. The sudden introduction of a sly breeze woke the few lit candles from their lazy slumber and long shadows danced, stretching around the walls, fluttering wings of light beating across her face. She drew a steadying breath and, in this flickering, capricious glow, inspected the scene of her imminent ruination.

A low table stood in one corner, holding a ewer and washbasin, a chipped chamber pot beneath. There was evidence of some effort to make the room appear more luxurious: a pair of threadbare, moth-nibbled tapestry curtains draped around the bed and even a small bowl of dried rose petals set nearby to sweeten the air. After all, this was the finest whorehouse in Norwich. Apparently.

Mistress Comfort, eager to impress, had carried up a jug of wine on a tray with two dented pewter cups. Unfortunately her lurching, crook-backed gait was not conducive to an even hand, and as she shuffled by Lucy to set her burden down, several puddles of vinegary liquid sloshed onto the tray. A shiny black beetle, caught napping on the small table beside the bed, was too slow to escape its doom when she brought the tray down with a clatter.

"A little something extra, madam," she grunted, hobbling back to the door. "Free o' charge."

Free of charge, indeed! She'd paid a small fortune for the use of this chamber and the old crone's discretion.

Fingertips tentatively pinching the dusty folds of the frayed bed curtain, contemplating a damp patch on the wall, Lucy muttered, "Well, now I've come this far, I may as well proceed."

She was aware of Mistress Comfort's beady eyes assessing her critically. The old hag must be wondering why she wore a leather mask over the top half of her face and why she was there to buy a man for the evening. Lucy certainly wouldn't tell her.

Releasing the curtain, she whirled around. "Bring him to me, then!" As always, when she was anxious, Lucy's voice grew tight and clipped. She heard the tone, but could do nothing to soften it, Her mouth was dry, her tongue might seize up at any moment. Eager to get this over with, she jerked off her hood. "Make haste, woman!" she added, pretending not only that she purchased a man's company every evening of the week, but she didn't hear the little skip of panic in her own voice.

Mistress Comfort retreated quickly, closing the door behind her, and Lucy began to undress before she changed her mind.

He'd better have clean hands. She didn't want him getting any dirt on her. A quick glance at the ewer assured her there was enough water to make him wash them. Good. And he could wash his other parts too, thank you very much, before they came anywhere near her. She looked at the bed, nervously pacing around it. There would be fleas, more than likely. She itched already at her arms and the back of her neck.

Lifting the wine jug, she sniffed daintily and immediately wrinkled her nose, almost retching. Stale, as she suspected, and there were flies floating there, merrily drowned. She set the jug back on the tray with trembling hands and ran to the window, afraid she might be sick. It was nerves, of course. Taking a few deep breaths, she bolstered her courage with a hasty self-lecture, for this was no time to be squeamish. At six and twenty, with only days left before her wedding to a man she despised, it was high time.

At least, this was her choice and on her terms. Lord Winton, that pompous old windbag, would be exceedingly miffed to find he'd bargained for used stock, but Lucy gained some satisfaction from this small protest. Her father would soon hand her over to Winton, the man he'd chosen, but she'd have this experience first, one last rebellion.

For once in her life, she did something for herself, her own way.

She knew the risks she took. Anything might happen to her at the hands of a stranger, but then Lord Winton was also little more than a stranger to her and nobody was concerned about her fate at his hands. At least this stranger was her choice.

Of course, there were other dangers. Once Lord Winton discovered she was no maid, he might take his fury out on her, but he was more than twice her age and had a bad leg. He certainly would never catch her if she ran. And she was no stranger to the sting of a cane or her father's belt. It had been a frequent occurrence for much of her childhood. Hardened by it, numb to it now, she would cope with her punishment, as long as she had this to comfort her later, a memory of one last mutinous act.

Sometimes, for women, life was only tolerable with occasional doses of victory, especially when there was no hope of winning the entire war.

She scratched her shoulder, glancing pensively at the bed again. Now where was this man she deigned to honor with her maidenhead? How dare he keep her waiting?

* * * *

"Yer wanted upstairs. Last chamber on the right. Lady willing to pay three sovereigns. She says yer to make haste, young feller."

He thought she addressed another, but as he shifted his gaze upward, merely out of curiosity, he found the old proprietress directing these words at him. Just to be sure, he glanced over his shoulder, but there was no one behind.

"*Me?*"

"What ye waitin' for? The queen's permission?"

Yawning loudly, John Sydney Carver sat up, running a splayed hand through his hair. "Most amusing. Where is he?" He waited, certain his cousin would leap out of the shadows, convulsing with laughter.

She sniffed at him with her hooked nose. "What yer sitting there gaping at me for? I don't know any feller who'd look this fine gift horse in the mouth."

He was still skeptical. While his mother claimed Cousin Nathaniel's practical jokes, however tiresome and often ill-timed, were never planned with spite, John wasn't entirely certain. Nathaniel would go to any peculiar lengths to make a point and win a wager.

"I know my cousin's behind this," he said evenly. "He told me to meet him here."

"Never mind that now, young feller. If yer don't get a move on, yon fine pigeon will fly the coop!" She prodded with her stubby thumb upward. "She's waitin' and she's none too patient. Proper little madam."

Eyes narrowed, he studied the low beams above and sighed deeply. So what did Nathaniel have up his sleeve this time to challenge John's new vow of celibacy?

He supposed he'd have to go up and find out.

* * * *

Before she left the house, Lucy had her maid loosen all the necessary points and laces, preparing herself for haste. In her long, hooded cloak she was discreetly covered and no one noticed her state of half-undress. Now her clothing fell away easily, as planned, and she was soon down to corset and shift. There was nothing left to do but pace, listening to the muted laughter from below.

Now she was struck by another troubling thought.

He might not be willing. There to enjoy a few ales, possibly choose his own woman for a sixpence, he might object to being the prey instead of the hunter.

Her heartbeat raced, straining within the confines of her corset, but just as she considered slipping her cloak back on and leaving, the door opened and he entered.

She almost heard a drum roll heralding his appearance. Her brother was right, she'd watched one too many plays.

Clutching the nicked, scratched bedpost, she looked at this man she'd chosen and discovered, to her shame and frustration, a wretched streak of cowardice threatening the fulfillment of her grand plans. She'd never felt so apprehensive in the presence of a man, but then she'd never been alone with one, other than her father or brother, before this. Under normal circumstances some form of introduction would be expected, but in a situation like this, were there any rules?

His restless gaze darted around the room, one hand on the door latch. "The old woman sent me up here." Finally his perusal came to rest on her in her leather mask. "What do you want with me?" he demanded.

A scratchy laugh spilled out of her dry mouth. "Well, let's see. I'm in a whore house and I'm almost naked." When he merely glared at her, she quipped, "I'll give you another clue. I'm not here for a dress-fitting." Waiting had pinched her temper, drawn her nerves very thin. He was clearly a peasant and should do as he was told.

Still his fingers played over the door latch, his brow creased in a deep frown. "Is this some sort of jest? Who put you up to this, Nathaniel Downing? Better put your clothes back on, woman. I'm flattered, but I do my own choosing and I prefer a wench with more meat on her bones."

Lucy took umbrage immediately. She straightened her spine, head up, shoulders back, and so what if her fingers held the bedpost a little tighter? He wouldn't notice. "Indeed, this is no jest, certainly not at these prices. I paid good coin for this chamber and I trust Mistress Comfort informed you I'm willing to pay three sovereigns for your company. Quite a bit more than the going rate for trysts in this place, I understand." Angrier by the breath, she added, "Surely that's inducement enough to overlook any lack of *meat* on my bones!"

"Three sovereigns?" he said in a faintly appalled tone.

"And I mean to get my money's worth."

Her intentions laid out in these plain terms, surely clear enough even for a peasant to understand, she turned her back and demanded he unlace her corset. Accustomed to the services of a maid, tonight she must make do with this complete stranger. If he stayed, of course, and didn't leave her standing there looking like a fool. Should he leave, Lucy wasn't sure she had the strength to start again and find another man. Besides, he ought to be damned grateful for what she offered him.

A moment passed. She heard the rusty bolt drawn, then his long stride echoed across the floorboards toward her, loud and menacing. Even the ill-fitting windowpanes rattled slightly in their lead casings. Her eyes flew open.

He was staying. This was it.

Another drum roll.

She flinched, expecting the cold touch of his fingers.

Nothing.

No tug on her laces.

No hands anywhere.

Had he forgotten his directions?

Swiveling impatiently, she found him very close behind her, wearing a scowl like thunder. Tripping back, she sat heavily on the edge of the bed.

"Who the hell are you?" he demanded.

"I'm afraid I can't tell you." She held up one hand, adding hastily, "I don't want to know your name either, plowman. It really isn't necessary."

As he stood over her, hands on hips, she drew in another shallow, tense breath and swallowed his scent. Leather, horse and hay. She'd never been this close to a country peasant before, never been outside the city walls of London, in fact, and only rarely ventured far from her father's house and grounds, until a few days ago when she'd been brought here to Norwich, for her wedding. This man, though he had the appearance of a rustic, didn't act like a rampaging, rapacious savage, which is what she'd been raised to believe of all men who lived in the country and didn't possess a coat of arms to their name. Her father, a stern man who ruled his household with an iron hand, terrified his daughters regularly with dire warnings about life outside his domain. It was a very effective method of keeping them under his control. At least, it was while Lucy was still a girl. But she was old enough now to understand that not everything was exactly the way her father taught her. Indeed he had a very skewed view of most things, including his eldest daughter's worth.

She cautiously studied the man before her. He seemed much larger now they were in the same room. His shirt was stained, the cuffs hanging over his broad wrists frayed and discolored, his boots thick with mud.

"Can we proceed?" Once again, she tried to conceal her nervous tremors under a haughty tone. "Would you like the money now or later?"

Because he stood so close, looking up into his face made her feel small and vulnerable. Instead, she stared at whatever reached eye-level. This, she discovered, was a mistake, drawing her gaze to the part of him for which she went to all this trouble, and subsequently reminding her that he was still fully clothed, while she was half-naked.

"Well, farmhand? Three sovereigns are enough, surely? You may remove your breeches and begin." She glanced dubiously at his hands where they hung at his sides. "Try not to touch me too much. Beyond the necessary, of course."

Instantly defying her orders, he clasped her chin with one of those large, roughened hands, lifting it until she could no longer avoid his steady gaze. "How amusing! My sides split. Where is he, then?" His low voice rumbled all the way down his arm, through his fingertips and into her jaw.

"Where is...?" She was breathless.

"Nate Downing. He put you up to this, didn't he?"

She tried to knock his hand away, but his wrist was strong as iron, his grip unrelenting. The more she struggled and pulled on his sleeve, the harder he held on.

"I don't like to be made a fool."

She snapped out, "That makes two of us."

There was a fraught moment, when he stared down at her and she held his gaze, unblinking, furious. Finally he let her go, his fingers drifting away. It was almost a caress, shockingly gentle, despite the potent strength in his fingertips. She shivered, every pore on her body snapped awake and alert. There was a decidedly impish gleam in his eye, curiously taking her in, very thorough, as if *he* were the one paying three sovereigns.

He'd better not try mastering her, she thought. If he knew her, he'd never dare try it. But of course, he didn't know her, did he? That was the point.

"Look, if you're going to be difficult about this, you may as well leave now. If you want your three sovereigns you'll get the dratted thing out of your breeches and get on with it."

His eyes were startling, a color hovering between verjuice and azure blue. She'd noticed them immediately when spying on him through the peephole and perhaps they were the reason she'd chosen him. He'd entered the place alone that evening and was by far the quietest, most subdued of all the men she considered. This led her to think him safe. Now, observing several fierce, treacherous tides churning away behind the formerly tranquil waters of those eyes, Lucy feared she'd been deceived.

He smiled, wolfish. "You're not one of the usual wenches."

"How do you know?" she demanded, chin raised. "Come here often I suppose."

When he chuckled it was almost a purr, but not of a household cat. His was the warning, heart-stopping rumble of a leopard she'd seen in the queen's menagerie. "For one thing, you're too damn clean."

Lucy stood and walked away from him to the foot of the bed.

"And for another thing, most whores don't give orders. Or pay their customers. It somewhat defeats the purpose of the job." But despite his mocking tone, the hard lines of his face softened, his eyes brightened.

Definitely interested—despite her lack of meat. *Meat!* She still couldn't get over his deplorable lack of manners.

But if he liked her, that was good, wasn't it? For her purposes?

Lucy wasn't so sure. The mischievous glint in his eye was troubling.

Better set him straight at once, before he got any ideas above his place. If he didn't like her rules, he could damn well leave and she'd go home. Might be for the best, after all. Not that she'd lost her gumption, of course.

"Are you *questioning* me?" she exclaimed. "How dare you? Perhaps this will be more trouble than it's worth."

He flexed his arms, shook out his hands. His slow, heated gaze wandered, contemplative, up and down her semi-naked length. And then he cracked his knuckles. "Wouldn't be changing your mind now would you? Looking for a way out? Looking for an excuse to withdraw the offer?"

Uh oh. She had indeed made a mistake. She'd expected anyone found in this place to do exactly as she commanded and willingly for the money, yet there was a powerful, obstinate strength oozing out of this man, like treacle from a broken pot. He now advanced a few steps toward her, not in the least discouraged by her icy frown. An expression notorious for freezing well-intentioned suitors where they stood, it seemed that tonight it held no power.

This was not going to plan. In fact, she considered abandoning her mission altogether.

As if he read her mind, his gaze slid sideways to the bolted door and then back to Lucy. Standing between her and the exit, he leveled his footing—a pre-emptive motion, the implication obvious.

"I've seen you before," he said very softly, a slight uplift to the end of the sentence, making it a question as much as a statement.

The same strange idea had passed through her own mind when she first saw him.

"Have I?" he demanded.

"Certainly not," she scoffed, although she sensed he wasn't asking her, merely puzzling over it himself.

A little bit of a grin tugged at his lips, breeze-blown candlelight toying with his rugged features. "Must have been in my dreams, then." There was a challenge in that smirk, daring her to make a run for the door.

She knew who'd be there first. And what would follow.

Mistake or not, the upward twist of his lips assured her it was too late to back out now; he was there, so was she, and sand already slipped through the hourglass.

Her resolve hardened again. "This arrangement is just for tonight, you understand? You'd better not get any ideas, for this is on my terms or not at all."

He devoured her with his gaze, moving intently over her mask and then downward, leaving no part untouched. Something inside her began to melt. She was very warm, her throat tight, her breathing too scattered. Further annoyed by his silent perusal and her body's involuntary reaction to it, she raised her voice, as if to a disobedient servant. "You'll do as I say, no more, no less." Though aware she was talking too much and too quickly, she couldn't stop herself. "I need this thing done properly. I trust you know what is required? Might we begin at once? Remove your clothes and there is water over there with which to--"

"I'm not accustomed to uppity wenches making all the decisions."

She huffed. "You surprise me." Naturally, he was merely bothered by a woman in charge--that *she* paid the coin. Nothing else troubled him. Tonight the injustices of life wore on her temper like flint on a knife's blade. "You can tolerate a woman's commands, surely, for no more than a quarter of an hour. I won't keep you long."

His eyes gleamed, his nostrils flared. Slowly he walked around her in a full circle, taking it all in again, before he dropped to the bed, sprawled against the bolster and lifted his foot. "Boots!"

"What?"

"Take 'em off for me, wench."

Wench? How dare he?

When she froze, he added with the quick flare of an insolent grin, "Unless you want me to keep 'em on while we do the deed."

She frowned at his muddy boot. "Are you cup shotten?"

"No."

"Then you can remove your own boots, man."

He tucked his arms behind his head. "No. You do it, wench!"

"Keep them on, then. This won't take long in any case. You won't be staying."

His eyes widened, then narrowed. "I'll have the boots off. If you've no objection. *Ma'am*." It was definitely not a question this time.

She sensed he was testing the waters, deliberately prodding her temper for his own sport. But what else could she do? Go back and find another man to take his place? There was no time and she was already half-undressed.

Yet there was another matter for consideration, far and above the practicalities.

She wanted him.

Lucy realized it then, as he lay on the bed, waiting for her.

Oh yes, she wanted him.

It was almost a challenge now. He dared her, thought she wouldn't go through with it, was ready to call her a coward.

But he didn't know Lucy Collyer, did he?

He soon would.

Chapter 2

So he was impudent and had a saucy mouth. What did it matter? Only a temporary hire, he was not one of her father's servants to reprimand. Besides, she rather liked his smile, not to mention that superbly carved body. Lying across the bed, seething with raw energy, he was a gift ready to be unwrapped. Simply put, she'd never seen a man quite so appealing.

She'd rolled the dice and this is where they'd fallen. It was her fault he was there, after all.

Perhaps, just this once, under the anonymity of that leather mask, she could put her hands on his filthy boots, another novel experience to be sure, but over in a few minutes. She grabbed his foot and pulled.

"The laces," he chided her. "The laces, wench!"

He lay back against the bolster, watching her, offering no assistance whatsoever, just an amused critique.

Once she'd tossed his boots aside she moved on to his breeches, but he sat up, grabbing her hands as she leaned over his sprawling form. "This I'll do myself," he warned, serious again.

Walking around the bed, she watched him undress. He was stocky, his thighs were thick and powerful. Afraid to look at anything else, she carefully averted her eyes to the floor boards, but he took a knife from his discarded belt, jumped up and came toward her with a determined stride. She backed away to the wall, alarmed.

There was a small diagonal scar across his left eyebrow, an interruption of the symmetry of his face lending a slight quirk to his expression which prevented those clear, sculpted angles from looking too stern. Even so, with that knife in his hand, when he commanded, "Turn around," she contemplated running for the window and leaping out.

"Turn around," he repeated. When she hesitated, he held the knife in his teeth, put his hands on her shoulders and spun her to face the wall. Then he slid the knife's blade under her corset laces and, with one ruthless motion, cut her free.

Evidently he was not the sort to trouble himself with knots and bows. In a quick burst of wry amusement, Lucy thought of her maid's face tomorrow when she saw the corset's sad fate.

With one impatient tug he freed her likewise of her shift. It tumbled down to her wrists and hips, where it came to a whispering halt. She closed her eyes, gathering her courage again. For just a few startled moments, she'd relaxed her guard and likewise the reins. Now her nerves galloped in every direction, almost out of reach.

His breath was on the nape of her neck. And then he touched her. Oh.

She'd forgotten to make him wash his hands.

He stroked lightly down her spine with his fingertips, to the dip of her waist and back again. Then he spread them to her shoulders and down her arms, as if he measured her, as if she were a young filly at auction and he a prospective buyer. It was not at all the way she imagined. Having received a brief theory lesson from her knowledgeable maid, she was prepared for a quick "in and out" that might take no more than five minutes at the most.

Head bowed, eyes closed, she murmured, "Blow out the candles."

"No," he replied gruffly, "I want to see."

She repeated her command, louder this time.

He kept his hands around her naked waist, fingers spread. "I'll keep the candles lit."

Lucy was accustomed to being obeyed by servants. This man, in her eyes, was simply another who should do as she bid, without question. "Do as I say. At once! I'm paying you, remember? This is on my terms! Mine!"

In reply, he jerked the sleeves free of her wrists, and then only the curve of her hip prevented the silk shift from falling. She felt it ready to drop, hanging there to save her modesty as if by its own willpower.

"Blow out the candles," she repeated.

This time he must have noticed her tremble, for his voice softened, turned husky. "Say please, then."

After a short struggle, she breathed the word, rare on her lips, and he finally complied with her wishes, extinguishing the candles, one by one, until there was only light from the young spring moon. He moved his hands around her from behind, his sinewy arms under hers, strong fingers splayed to cup her breasts. No one had ever touched her like this. He hadn't even asked permission. She felt marked already, despoiled, merely by his forceful hands on her breasts, the rough pads of his brazen fingers caressing her nipples. She worried he would hear her heart thumping away--surely it vibrated along her backbone. There was no way to hide it. She could mask her face, but not those emotions pounding through her like galloping horse hooves.

His lips were on the nape of her neck, his teeth gently nipping. His warm breath stirred the little hairs straying from her caul and, with far greater alacrity than she, a woman never before touched so intimately, might expect, the anxiety faded. He kissed her ear, the side of her neck and her shoulder, his mouth moving wetly over her skin. Perhaps there was magic in his hands and lips, some elixir rendering her calm, soothed.

Ready.

"Where shall we begin?" His unshaven chin grazed her shoulder, while he slid a hand down her naked belly and gripped the silk shift where it bunched around her hips.

She gasped, a sharp burst of nervous laughter shooting out. How did she know what to ask for? She circumvented the question. "I'm spoiled for choice. With so much on offer how does one begin?"

"A smart-mouthed wench, eh?"

"A very wicked and disobedient one, I'm afraid. Will you get on with it, or are you all talk?"

He drew a quick, sharp breath. "I can see I've got my work cut out for me. Since no other man has taken you in hand, I'd best see to your guidance."

Anticipation rippled through her every nerve, the touch of his hands and his words somehow communicating with parts of her which until now had lain dormant.

In the next beat of her heart, the shift fell from her hips, slithered over her thighs, stroked her knees and pooled soft around her feet. Immediately he was there, hard and warm, pressed to her bottom and the small of her back.

He moved to unpin the caul, a gold mesh net holding her bound hair.

"No," she gasped. "Leave it."

"I want it down."

"And I say it stays." She mustn't be in too much disarray upon her return, in case she encountered anyone other than the maid.

Hands resting lightly on her shoulders, he turned her to face him. "The mask then. Take that off at least."

"No!" Bracing for another argument, she tried to ignore the heat radiating from her nipples, where they brushed his chest.

"Is there any part of this we can agree upon, do you think?" He sounded bemused rather than angry. "Are you going to let me do this my way, or not?"

"I'm the customer," she pointed out tartly. "Shouldn't it be my way?" He would fight her for control, she knew it. This man was no fool, neither was he afraid of a challenge. A strange excitement bubbled and whispered within her. Like recognized like, she thought. Here, in a Norwich bawdy house, of all places, she'd found someone as stubborn as herself.

One hand to his mouth, he hid either a curse or a chuckle. More likely the latter, since his eyes were very warm, his lashes lowered slyly.

Lucky for him, the contrary fellow was really very pleasing to look upon. To her surprise, even better naked. "We'll compromise," she conceded breathlessly. "You may take down the hair. But not the mask." If only he knew how great a concession that was. She never willingly gave any man even her hand to kiss.

He tugged a pretend forelock. "Why, I thank you most humbly ma'am!"

"I'll change my mind if you don't hurry."

His blue eyes gleamed in the moonlight. "Impatient for me?"

"No," was the curt rejoinder, "Just impatient."

The pins were speedily discarded, gold mesh tossed aside. Her hair tumbled free and as the heavy lengths fell to her shoulders, over her bared breasts and down to her hips, she cursed herself for giving in. He was a persuasive fellow. His smile, oddly endearing, brought out a softer side in her she never knew existed.

Wrapping her hair around his knuckles, he brought it to his face, murmuring softly, as if he'd never seen or felt anything like it. While he explored, she remained still, her hands at her sides, resisting the urge to cover herself now, although wearing only her stockings, garters and her favorite pearl earrings.

He ran his thumb across her mouth, pressing down on the lower lip. She had time for only one quick breath, and wondered if he inspected her teeth now too, before his lips descended to hers and pried them further open. Lucy had never been kissed on the mouth. Never. Astonished, she stood quietly and let him do it.

His ale-spiced lips were firm, certainly knew what they did and were not at all objectionable. The tongue, however, was an alarming development. With his hands around her face, she couldn't pull away, so she tried to quell the anxiety, chiding herself for it. Let him have his kiss, if he wanted it. She supposed it would do no harm.

Brushing her hair aside, he gazed down at her breasts. Again she waited, glad of the semi-darkness to hide her hot cheeks. With an odd sound, deep in his throat, he ducked his head and took her nipple in his mouth, sliding his hand down her back, holding her close.

What the devil was he doing? This was supposed to take no more than a few minutes. She knew the basics of what must be done, but he seemed to be taking the long way around to it. He stroked her bottom, pressing her even closer so she felt his erection, hard and hot against her stomach. Her blood fizzled and sparked, as if laced with gunpowder. But again he delayed. Slowly he sank down, licking a meandering course down her body. Lucy bit back the cries singing in the back of her throat. She must not get carried away. She must not...

He licked her belly.

His mouth grazed her hip.

He kissed her inner thigh.

And when she moved her hands finally, knotting her fingers through his hair, she felt his tongue dart out, touching her most private place, his lips kissing her where she'd never dreamed. He was now on his knees before her, his hands around her thighs.

Oh.

She held her breath, almost lost her footing.

Oh.

This was most definitely not to plan.

Holding her firm, he tasted her, while she trembled like a newborn lamb, amazed by his audacity, but also at herself for allowing it. This was too much. She would shatter into a thousand pieces if she let him continue like this.

She should never have...

With a small, breathless cry, she arched, waves of pleasure flooding her body, every tiny hidden part of her too sensitive and all of it, every inch, at the mercy of his tongue. Her knees weakened until she almost tumbled forward and only his powerful hands, clasped around her stockinged thighs, kept her upright. When she attempted to pull his head back by the hair, he grunted in protest and another rush of heat overtook her, stealing the strength from her limbs.

"My good fellow, this is not necessary, you know. Stop that!"

He did as she asked this time, looking up at her, moonlight shining in his eyes. He was breathtaking. Not smoothly well-favored like other gentlemen she knew, but like a barbarian, hard, unrefined, even brutally handsome.

It was tempting to let him continue as he wished, to let him take all the time in the world he wanted; however, there must be no deviation from the plan. Time was wasting. He, of course, knew nothing of any plan. Nothing about the maid waiting anxiously to let her in at the servants' entrance before first light crept over the sky, nor about her strict father, who sat up late to read and rose early to walk, no matter what the weather.

"Hurry and get on with it, then," she exclaimed. "Take me to the bed and…do what needs to be done. No more of this delay."

His expression, so easily read, told her she was lucky. He wouldn't usually hear a woman's commands. She was trying his patience and he was primed. Yes, this too was gloriously evident as he stood again before her, not bothering to hide. In fact, he showed off, boldly confident in his raw male beauty.

The only other naked man she'd ever seen was her brother, when she once burst in on him by accident as he dressed. At the time, it made her laugh, much to her brother's chagrin. As a young girl, she'd thought how glad she was not to have such an unwieldy burden to hide away. Women were fortunate to have everything neatly tucked out of sight.

But now she thanked the good Lord for giving her some idea of what to expect. She also had her maid's careful explanation of its purpose, so she was not utterly at a loss, however, to have this stranger's large appendage thrust upon her was quite another matter. Under no circumstances would that thing fit anywhere…she couldn't even finish the thought.

He took her by the waist, holding her hard against the item in question. "Are you ready for this now?" he whispered, leading her hand to his erection, watching her lips, which had yet to recover from the invasion of his kiss.

"I don't think it will fit."

He laughed. "I'll make it fit."

She swallowed hard, grateful for her leather mask, which hid most of her expression, but whatever he saw in her lips made him press another gentle kiss to her hot cheek. "You leave it to me, my lovely wench." There was the slight twist of a question in his tone, as if she puzzled him and he still couldn't make out her purpose there in his arms.

She struggled to remain aloof. "Very well then. Proceed."

Dipping his head, he put his mouth to her other breast, teasing her nipple with his lips and tongue, relishing, savoring. He was in no hurry, intent on taking his time. With one timid hand, Lucy touched his manhood again. Instantly he reacted, the broad head swelling further, thick veins pulsing, pushing against her tentative, exploring caress. He closed his fingers around her wrist, as if he meant to stop her, but then he was guiding her hand, up and down, setting the pace to a slower tempo, even as his breath quickened.

Alas, through the open shutters, the sound of church bells rang out. "'Tis the hour of nine already," she groaned, turning her face toward the sound.

At first, one hand still pacing her strokes, he seemed not to hear. Then, waking himself, he muttered, "Do I keep you from more important business, wench?"

"Yes. I can't stay long, so make haste."

There was a sharp silence, cutting the cool air. He dropped her wrist. When she looked at him, his eyes were afire, his breath exhaled in short, shallow gasps.

Fearing she might have insulted him in some way, trying to ignore the warm strength of his hand spread across her bare back, which, for some reason, seemed just as intimate as when he'd touched her between the thighs, Lucy tried to coax him forward. "You may as well get on with it." Still holding his manhood, she now grew bolder out of desperation, stroking up and down, faster without his guidance. "This item is all we need, is it not? It seems...prepared."

His mouth opened, but nothing came out.

"I'm only here to give away my maidenhead. It won't take long will it?"

She might have slapped his face. It surely couldn't have achieved that expression of shock and horror in any other way. Afraid he might leave, she grabbed his free hand, placing it over her breast.

"Don't mind me," she said. "You may continue."

Chapter 3

John Sydney Carver concluded he must have drunk more than he thought. Or else he'd fallen through to an alternate world, where women made the decisions and men were expected to obey like mindless playthings.

Or someone was out to play a trick on him. Cousin Nathaniel, for instance.

He exploded. "Your what?" He snatched his hand away from her breast, as if her skin was scalding hot. "A virgin? You'd best explain yourself, madam!"

Wide-eyed under her mask, she said nothing. This sweet-tasting, naked young woman, who should be guarded with greater care by whichever male was responsible, had nothing to say for herself.

Appalled, he spun away and sat on the edge of the bed, hands on his knees, shoulders slumped. "A virgin?" he repeated, as if she'd just announced she had the French pox.

"I want you to take my maidenhead. I thought you understood." She sounded annoyed, frustrated. Feelings that were surely all his domain.

Amid all these muddled thoughts, one stood out. Today was his thirtieth birthday. Was it possible this ripe maiden was Nathaniel's gift to him? His cousin didn't generally remember birthdays, but it was just the sort of thing Nathaniel would do, present him with a virgin to deflower. Nathaniel refused to believe him capable of celibacy and with this beautiful, bold creature for bait, he must have set out to prove it, once and for all.

Aware of her gaze pinned lasciviously on his erection, he covered it protectively with both hands, glowering at her, suspecting she might try to separate it from the rest of his body. How did he know what her true intentions were? Was his cousin under the bed, waiting to jump out and surprise him in the act?

"This prudishness didn't trouble you so much a moment hence, farmhand."

Why did she keep calling him "farmhand" in that snooty voice? As if he should be insulted by it, or ashamed of working for a living.

When she tipped her head back, moonbeams caught on her bare shoulder and framed her tumbled hair. Earlier, there had been a reddish tint to those long, thick locks, and the candle light before it was extinguished had played warmly over her bound tresses, but now, in the cool moonlight, her hair was mostly a dark mass, a mystery to be explored.

"You were ready enough to do your worst just now," she snapped.

He stubbornly looked away from the temptation. "That was when I thought you were..." he stopped, shaking his head again.

"Because I'm a maid, you won't continue?"

"No. I mean...yes." He liked to think he was a reformed character now, a hard-working man of responsibility, one day soon to marry a young lady of moral fiber and good family. He was not in the habit of casually deflowering bossy maidens in whore houses. However lovely they were.

And she was. She was damned lovely to look at, at least, the parts of her she let him see. She smelled sweet, tasted even sweeter. If he stood, she would see for herself how much he ached to continue.

He couldn't get the idea out of his head that he'd seen her before in his dreams. He seldom remembered dreams, but these stood out in his mind, little disjointed flashes, broken shards of glass, glinting in sun as they fell through the air.

Ah, he was just being a hare-brained fool. Wishful thinking wasn't enough to bring a dream to life, was it?

He cursed again under his breath. It had been Nathaniel's idea to meet at Mistress Comfort's. A frequent customer of such houses, he'd teased John that he shouldn't be so ready to shut pleasure out of his life. No doubt this was the sort of pleasure his cousin had in mind.

A brand new whore. How much did she cost Nathaniel, he wondered. Probably more coin than his cousin should have at his disposal, considering the number of angry people to whom he owed money. But whenever Nathaniel was flush with coin, he spent it on frivolous luxuries instead of paying off his bills.

"Listen, plowman." She stooped, gathering her shift and holding it over her pert, moonlit breasts. "I was told this should only take a few minutes. If you have no inclination for the job, I may as well find another who does. You waste my time."

He stiffened, incredulous. This was getting worse and worse, or better and better. He wasn't entirely sure which it was and whether he should be angry or laugh. Hands pressed down on his thighs, he regarded her fiercely. Go to another, would she? Leave him in this state?

"If you won't perform the service to my satisfaction," she added snippily, "another will."

She was either very brave or stupid to provoke his lust and then his temper. He squinted, trying to hide his thoughts, not wanting her to know his mind was made up already and under no circumstances, except over his dead body, was she leaving now until he'd had her. Had her to *his* satisfaction. She wanted a "service" performed? The malcontent wench would get that and more besides.

In all likelihood she was no maiden. It was probably an act meant to titillate his interest. As if he needed any additional incentive to bed her.

"I'm not even to know your name?" he demanded.

"That's correct. It's all very simple." And she punctuated her answer with a condescending smile. Even as it roused his anger, he felt his cock shift and pulse, stretching another half inch, eager to conquer and subdue this haughty creature.

Still he pretended to consider his choices, rubbing his chin slowly with one hand, while leaning back on his elbow, letting her look at him.

Her eyelashes fluttered against the holes in her leather mask, her lips parted with a sudden breath of excitement.

"Well?" She clutched her shift around her. "Must I go down and find another man?"

It must be part of her act, he mused, this prim formality. It matched the fine look of her, the soft, clean skin and well-kept, fragrant hair. Her perfume was obviously an expensive blend. He recognized ambergris, musk and sweet marjoram. Thanks to his sisters he had familiarity with these things, more than he ever wished to. Her teeth were clean, her breath flavored with aniseed and mint. She was, as he'd said to her already, not one of the usual wenches. Must have cost Nathaniel a fortune, in addition to those three sovereigns she kept offering, just to make her fine, ladylike act more convincing.

"I think you know what my answer is," he said softly.

But still she waited, as if she didn't, in fact, know. As if the sight of his proudly erect cock wasn't answer enough. Exquisite, teasing little whore. Virgin or not, and there was only one way to find out, since she played her part prettily. He wondered if this was good fortune or wicked mischief. Perhaps it was both.

One thing was certain: this woman had a rarefied loveliness no man could pass up. His cousin had excellent taste and evidently knew exactly what would tempt John. Her high and mighty manner was just annoying enough to set him a challenge. The way she talked down to him, tossed her head and set her full lips in a disdainful sulk made his shaft harden until it almost hurt. Even before he touched them, her nipples were tight, budding in readiness for his tongue, and between her thighs, tender treasure blossomed eagerly, sending out signals he couldn't ignore. She was irresistible and, as she said, it was only for the night, no complications. Was this not every man's fantasy?

"All right, woman, I suppose I'd better service you, now you dragged me up here away from my ale and that warm fire." Lurching upright, he crossed the room to where she stood, lifted her in his arms and carried her to the bed. "But there is one thing," he said, as he dropped her to the mattress and knelt beside her, tossing the bolster and sheets aside.

With foolish modesty, she clutched her crumpled shift to cover her nakedness. "What would that be?"

"I want all night." He held back a smug grin as her prim lips parted again, ready to argue. "Not just a few minutes of your time," he added, "thrown from the high table like scraps to a dog."

"But it won't take long. It's all over in a moment, my... I was told by a reliable source with experience in these matters."

He tugged on her shift, prying it from her clenched hands. "You were misinformed. I see I must set you straight." Tossing her shift to the floor, he sat back on his heels at her side, running one hand slowly up and down his eager manhood. "Now...do you want this or not?"

Her lashes fluttered again through the eye holes of her mask. Her lips rolled inward and then popped open as she drew a wistful breath. That silence was eloquence itself.

"Then you'll let me take my time." He released his grin fully now. "Perhaps, where you come from, it only takes a moment. Where this simple plowman comes from, pleasures are few and generally hard won, so they're relished and properly appreciated."

"Oh," was all she said.

He'd noticed a small dimple in her right cheek and now saw it was the herald of a polite, painfully dignified smile.

He tipped forward, a hand on either side of her shoulders. "Let's proceed, shall we?"

Her lips pursed and she stiffened.

"You've a lot to learn," he remarked coolly, waiting.

There was a small movement in her throat. Her tongue darted out, dampening the soft, fragile rosy blush of her lips to a deeper, more exotic hue.

"Arms down then, madam."

Slowly she uncrossed the arms to reveal her breasts, two pert, dainty things, lush mouthfuls crying out to be lavished with more of his attention, nipples waiting like precious little rubies on creamy silk pillows. He paused a moment, taking a breath, reminding himself not to rush in clumsily, however badly he wanted to claim the prize.

No need to act like a barbarian, he cautioned. She'd still be here in ten minutes, in twenty, in two hours.

No need to abandon civilized manners altogether, just because....

Too late.

He gave in to the desire pounding through his body like a blacksmith's hammer against an anvil.

* * * *

With his weight over her, his tongue caressing her skin, Lucy struggled to remember that she must be home by daylight, before she was missed, or her maid would be in trouble.

"All night," he insisted again, pressing his words to her breast like a branding iron, his deep voice choked with passion. She guessed he was rarely refused in such instance. Who would refuse all this? As he rose up again, his body poised above her, staking her to the bed, she noted the sharp contrast of her smooth, white hand against the sun-browned planes of his hard chest. Then, slowly, she returned her gaze to his face, finding his eyes, warm with mischief, watching her hand, too.

"Why? Have you nothing else to do tonight?" she asked wryly, relaxing a little, her voice warmer, throatier. "None other to entertain with all your delights?"

"No. You're a lucky wench, to have me at your disposal this evening."

"Am I indeed?" She wanted to laugh then. It was a pity she didn't know his name. She could have sent him a gift later, to thank him, perhaps wine or oranges, or a brace of birds from her husband's land. Or a token more intimate, like a ring. She looked at his fingers now laid over hers, where she held them to his chest. He wore no jewelry. Of course not, he was but a peasant.

Pity he wasn't a permanent fixture in her life, a secret lover.

He drew her hand to his mouth. "Perhaps we're both lucky tonight." He kissed her fingertips, one by one, his gaze never leaving hers. "The least you can do is stay with me all night, wench." A slow, provocative grin melted her further still, until she was liquid under him. "If you want this thing done properly, as you first claimed."

Already sensing the danger of looking into his breath-stealing blue eyes too long, Lucy closed her eyelids tightly, stretched out her body and impulsively flung her arms over her head, finally and completely offering herself up to him.

And as his brawny thighs eased her knees apart, he whispered in her ear that a job worth doing was worth doing well.

He lived up to this maxim, kissing her from head to toe, touching her tenderly, until she was utterly desperate to have the rest of him. Even then he made her wait, lowering his body with infinite care. When he entered her at last, she would have cried out, but he kissed her quickly to quell the sudden sharp sound.

It rained that evening. The first drops were light, spattering against the open shutters, but by the time he crossed her threshold, it had become a steady downpour, muting even the sounds of the tavern below.

Through the rain, she heard her own gasps and his breathy, soothing whispers, telling her the pain would pass. He lay still while she trembled under him and then, when she relaxed, opening like a bud in spring, he filled her a little more, gradually easing his way deeper. His whispers changed to soft groans of pleasure, resonating deeply within her, teasing her further open. He buried his lips in her hair and the side of her neck, while she stroked his broad shoulders and kissed his ear, letting him know the pain had indeed passed. And she wanted him, all of him. Bracing his torso above her, arms tense with strain, he was foggy-eyed and ground his jaw. Shyly she stroked the clearly defined muscle of his arms, soothing him as he did her, with gentle, encouraging whispers. Then as he still paused, holding steady, more urgent needs overcame the limits of her patience and she arched up, lavishing his chest with hot kisses, licking his sweat-dampened skin, winding her fingers through small curls at the nape of his neck, pulling him down.

Encouraged, he rocked forward the last little distance, until she held all of him within her and she wanted to weep then with joy, wrapping her legs around his lean flanks, making certain he had no plans to withdraw from her yet.

Briefly they lay thus, she growing accustomed to his size, he whispering apologies for hurting her, but when she rubbed her leg along his side, he felt the fine lace of her garter, which seemed to have the curious effect of banishing his fears. He stroked her leg, under her knee to her thigh, and she felt the quickening heavy thud of his heart pressed to her bosom. He slid his hands under her bottom, lifting it slightly so that his cock thrust even deeper yet, and his breathing became labored as he moved his hips, his eyes narrowed, fixed. Already tonight he'd teased her to the peak several times, keeping her in a state of low-burning arousal. Now the steady friction brought her quickly back to that fevered stage, more intense than ever. Faster now he moved and, as she opened and contracted around his hard, thick shaft, Lucy felt the glow he'd lit within her expanding rapidly, ready to burst into flame.

It wasn't supposed to be this way. The act of coupling was for procreation only, not for pleasure, a lecture that had been instilled in her for years. Yet here she was, blatantly enjoying herself with a man who was not her husband and whose intention was not to impregnate her with his seed.

Alarm shivered through her. They hadn't discussed those practical matters. Would he withdraw? Should she remind him?

What was the proper etiquette at a time like this? It might be indelicate to mention it, but...

Opening her eyes, she met his blue gaze staring down at her, fierce and hot.

He tensed and then his strokes became longer, harder, slower. Gasping with every forward plunge, she felt the bed shudder beneath them. The lines of his face sharpened as he breathed in so deeply. Watching him lose control was almost as arousing as the thrusting and withdrawing itself and when he bent his head to take her nipple in his mouth, it took only three gentle sucks before she was over the highest peak yet, losing herself gladly in his arms. She clung to him, fearing she might drown without him there to keep her afloat. Her body flexed against his, molded to him, the sweat on her skin mixing with his, making a potent, sensual elixir.

He bucked, pounding into her as she rode the crest of that wave. Finally, at the very last minute, he withdrew, spilling onto her belly with a low, guttural roar.

It was over. His weight was gone from her so thoroughly, she felt cheated. She hadn't reminded him of the danger, yet he withdrew of his own accord and now, despite the sheer, reckless stupidity of it, she actually wished he'd stayed inside her and finished there. But she shook off this wanton, ridiculous idea, returning to more sensible, even-tempered thoughts. She was lucky he had more willpower than she did, it seemed, and even at his peak he thought of her safety. Her heart warmed to him and an unexpected tear bristled in the corner of her eye, stinging spitefully.

Still throbbing from the intensity of his thrusts and her own tremors, she lay mutely while he wiped his seed from her stomach with his shirt, sacrificing the only thing he had at hand for the task. She was moved by his thoughtful, selfless action and when he couldn't meet her gaze, she stayed his hand, still bunched around his shirt, and reminded him, in a quaking voice, that this was her idea from the very beginning. This was what she wanted, he was the man she chose and there were no regrets to be had.

He threw his shirt to the floor and gathered her into his arms, holding her, saying nothing.

With her face pressed into the steadily-pulsing contours of his chest, she whispered, "Was it...was it not good?"

Discerning a slight tremble, a disruption to the firm rhythmic thud of his heartbeat, she pulled back, looking up at his face and found him chuckling. "Yes." He cupped the back of her head with one hand, drawing her up for a kiss, caressing her mouth with his words. "It was too good."

"How can something be too good?"

There was a pause. "I don't know. I never knew it was possible until tonight."

It was rare for a man to confess there might be something for which he had no answer. How honest and sweet he was, she mused, how very different to the other men in her life. The men in her life. Now he was one of them, a delicious secret, a memory to be cherished.

The rain finally eased, falling away to a gentle pitter-pat, soothing as a lullaby. She looked up, her gaze trailing dizzily over the damp stains on the slanting ceiling of that little bawdy house bedchamber. She imagined her father and her future husband looking down at them, coldly dignified, demanding to know what she thought she was up to.

She's always been trouble, she heard her father exclaim haughtily. *Now look at her.*

And the image of her fiancé, Lord Winton, watching without emotion, repeated those same words she'd overheard only a few days ago, when he hadn't known she was behind the door of his library.

"I would much rather have had her sister, but if you think Anne is yet too young, I suppose I must be satisfied with Lucasta, as long as I might be assured she's a maid. I never cared for redheads. She's too old for me in truth and thin at the hips, but at the very least, you can promise me she's untouched?"

Of course he would rather have her passive, sweet-natured, half-sister Anne, but little Anne was lucky. Their father had higher expectations for his favorite younger daughter and was much more eager to be rid of the troublesome, past-her-prime Lucy to the first man remotely willing. Lord Winton was also "old nobility," something her ambitious parvenu father looked up to and aspired to be. Thus the marriage was all arranged and Lucy, however hard she prayed, had no more chance of preventing it than King Canute had of turning back the tide. Her prayers she'd learned while still a child were not heeded. She must have done something very wicked as a babe, something unforgivable in God's eyes.

It was years since she'd cried, twenty at least, but tonight sobs choked in her throat. Salty tears seeped into the leather mask. She lay with her head on his shoulder, one hand stroking the contours of his hard, sweat-dampened body, consigning it to memory. After having worried over the time all evening, she now forgot it completely, for in his arms she felt needed, desired for once. She wanted to make it last longer, as long as she dared. Nothing existed beyond the two of them, nothing but the moon, the stars and the rain.

Gone was anxiety and practicality and reason, gone was one frost-hardened, affection-starved, tightly-wound maiden. Lucy sensed the unfurling, the thawing. She was now a woman undone, awakened to passion.

"Can we do it again, soon?" she whispered, needing all other thoughts erased by more of those wondrous, intemperate sensations. "Please," she added, remembering he liked her to say that.

* * * *

With his fingers, John slowly traversed the steep valley of her waist.

"Again already? If you insist, wench." He rolled his eyes, feigning weariness, but the heat was already rekindled. This could be dangerous. He glanced down at his rampant shaft, incredibly eager for more. Good thing it was only for one night.

"I do insist," she exclaimed. "Please," she added belatedly.

He lifted up onto one arm, looking down at her, quizzical, trying to get her straight in his head. Appearances deceived, for while she seemed fragile, she was delightfully limber, supple and, so it seemed, tireless. If she were sore, as she certainly should be, the wench made no complaint. Instead her only concerns were whether he'd enjoyed himself and how quickly they might play again. He wound a lock of her hair around his forefinger while he pondered the enigma in bed beside him. "Will you take off that mask this time, woman?"

"No." Her hands flew up to hold it. "Please," she added again, a quick pupil.

"You're being very polite now," he observed dryly.

"Yes. I'll do anything you ask, but

not that."

The sadness in her voice made him relent. This kind streak, he thought dourly, would be the death of him one day. But still, the offer of anything else he wanted from her...that wasn't easily passed up now, was it?

She was dewy, tender, pliant and ravishable. Even so, she held something back, kept her secrets behind that mask. It troubled him, but there was no time to let worries linger when other primal needs took precedence.

What just happened to him was new and unexpected, even a little frightening. It took all his willpower to withdraw from her in that last heart-stopping minute, when he longed to spend inside. Yet he'd always been careful before with women; he never got so carried away he forgot the danger. Tonight...tonight was different in many ways.

So she'd been a maiden, after all. It hadn't been a trick, or part of an act. He hadn't been entirely sure until he breached her tender barrier, and now he didn't know what he felt about being her first. It was a first for him too. He'd never had a virgin.

With her head cradled in the curve of his shoulder, her slender form locked against his, her feathery breaths caressing his chest, he celebrated his amazing good fortune and smiled a little into the shifting shadows of the rainy evening.

Anything else? Well now, let's see...

Grabbing her around the waist, he dropped onto his back again and let her lie over him.

Hmm...he gazed at her full lips, at her pretty breasts pillowed against his chest, and as she moved restlessly over his body, he let his hands sweep down to hold the smooth, firm curves of her sweet little bottom. She was perfection. He couldn't have dreamed anything this fine, surely. He didn't think his imagination was that good.

"Let's do it all," she whispered, endearingly winsome now, her hands on his shoulders as she settled over him. "All those things you said before. Everything. Anything you want."

Her words enflamed him. He tightened his hold on the cheeks of her bottom and when she kissed his chin, her tongue licking his stubble, the effect on him was not unlike that of his mother's deadly plum wine. And he was ready to wallow in it. She was incredible.

Everything? How much, exactly, had Nathaniel paid her?

"Take all of me." Her voice was smoky with yearning. "Leave

nothing for him."

She didn't have to implore like this, but apparently she thought it necessary and who was he to correct her?

Everything?

He would gladly, and very ably, concede.

After all, it was only for one night. He'd manage without sleep.

Chapter 4

Take all of me. Leave nothing for him.

He woke with a start, sitting up in bed. His head ached, his tongue cracked as he forced it to unstick from the roof of his mouth. How much had he drunk last night? He often suffered vivid dreams as a result, but this one had been a wonderful fantasy indeed.

Anxious, he looked down at his body. The parts were all exactly where they should be, but there on the mattress, and on his crumpled shirt, discarded on the floor, was evidence that he'd not spent the night alone. So she wasn't a dream this time. In fact, he couldn't have been asleep for long. Although shredded gray clouds streaked across a dirty yellow sun outside the small window, he knew he'd only finally closed his eyes to sleep a short while ago, no more than an hour or two. They'd spent all night long exploring and entertaining one another, discovering new paths to pleasure. They'd been tireless, the sensations too intense to let go, time too precious to waste in sleep.

He fell back on his elbows, blinking, waiting for his head to clear. The three sovereigns she'd promised were on the table beside the bed.

This arrangement is just for tonight, you understand.

As he swung his feet to the floorboards, still scratching his rumpled head, he stepped on something hard. A pearl earring. It must have dropped from her ear last night, or else, leaving in such a hurry, she accidentally left it behind.

The sun was a tired weakling, barely having the strength to pass through those dingy clouds and there was a damp bite of cold in the air, lingering from last night's rain. Encountering such a dreary day, most folk would curl back to bed and steal an extra half hour's nap, but not him. He'd never lain abed a day in his life and on this particular morning he had a very important cause to be up.

He had a woman to find.

Take all of me, leave nothing for him.

He didn't like the sound of it, not a bit. She wasn't going to any other man, not now. She belonged to him, damn her. He couldn't bed a virgin and then arbitrarily let her go with no further concern. He was a reformed man now, no longer a rogue whose first interest was his pleasure and second interest escape from consequences.

Throwing on his clothes, he relived their conversation in his mind, searching for clues. She seemed to think he would have no more curiosity, would make do with one night and never think of her again. Last night he'd even let himself believe he might do that.

Wrong.

Stumbling down the narrow staircase, he was immediately cloaked in thick, woolly wood-smoke and the stink of stale sweat. A handful of fellows still sprawled across the lower room in varied states of drunkenness, while Mistress Comfort genially pushed at their groaning forms with her broom.

"Wake up yer lazy buggers," she chirped. "Rise and shine! Off out of 'ere with the lot o' yer." Having taken their coin, she wanted nothing more to do with her patrons until they had full pockets again. Catching sight of the man lurching down the stairs, she shouted that she hoped he had a good night and would return again soon.

He groggily negotiated the last step. "Where is she this morning? Where did she go?"

"How would I know?" She resumed sweeping.

"She's one of your girls."

"I wish it was so. Could raise my rates then."

He tried to get his breath back. A great, heaving hollow opened up in his gut, as panic, a rare sensation in his life, reared its head.

"First time a lady ever paid for the use o' one o' my guests," she exclaimed, clearly amused. "Perhaps I might start a new trade, eh? Lonely widows and bored wives looking for forbidden fruit." She eyed him speculatively. "I suppose she wanted some very strange things, eh? The hoity-toity types often do."

He swore. "You're telling me you know nothing about her? She didn't just appear in a puff of smoke."

"Might as well have. Yer won't find her again. She ain't from around here, 'tis for certes. A lady like her won't have naught to do with the likes o' yer sort. Not in daylight anyhow. She took what she wanted from yer, lad."

As she shuffled away down the alley, he followed close on her heels. "When did she leave?"

"First light. Told me to let yer sleep on as long as yer wished and tipped me a few more coins to let yer rest." The old lady cackled. "Wore yer out did she?"

Frustrated, he exclaimed, "Did Captain Downing come here last night? He must know who she is."

Mistress Comfort spat over her shoulder. "A fine lady like that would have naught to do with Nate Downing, my lad. No, whoever she is, yer won't find her again."

John stared at the wall, the anger mounting from a small, smoldering bonfire to a raging inferno.

Whoever she was, she'd used him and cast him aside like a dry, stale crust.

"Best forgotten, lad," the old lady added. "I daresay she's forgot it already."

His pride didn't want to believe it, but she was probably right. A woman who discarded her virtue in the bed of a complete stranger was obviously trouble.

But those words haunted him.

Take all of me. Leave nothing for him.

* * * *

He spent the morning searching Norwich, making inquiries around the town. Unfortunately he had no clear description of her face, only her lips. As for her hair, there might be fifty women with red hair in the town and everyone had their own opinion as to what was red, what was ginger, chestnut, fair or auburn. He was whistling against the wind and he had work to do at home. Spring plowing and planting wouldn't wait. Turning reluctantly to one last matter of business before he left Norwich, he drove his cart to the large, rambling house of Lord Winton, a notoriously slippery old character who owed him for several weight of good fleeces.

A harried servant finally came in answer to the seventh pull on the bell cord at the gate. Fortunately he knew John by sight, knew him to be a good fellow who always bought a round at the high street tavern on market day and who had, more than once, helped out in a fight. When John explained his purpose, the servant unlocked the gate and let him in, warning he'd be lucky to get a penny.

"Until after tomorrow," he added with a sly wink. "Then I daresay the old man will be flush again for a while. Should come back after Friday, young feller, after the wedding."

"Wedding?"

"Aye he's to be married again on the morrow. Rich young lady with a weighty dowry."

John shook his head. "I can't wait here until Saturday. He'll have to pay up today."

The servant led him through the great hall, currently being decorated with bowers of greenery in preparation for the feast, and into a small, paneled chamber off to one side, where three busy, overworked tailors gave Lord Walter Winton a final fitting for his garish wedding clothes.

"Master John Carver is here, my lord," the servant intoned solemnly. "A matter of business regarding fleeces."

The old man didn't need to be told. He knew who John was and why he was there, but when it came to matters of money he maintained a curiously frangible memory. Bills due had a tendency to cause sudden illness, but the old man was far stronger than he looked. His gnarled, trembling hands, the wrinkled skin thin as gauze, might seem feeble, unfit for any purpose, but it was all an act. Those claws held onto his money purse with the deadly grip of an iron-toothed mantrap.

Irritably regarding John's arrival that afternoon as a great inconvenience, his eyes misted over, his back stooped and he snapped out for a chair, exclaiming he'd stood too long and his knees would no longer bear the strain. "I cannot think why you bother me with this today, of all days," he muttered in John's direction. "You young people have no sense of decorum, no manners, no respect for your elders."

"I'll be on my way and disturb you not a moment longer, Lord Winton, once you pay me what I'm owed for those fleeces, fair and square."

"Fair and square indeed! You cheating young scoundrel. I know you look to overcharge me," the old man grumbled, "and I suppose you come here today, thinking I will be in a charitable mood on the verge of my forthcoming nuptials."

Accustomed to Winton's delay tactics, he waited, saying nothing, looking down at his fists.

"Can you not see this is the very worst of times to come begging for coin, Carver? I have far more important matters at hand." With a groan, clutching his chest, the old man stumbled back into the chair he was provided. A loud ripping sound caused one of the tailors to throw up his hands in despair and this too was blamed on John's presence. "There, now. See? I split my dratted breeches."

Stepping up to his chair, John leaned over the wrinkled fellow and hissed, "I'll take what I'm owed, Winton. Or your tailors will have more to fix than that hole in your backside."

"How dare you threaten me, you young rapscallion!"

"How dare you steal from me!" After the morning he'd suffered, John's temper was easily baited.

"Steal?"

"To take without paying is stealing.

You're no better than a common thief."

Now the old man shriveled in his chair, falling back on age and decrepitude. "To be so spoken to and threatened in my own home. What is this town coming to?"

John held out his hand, palm up. "The coin, Winton. Give it to me, as agreed yesterday, and I'll be on my way."

"I can pay you a third today and the rest at the end of the month."

"I'm not coming all the way back to Norwich just to collect what you owe me."

"Then I'll send it."

"As if I'd trust you again."

The old man's gaze turned sharp, greedy. His dry lips curled, showing small, pointy, yellow teeth. "A gentleman's agreement, Carver. Is that not what you aspire to be these days, a gentleman farmer? Did you not vow to turn a new leaf? Your mother swears you've changed. The last time she pleaded for you, when you were up before me for brawling yet again, she promised you were a reformed man, tending the family farm, looking after her, ready to settle down. Did she lie, Carver? Did your mother perjure herself to me?"

Squinting, trying to restrain his temper, John straightened up, hands on his hips. Winton knew all too well what the mention of his mother would do.

"Take one quarter and you will get the rest when I have it," Winton continued, spitting out his words, "when I am satisfied those fleeces are the quality you claim."

"You haven't looked at them yet?"

"I haven't the time, Carver," the old man exclaimed. "I have a wedding tomorrow." Waving his hand weakly, he coughed. "Now get out of my house or I shall have you banned from trading in the market here. No one in this county will touch your wares, if I spread the word. I've ruined better men than you."

He knew it was true. Winton was a foul, spiteful, cunning old wretch who must have made a pact with Satan to live this long. But he was also the local Justice of the Peace and it was not wise to make him an enemy. Although most folk in Norwich hated him with a passion, they avoided confrontation and simply waited for him to die.

"I'll get my payment from you, Winton. One way or another."

The servant held the door open for him and John swept out.

* * * *

Lucy thought she'd heard a door slam somewhere in the house, but none of the other women noticed. Seated in a small, tidy circle, bent over their embroidery, they worked without pause, occasionally whispering to one another, but mostly silent. Turning her head, she stared at the dull sky through the solar window, betaken with a sudden whimsical idea of leaping out and stealing a ride on one of those rippled clouds.

Even the pensive sigh she exhaled went unheard by her companions, or at least ignored. Her half-sister, Anne, kept her head bowed as she worked, her pretty eyelashes occasionally blinking, the only part of her, other than her fingers, that showed any movement. Lucy often wondered what went on inside Anne's head and amused herself by picturing a world of bright rainbows and skipping coneys. Of course, it was more than likely that absolutely nothing went on inside that head, but there was always hope. Anne's mother sat beside her, struggling with plump fingers to thread a needle. The other women, Lord Winton's aged sister and two sour-faced nieces, huddled together, hands working in unison, never faltering, even when one of them flung a cold, resentful glance in Lucy's direction.

Horses whinnied in the yard and wheels rumbled over cobbles.

Probably another tradesman bringing items for the wedding feast tomorrow.

She heard a curse, whipped out low and furious. It came from directly below the open window. Her companions remained undisturbed. She was apparently the only curious soul among them. Rising quietly, she moved to the window and peered down over the ledge. The window squealed violently as she pushed it further open, but the man below was too annoyed, too busy talking to himself, to hear.

She saw the top of his dark head, the broad musculature of his shoulders, his rough hands reaching for the reins of his horse. A brief gleam of blue was apparent, even from that distance, as he looked up, tracking the flight of a pigeon. On instinct she ducked aside. Had he seen her?

Her stomach tightened.

It was him. He'd come for her.

She ought to shout down a warning, tell him to leave, but nothing came out. Her tongue was too thick, blocking the sounds. Panicking, she turned away from the window too quickly, her kirtle knocking over her chair.

Anne finally raised her lashes and asked if she were quite well. "You look very pale, Lucy."

With quaking hands, she set the chair upright and lowered herself to the seat. "It was naught," she muttered, straightening her skirt. "Just a little dizziness."

"Must be the excitement of your wedding," Anne cooed, smiling foolishly.

"Yes. That must be it," said Lucy, who had never been excited by anything in her life, except the man in the courtyard below.

He must have followed her there.

She was sick, her palms damp and hot.

He had come for her. It was sheer folly.

Ruth, her maid, silently passed the sewing she'd dropped and then, at the urging of one of the other women, closed the window.

"We don't want you getting ill, Lucy dear, the day before your wedding," Anne said. "Fresh air can be so very bad for one's complexion and sunlight causes freckles."

Lucy faintly heard her stepmother muttering that more freckles were one thing she didn't need. Lord Winton's nieces sullenly agreed.

Licking her lips, she glanced over at the door. Any moment now, all hell would break loose. Would her father arrive first, or would her lover dash in, sword at the ready, to fight for her? Just like a play.

What would she say? What would she do?

It was absurd. He was a peasant; she was the daughter of a wealthy, upward striving merchant and soon to marry into the nobility. She couldn't possibly go with him. Was he mad to come there and try to find her?

Anne would say it was romantic, but then Anne was sadly quite stupid and desperately naive.

She watched the door, nerves stretched taut, expecting it to burst open, to hear her name shouted in fury.

The moments passed. Nothing. No footsteps charged down the corridors of her fiance's house, no enraged voices were heard.

"Ruth," she turned to her maid, "is there anyone in the yard?"

The maid checked and shook her head. "No ma'am."

Her shoulders sank. Had she imagined him there?

"Just one of the tradesmen leaving on a cart, ma'am."

Leaving.

Leaving her behind.

She picked up her needle. Well, that was it. Might have known. Men, she knew from observing her brother and father, never looked very far when searching for something lost. Never moved anything, or looked behind it, just stood and gazed about indignantly, expecting the missing item to reappear. It was always left up to a woman to find it.

Her chance was gone.

She supposed she could run after him, scream through the window. But what would she scream? *Oy, Plowman? Shepherd? Yokel?* She didn't know his name.

No, it was wiser to remain where she was. At least she wouldn't starve or freeze to death in some humble, drafty, stone cottage. Here she had a fire, warm clothes, plenty of food, music, dancing and entertainments, such as he probably never even knew existed. Everything here was predictable and safe. There were many folk in the world far less fortunate than she was. She'd watched beggars fighting for scraps outside her father's gates in London.

And she'd had her night of fun.

If she ever wanted to experience another world again, all she need do was go to the theatre and watch a play, living love, tragedy and comedy all from a sheltered distance.

Much more prudent and practical.

She jabbed her needle into the cloth and pulled it slowly through. Another neat stitch in its place. Another moment of her life gone by. Years from now that stitch would be all that remained to prove she ever lived and breathed.

* * * *

Perhaps it was better this way, he thought. Evidently she didn't want to know him. She'd made it clear what happened between them was for one night only.

Did she think of him at all tonight?

It felt a lot longer than twenty-four hours since he'd walked into a bedchamber and seen her there in her leather mask. Sometimes he still thought he might have dreamed it, but of all the women to conjure out of his dreams, why create one like her? Why not a gentle-tempered, demure, unquestioning woman who let him make all the demands, the way it was supposed to be? Plenty of pretty lasses at home competed for his notice, and there was Alice Croft, a good girl, just the sort he should find in his dreams, now he was reformed.

But instead there was this determined, deliciously abandoned creature, who had the gall to throw three sovereigns at him, supposedly in exchange for the services of his cock, probably another of Nathaniel's jokes, and never wanted to see him again. She was the one who would haunt him forever; he knew it as surely as he knew the sun would rise and set again tomorrow.

She was insatiable. Wildfire.

If only she'd stayed longer, he might have persuaded her to take off the mask. They could have talked, made better sense of it all. He'd never felt such a connection with any other woman, never really cared to know what they were thinking, what troubled them, what made them laugh, or what made them cry. With her it was all new.

He couldn't get the vixen out of his mind. All the things they'd done, sometimes savage, sometimes gentle. He remembered the cries of wanton delight from her lush lips, the funny, refined way she had of saying "please," once she'd learned what it won for her.

He concluded that this must be some form of self-punishment. His conscience tried to make him feel guilt for the lackadaisical way he'd treated women in the past. This curious event at Mistress Comfort's proved how little he liked to be used and then forgotten. Women, he supposed reluctantly, must feel the same way when a man turned his back, or left the bed before they woke and never bothered to say goodbye.

Just as *she'd* done to him.

Shaking his head, he flipped the reins lightly, urging the horse onward and homeward.

"Red sky at night," he muttered, looking up at the setting horizon, "shepherd's delight."

Chapter 5

What a curious color the sky was this evening, almost blood red. In an unusual, day-dreamy state, Lucy stared out of her bedchamber window, watching a slow, hot blush spread above the rooftops and chimneys. Finally she focused her drifting gaze on her stepmother's face, crookedly reflected there beside her own in the leaded glass, and then she came back to earth with a thud.

"Truly, it matters not to me," Lucy exclaimed. "You need not fuss." She brushed away her stepmother's plump hands, where they hovered around her shoulders like two nervous, over-fed sparrows. "I don't need the necklace in any case." This woman had never been motherly, and her last-minute attempt to be so now made Lucy's skin crawl.

"But I wanted to give you something for the wedding, Lucasta."

"I'm sure Anne will get more use out of it and besides, she has the bearing and the beauty for fine jewels. I would only lose it, no doubt, or break it."

In the window, she watched her stepmother turn away, wringing her hands, making an extravagant show, when, to be sure, there was never the slightest intention of giving Lucy her necklace.

"I really don't mind," she repeated firmly. "Anne should have it when she marries. I would never do it credit."

But when her stepmother suffered guilt, she talked herself from one lie to the next and there was no stopping her. "I always meant for you to wear the necklace when you married."

Lucy smiled wryly, turning away from the window. "I thought you expected me to die an old maid."

Her stepmother feigned affront, as if the idea of Lucy remaining a spinster, financially reliant on her father, never once occurred to her. "I knew you would marry eventually, Lucasta, of course, despite that willful temper."

"As soon as father found someone desperate enough to take me on."

Although she should be accustomed to Lucy's sharp tongue by now, her stepmother made a show of being shocked and appalled by it. "You should not speak so, Lucasta. If only you might have learned a little softness, for I fear that cold tone will not please Lord Winton. It makes you sound ungrateful and churlish."

God forbid. "Keep the necklace until Anne marries. Is there anything else you wanted?" After the exertions of the previous evening, she looked forward to her bed, her last night of freedom. Her stepmother being all "concerned" for her only multiplied the dread of what tomorrow would bring.

"Well, I'll bid you goodnight then, Lucasta." The woman finally retreated.

No sooner had the door closed behind her then there was another loud knock. She thought it was Anne, come to make certain that necklace was still hers, but it was not her half-sister, it was her elder brother, Lancelot, in a cheerful mood, eager to pinch her cheeks and tease.

"I don't know why you ever agreed to it, Luce," he exclaimed, pushing his way in. "I thought you'd die an old maid."

She knew this was exactly what they all thought, although only Lance would have the impertinent guts to say it. Her brother might wonder why she now agreed to go like a lamb to the slaughter, but Lucy understood the way the world worked, even if she didn't agree with it. Unless she married, there was no use for her. It was so for all women and the older she became, the narrower the pool of potential husbands. As her father had kindly pointed out, Lord Winton's might well be her last offer.

She'd had her share of suitors over the years, most attracted to her bridal purse, none pleasing enough to encourage. With one cool, imperious glance, one sniff of contempt, she erected a set of forbidding, barbed walls before which even the bravest of knights would fail. She had exhibited no desire to please her suitors, showed none of the meek subservience expected of a wife, and was often reprimanded for a "smug and superior" facial expression. Few men would tolerate her disagreeable manner, when there were other women, younger, more pliant, biddable and willing, not to mention grateful. In the eyes of many she was an old maid now, a liability and a burden on her father, whose patience she'd worn beyond its limits. Not that he'd ever had much for her in any case. Finally, since she'd continued to hold suitors at bay with her icy demeanor, he'd chosen a husband for her.

Lucy's dowry would compensate Lord Winton for the inconvenience of marrying her and he was willing to overlook her many failings, as long as she was a virgin. Ironically, this man in his sixties considered her, at twenty-six, too old for him. She'd heard he kept a mistress, so it was unlikely he would share a marital bed with her very often, if at all. Thank the Lord!

All things considered, she didn't expect this marriage to trouble her unduly. She would survive in a loveless union, she supposed, as other women in her shoes managed. If they did it, so could she. Her choices, she believed, were practical, made with a cool head, no fanciful expectations of the slightest happiness. Once married, her life wouldn't change much from what it was now, except she would have her own home to manage and no longer be obliged to witness her father's disapproving face each day, or hear her stepmother making loud, awkward excuses to all and sundry for why she remained unwed.

Neither would she need to put up with her brother's teasing.

Striding across the room, Lance asked if there was any advice she might need for the wedding night. Seven years her senior, he often took it upon himself to counsel her, whether she welcomed his "wisdom" or not. Tonight she was tempted to reply that there was nothing he could tell her. After her romp at Mistress Comfort's, she was certainly no longer a blushing innocent. The memory of it brought a slight smile to her lips, which, fortunately, Lance, who could be extremely straitlaced and disapproving, didn't see. Throughout the day, she'd caught herself reliving the previous evening's adventure and smiling stupidly. But then something would intrude to bring her feet back to earth and her lips would straighten at once into the somber expression she usually saw staring back at her in any reflective surface.

Why had her mystery man come to Lord Winton's house that day? Fearful of rousing suspicion, she daren't ask anyone about him, and her maid had been unable to find anything out.

She sat by her mirror, one trembling hand reaching for the hair brush, anxious for something to quell her restless fidgeting. "I don't suppose old Winton will trouble me often," she murmured, while Lance critically surveyed his own reflection over her head. "He has a mistress, a fat ale-wife in Cambridge, I understand."

"Ah, but he needs an heir to inherit his title and estate, sister." He winked at her in the mirror. "Best get to it at once. We wouldn't want him bringing you back again, if you fail to fulfill your duty. No returns!"

She smiled stiffly. "Thank you for your counsel, Lance. I shall, as always, pay it the reverence it deserves."

"Now, now, sister. I warn you only for your own good." He ran a hand over his closely cropped hair. "And make sure it's a son. Girls are next to useless, as you know."

Frowning, she slammed her brush down on the dresser. "And when will you consider marriage, Lance? When will you fulfill *your* duty?"

He threw back his head, laughing loudly. "At the last possible moment before they put me in the ground." Although their father had not so subtly pushed Lancelot in the direction of marriage for the last few years, her brother still dug in his heels. Being a man, he might take his time choosing a wife and his standards were impossibly high. Lucy knew why. With such ridiculous requirements and expectations to be met, Lance always had an excuse not to fall in love. Like her, he saved himself from heartache. In the Collyer family, emotions were anathema, a weakness they couldn't tolerate in themselves or anyone else. For Lance, of course, it was more acceptable he behave that way. Men were supposed to hold their emotions in check and, as he often said, "A man is only as strong as his stiff upper lip."

But Lucy, previously as impassive and impenetrable as her brother, currently suffered some strange, unwanted feelings. They careened in circles within her, like playful, rambunctious kittens escaping a basket. No matter how many times she caught them and put them back, the little rebels found a way out again, eager to go exploring. Her notorious Collyer indifference was apparently thawing.

Leaving her brother worriedly inspecting his faultless appearance in the mirror, she wandered back to the window and contemplated the bloody sunset dripping over a cluster of Norwich rooftops.

Where was her farm-hand now? Would he go back to the bawdy house? She didn't like to think of him with another woman and that annoyed her. Until now she never knew herself to be the fussy, possessive sort and certainly had no right to be in his case. Oh, but the mere thought of him smiling at another woman sent her belly into a rapid churn.

While her brother chatted away behind her, she ran a fingertip along the lead strips in the window. All her life she'd stared out of windows like this one, wondering what happened on the other side. Now she knew.

As her father would say, *knowledge can be a dangerous thing in the wrong hands.* In her case, Lucy was inclined to agree.

After her nighttime exploit at the bawdy house, she'd expected to feel less stifled anger toward the hypocrisy and double-standard, yet the experience only made her view life with even greater dissatisfaction. Rather than diminish the hidden flame of rebellion, her one night with a stranger breathed more air into the fire, like a hearty pump of the bellows. She was afraid she might let something out if she didn't soon manage to control it again, smother it along with all her other needs, wants and emotions.

"I suppose I'll miss you, Luce," Lance said, struggling to express a feeling he barely allowed himself. "If you need anything, you must write to me."

He'd always been protective of Lucy, but in recent years she'd felt him drifting away, his sex giving him many freedoms to come and go, while hers kept her confined. Still, she realized helplessly how much she adored her brother, despite the inequity. If only he relaxed once in a while. What he needed, she thought with a sudden devious smile at her own reflection in the window, was a night like the one she just enjoyed. A night of anonymous pleasure, of letting go at last.

"I'm sure you'll soon forget me, Lance. When you return to London you will have many distracting entertainments." Swinging around to face him, she teasingly named the many and varied young ladies who chased after him, much to his mortification. "You won't be able to avoid our father's ambitions much longer, you know," she added. "He grows more and more keen on the idea of you marrying Lady Catherine Mallory and you won't wriggle out of it forever. You and Lady Catherine, the Earl of Swafford's eldest daughter..."

His face reddened, his shoulders squared, and then he was off on a familiar tirade against that particular young lady, whom he swore he would not marry if she was the last woman left standing. She was, he declared, a vengeful harpy, a savage, with a very bad temper and possibly a tendency to insanity. He had not, in actual fact, seen the girl in some time and, as far as Lucy knew, all this fuss was simply because, years ago, Catherine Mallory bit him on the buttocks, right through his breeches. There was hardly a soul left in England who hadn't heard the tale, or been shown the non-existent teeth marks. An elderly maiden aunt once fainted into her supper when Lance dropped his breeches abruptly to illustrate the story. He would never let anyone forget, nor would he ever forgive the miscreant, and although their father was eager for a match binding the upstart Collyer name to an ancient, noble family like the Mallorys of Dorset, whose pedigree reached back to the Norman Conquest, it would be an uphill struggle indeed to change Lancelot's stubborn mind.

In the meantime, their father appeased his need for control by marrying his eldest daughter off.

Lance took her hand, bowed his handsome head and planted a kiss on her knuckles. "Now don't forget. Write to me, Lucy, if you're ever in need... of...anything."

"And what shall you do?"

He straightened up, face flushed. "Help you, of course! You're my damned little sister, after all. No matter how irritating."

"Thank you, brother. I'll remember that."

"Yes...well." He nodded, frowning. "Good night then and...good luck."

Once her brother departed, she turned thankfully to her bed again, only to be stopped by yet another late-night visitor.

Sir Oliver Collyer was a tall, spare man with graying hair receding a good few inches from his brow, giving his head the appearance of a goose egg. To make up for the lack of coverage on top, he wore a bodkin beard and let his hair grow longer down the back, so it sat upon his shoulders and his wide, lace-trimmed ruff in a thin straggle. His second wife, for whom appearances were so important, constantly fought to make him cut his hair, but he stubbornly prevailed in the battle. He would not be told what to do, or how to cut his hair, by any woman.

His fortune was acquired through overseas trade and further increased by a successful money-lending service to various needy gentlemen, even the occasional peer of the realm. Twenty years ago he reached a pinnacle when he earned his Knighthood. Now he forgot how his own father was a mere shopkeeper, his mother an illiterate worsted weaver. Nothing was ever quite good enough for him. Other people disappointed more often than they pleased, and his eldest daughter knew she was the worst offender.

Rather than enter her chamber, he stood at the threshold, hands behind his back, head stooped so as not to bang his forehead on the lintel.

"I trust you're well prepared for tomorrow," he intoned gravely, his gaze skimming the room suspiciously, expecting, no doubt, to find several pots bubbling over with witches' potions. All women were a mystery to her father, but none more than she. He never looked at her, she knew, without remembering she was the reason her mother died. Lucy had heard the servants say his first marriage was a love match, a most unusual thing, and her father had never fully recovered from the loss. In his eyes, it had been all Lucy's fault. But surely, she thought sadly, since her mother almost died after Lancelot's birth and had been advised by the physicians never to attempt another child, their father was at least partly to blame for the pregnancy occurring seven years later, bringing his daughter into the world and taking his wife out of it in the same breath.

As a babe she'd been left to the care of nurses, given every luxury money could buy, but no genuine love or affection. She found his late effort now oddly unsettling, so, once again, like her stepmother's strange affections, his unusual attention fell upon cold, stony ground.

"Yes, thank you, sir," she said, as it was the only thing she could think to say.

Again he glanced around the chamber. "It is good you finally came to your senses and agreed to this arrangement."

It is good. Couldn't he say he was pleased?

She supposed he looked forward to concentrating all his efforts now on the much worthier Anne, who was bound to make a very advantageous marriage to someone far wealthier and more consequential than Lord Winton. Anne was a paragon of virtue, that most precious of all things, an obedient woman. She was beautiful, empty-headed, unquestioning.

Her father put out his hand and Lucy, seeing naught else for it, accepted the gesture. They were like two relative strangers sealing a matter of business.

"You're quite certain?" he asked.

"Yes, sir."

There was something wary in his eye. Alarmed, she thought he might know something of her escapade the previous evening. But it passed. He nodded briskly, turned on his heel and was gone.

Closing the door behind him, she rested against it, regrouping her spinning thoughts. Why would he say such a thing to her now, on the last night? It was surely too late for second thoughts. What would he have done if she'd said, *No, sir, I don't want to marry Lord Winton. If 'tis all the same to you, I think I'll run back to the bawdy house, find my lover and live with him instead?*

Having endured her fill of family concern, she bolted her door and blew out the candle, determined not to receive another guest tonight. She ran to the bed and leapt under the covers, eager to dream of her once-in-a-lifetime lover while she still had his scent on her skin.

* * * *

The morning passed in a flurry, everyone darting around her, fussing over her gown and headdress, all those things that didn't matter, but her mind was far away from it all, living in a strange fantasy, as if she still dreamed and nothing would wake her.

She imagined herself living on a farm with her lover. Her life was filled with work and she was never idle, but she was happy, as she'd never been before in her life, and she wanted to cry with gladness. She smelled lavender and honeysuckle. The sunlight was a warm kiss drifting across her brow and a tall iron gate cooed on its hinges before clanging shut, as if someone had just passed through it. She wore a loose gown, no crippling corset, and her hair was tied back with a simple, frayed, plunket ribbon. The image was all golden sunshine and the sweet song of birds, just as she thought heaven must be for those who deserved it, but she felt unworthy of her dream. Her heart, the organ she'd protected in a shell all her life, now ached. The barrier was breached. But she must have been happy before, at some point in her real life, surely?

No. Never like it was in her dream.

For as long as she remembered there'd been only fear, guilt and doubt crowding into her mind each day. Even as a child she'd had the worries of an adult pressing on her shoulders, no fancy for games and toys. There was no pleasure simply for the sake of it. There was trial, the constant struggle for her father's forgiveness and approval. From her earliest years she was aware of dark things most children still were not. Knowing her mother had died, she lived in fear that death would take her father, too, and her brother. If it took one important person away from her, it could take anyone, could it not? Their father married again quickly and seemingly put it out of his mind, leaving his children to founder with a great gaping hole in their lives, unexplained, a matter never to be discussed. Lucy, for many of her childhood years, believed she was entirely responsible for her mother's death. What else might account for her father's cold distance, the way his eyes avoided her, the disappointment in his countenance?

Yet in this strange daydream which began the night before her wedding day, she was fully content, blissful. And she knew then that she'd never been truly happy. Sorrow and self-pity, that most wasteful of all emotions, ripped through her, left her torn in a thousand ragged, bloody pieces.

This was all *his* fault, she thought angrily. His fault for giving her something she'd never known existed until two nights ago, forcing her to feel, forcing her to know what it was to be alive for once. The little pastoral fantasy lived in her head now and wouldn't come out. It was an infection, cruel and deadly.

But perhaps, finally, today she would raise a smile from her father's lips. By marrying Lord Winton she would surely please him. Surely.

This morning, however, his expression was grim and dour. He avoided her gaze. He was more concerned about who would attend the wedding feast than about the bride's welfare. There was no kiss upon her cheek, no whisper of pride, no tenderness. He looked over her gown briefly, ensuring she looked the part and wouldn't embarrass him. Then he turned away.

It didn't matter, she told herself. This was the way it was meant to be and she would go on as if the interlude with the stranger never happened. Feeling sorry for herself wouldn't help. Thinking of her stranger wouldn't help. He'd been for one night only. She knew that and had made the most of it. Now she must get on with her life, such as it was. This was the bargain she'd made with herself, so why was it so hard now to contemplate?

The more she tried to salvage her unraveled nerves, the more her stitches fell slowly apart.

"Are you all right?" Lance whispered in her ear, his breath gently moving the veil of her ornate headdress. "Luce?"

Looking down at her hand on his arm, she tried her best to stop trembling. Somehow her brother's anxious expression made it all much worse. Shameful, childish tears threatened. Taking another stifled breath, she squeezed her brother's hand until she must have crushed the bones in his fingers, but he was gallant today. For once he didn't tease her.

She pictured her needle making another stitch.

Here I lived once. Remember me.

But she didn't live, she existed. Only now had she opened her eyes, fully awake, to see the truth.

Chapter 6

The feast went smoothly. The toasts were said, the dances danced, songs sung and all the guests dutifully declared her a beautiful bride. They lied between their teeth.

Now she and her groom were carried to their bedchamber, amid much raucous hilarity, at which she must pretend to blush with maidenly timidity. Well, now Lord Winton would discover he was already a cuckold. Somehow it was not quite so amusing as it had seemed two nights ago. When the servants withdrew, the awful finality of her situation struck her.

Almost as hard as the back of his hand across her face, the moment his bedchamber door closed behind them.

Finding herself on the floor, dizzy and startled, she put one hand to her cheek and felt warm blood from the cut of his ring. A second blow and then a third left her numb, disorientated. She stared at his yellowed, over-long toenails. A long-legged spider ran by her line of sight, scuttling across the dusty floorboards and under the bed, narrowly missing his trampling feet.

"May that teach you a lesson, wife," he said sharply, standing over her in his nightgown and a long overcoat of heavy brocade. "From now on you will pay attention when I speak to you and you will look at me without that countenance of smug disdain. Do you understand?"

His voice echoed inside her aching head.

"Get up." He kicked her in the side. "I tolerated your rude manners all week, but for the last time. Yesterday you were still your father's daughter. Now you're my wife and your behavior is mine to correct, your discipline mine to maintain. We shall begin as we mean to go on."

He moved away from her, limping heavily on his bad leg, and perched on the end of the bed to soak his feet in a bowl of scented water.

Slowly she sat up, wincing at the pain in her side, wiping her bloodied cheek on the sleeve of her shift. If he'd given her this, just for looking at him the wrong way, what would he do when he discovered she was not the pure maid her father once guaranteed?

She'd not known he possessed a violent temper. He always appeared too frail to be any physical danger, and, of course, he put on a gentlemanly act for her father, but tonight she felt the spiteful strength of those mean, gnarled hands, willing to cause hurt for even the slightest reason.

Still dizzy, she scrambled to her feet. He was stooped over, rubbing his aching corns. The sight of his thin, bony legs, so pale they were almost blue, disgusted her.

"Get on the bed and prepare yourself," he instructed her grumpily. "I'll be with you in due course. Lie on your back and lift your shift. Up over your breasts. I'll need something to look at other than your sulky, defiant face." He spat his words over one crooked shoulder. "Surely your maid warned you what to expect. I've no inclination to tutor you."

Blood in her mouth. She must have bitten her tongue. She looked at that bed, an implement of torture, and saw the lump under the coverlet, where the servants forgot to remove the warming pan.

Lord Winton, apparently, hadn't noticed the oversight.

She pressed one hand into her side, as another, deeper breath burned through her ribs. Stupidly, she'd imagined she might be able to go through with this, for practical reasons and in some vain hope of pleasing her father, but it was impossible. All of it. However other women managed, she was not one of them. She simply couldn't do it, physically or mentally. There must be something wrong with her, but she was not willing to settle for duty, to lie down and have the life smothered out of her.

Winton was humming a tune, intent on the relief of his own aches and pains. She carefully removed the pan of coals from beneath the coverlet and stood behind him with it, her arms shaking.

"The consummation should not take long," he muttered. "Just lie still and don't fuss. I hope you're fertile and strong enough to carry a living son to full term. You look too skinny and thin at the hips, but your father assures me you're from hearty stock and likely to breed well. Six and twenty is older than I would have chosen to mother my first child. In fact you're too old in most respects. Still," he sighed heavily, staring down at his feet in the bowl of water, "I wasted my time and precious seed on the last four witless wenches, none of whom gave me a living heir, despite their youth. Thankfully they had the good grace to die quickly and leave me free to try again." He paused. "I recommend you try harder than they did, or else I'll have to deal with you the same as I did with them. A little hunger, I find, sharpens the appetite to please and a good beating makes every woman yield eventually. The occasional adoption of a scold's bridle will also cleanse you of that proud, superior expression, I daresay."

She swung the pan of coals at the back of his head.

* * * *

A hired litter took her through the crowded streets to Mistress Comfort's house on the other side of town. It was the only place she knew to look for him. She'd dressed hurriedly, thrown her hooded cloak over her shift and piled on as much jewelry as possible, any items of value she possessed. In half an hour, perhaps less, it would be curfew and then the streets would be empty, escape from the town impossible until daylight.

She had no thought of what would happen next or how she might explain herself, but she couldn't stay a moment longer with Lord Winton. It had all been a terrible mistake. Perhaps she was a coward and weaker than other women, but if she stayed there she would shrivel and die inside. She'd recently discovered that she was indeed a flesh and blood woman, not a block of ice. And she was not ready to go to her grave struggling to bring one of Winton's wretched offspring into the world. There was more fight in her than she'd ever suspected.

Mistress Comfort saw her enter the smoky parlor at once and scurried over, shoving aside her less well-heeled patrons. "Madam, we're honored again," she exclaimed. "Ye wish to choose another fellow from among--"

"No. The man I had before. Is he here?"

The old lady looked taken aback. "No, Madam. Like I told ye last time, he's not one of my regulars. I never saw him before. But there are..."

Desperate, on the verge of tears, she spun away and collided at once with a broad chest in a slashed leather doublet. He had black curly hair, peppered with gray, a wide, rather wicked grin and clear, silver eyes which took her in with one skilled and hasty appraisal. "Looking for someone?" he yelled above the noise of the crowd. "May I introduce myself? Captain Nathaniel Downing. At your service." He swept a low, extravagant bow, almost spilling the contents of his tankard.

Annoyed, she tried to pass, but he stood in her way, shaking a finger in her face. "Don't look at me like that, madam. Whatever you've heard of me, I'm innocent. I've done nothing wrong." And then he grinned again, eyes shining. "Yet."

Nathaniel Downing. Where had she heard that name before? And then it came to her: the stranger had mentioned his name. She decided to take a chance. What did she have left to lose? Here she was, escaped from her bridal chamber, probably a hunted woman by now already, perhaps even a murderess. Her brother had left for London several hours ago and she had no one else to help her, no one to trust in this town.

"There was a man here the night before last. I must find him." Her hood fell back as she looked up at the stranger. "Can you help me? I believe you might know him, since he mentioned your name. I'll pay you well for any information."

"A man eh? What sort of man?"

"Dark haired. About your height, but stockier. He wore the clothes of a farm laborer."

"Handsome, eh?"

"He had a small scar across his right eyebrow and blue eyes, sometimes green."

He stared at her thoughtfully. "What did he do? Manhandle you? Did he insult you or pick your pockets?"

She frowned. "No. He...." She stopped, leaning back. "Don't touch me!"

"What happened to you, then?" he demanded, turning her face to the light. No longer grinning, he was deadly serious, as he examined the marks left by Lord Winton's hand and the heavy ring on his finger.

She pushed him away, wincing as the effort caused another throbbing ache in her side. "Do you know the man of whom I speak or not? If you can't help me, I waste time here with you. He mentioned your name and I..."

"Who are you?"

"Lucy," she said simply. After all, she was not legally Collyer anymore and she couldn't bear to say the name Winton.

He took her arm, drawing her away to a quieter corner of the parlor. "I might know this man of yours and I might not. What do you want with him?"

She wavered. What did she want with her mystery man? He was evidently poor, probably an indentured servant. He might even have a wife. She'd not considered that possibility until now. In all likelihood he wouldn't welcome her reappearance, especially since she'd promised there would be no complications after their night together.

"Is he in trouble?" Captain Downing asked, eyeing her warily. "What has he done now, eh? Did he do that to you?" He gestured at her stiff, swollen cheek.

"Of course not!" Afraid she might burst into tears like a child, she turned her face away, swallowing.

She saw a flutter in her side vision and flinched, but he'd only raised his arm to signal for another tankard. "You look like you need a drink, young lady. Have this one on me. And if you tell me your troubles, I'll do what I can to help. I don't like to see a lady cry."

Having thought she'd succeeded in holding them back, she was shocked to find her tears already spilled. Her bruised face was so numb she hadn't felt them fall, but Nathaniel Downing wiped them away with his fingers. Irritated by her own weakness, she shook them off. "There's no time to delay here," she said. "Please take me out of Norwich now, Captain." She showed him a bracelet of pearl and amethyst. "I will pay you for your trouble, but we must leave now, before curfew."

* * * *

Captain Downing had a very understanding ear and, he readily confessed, a fondness for damsels in distress. When they stopped at a tavern on the road east, she finally lowered her defenses enough to tell him of the husband who'd struck her. Outraged, the captain was ready to return to Norwich at once, find Winton and beat him to a pulp, but she restrained him, both hands on his arm.

"No! I don't want to go back there. I can't. I just want to leave and forget. I want to go far, far away, where he can never find me." She was not even certain if Winton was alive or dead. When she'd dragged his unconscious body up onto the bed and covered it, she'd thought she heard him breathing, but perhaps it had been merely her own gasps of exertion, for he was heavier than he looked, as well as stronger. She'd quickly extinguished all the candles and then sent the servant, who waited outside the door, for another bowl of water, claiming the first had spilled. She blamed her own clumsiness for the great clattering noise he must have heard. As soon as he left on this errand, she'd simply walked out of the bedchamber, and out of the house by the servants' entrance. Most of the wedding guests had celebrated a little too heavily at the feast and were deeply asleep, or close to it. No one apprehended her and it might be some time before Winton was discovered.

If he were dead, she would be hanged. And the captain, so eager to defend her, had drunk rather too much ale, which, while granting him an overabundance of self-confidence, severely tested his balance, aim and eyesight. She didn't want him embroiled in her troubles when he'd been so kind to her already. Fortunately, his desire to beat Lord Winton's brains to a slurry could not compete with the need for more ale and she was able to distract him by ordering another jug.

"Perhaps, Captain," she said, "you might tell me where I can find the man I seek. If you do know him."

"Know him?" He blinked, swaying along the settle toward her and then away again. "Did he say I owe him money?"

"No. He thought you sent me to him, that you played a joke."

The captain frowned. "Some men don't know a good thing when it lands in their lap." He smiled slowly. "Boy couldn't get out of his own way. Too slow to catch cold, when it comes to women."

"What boy?"

"One I knew once." He lifted his hand to his waist. "So high. Little lad. Running in circles 'round the yard. Stark ruddy..." he burped, "...naked." Clearly he was too soused to make any sense. He thrust a finger at the ceiling. "Name's Harold. Aye, that's it."

"Harold?"

"No. No," he chided her, "not the one who burned the cakes. Algernon. You know, old Algy with the squint. Breath like a rotting carcass. "

She was silent, lips pursed.

"Married the glassblower's daughter from...Ipswich. Or was it St. Ives?" He stopped and looked at her cup. "Not drinking?"

"Thank you. I'm not thirsty." Better keep her wits about her, she mused.

Watching the captain drain her cup, Lucy decided not to press him any further on the subject. After all, her mystery man wouldn't want her turning up again in his life. This predicament wasn't his problem, it was entirely her fault. She couldn't make all this trouble and then run to him, like a feeble creature, hoping he might get her out of it.

But what could she do now? If she ran to her brother what would he do? Lance was employed as bodyguard to the Earl of Swafford and, as such, he traveled a great deal. He had no home of his own where she could stay and, if he tried to help her, it would only get him in trouble too.

Captain Downing exclaimed, "Best come with me, young lady. I'll take care of you." Perhaps reading the shadow of doubt on her face, he laughed, tweaking her chin playfully. "You're too young for me, girl. You could be my daughter! No matter how tempting you find all this manhood before you, best put that out of your mind."

Lucy made the decision to place herself in his care. What other choice did she have? If she wrote to her brother, he wouldn't receive the letter until he returned to London, and who knew how long his journey might be delayed. Even then, once he knew what she'd done, how would he react? He had a tendency to believe men were always right and he might make her go back to their father's house.

She'd made a scandalous mess of everything and it would be far better for all involved if she were never found again.

Chapter 7

July 1588

What items would an unmarried fellow of more than half a century in years, a man who spent most of his adult life at sea and never enjoyed more than the most transient of relationships with place or person, leave in the hands of his beloved cousin? This was the bemusing question on John's mind as he tore open the seal on his cousin's missive that morning and studied the uneven scrawl penned there. Captain Nathaniel Downing was not a great scribe, this being clear from his misspelled words, but his story might be told as much by what his list excluded, as what it contained.

One stool--two legs mended, third stuck in another place, but if that cheating fishmonger should ask, I deny all responsibility
Chest with lock--damaged by vengeful hussy
Pottery wine jugge--cracked, over my head by other vengeful hussy
Goose-down mattress--much abused, hey ho
Splendid Hat--chewed, straynes the rayne well enough
Best cloak trimmed with coney--ripped and stayned
Sundry pewter vessels--dinted
One brass pot--with hole, handle, none
Knyves--blunt
Turkish carpet--slightly worn
Goats two--ill-tempered unless fed timely
Wall tapisstry--moth-bit, good for spying through
Paire of very fine Italian leather boots--one half of, other lost over roof of the Pig and Whistle in the High Street
Comb of ivory--teeth, none
Friday winch--on loan, handle at own risk

Nathaniel had departed the shores of England to fight the Spanish Armada, and since he always assumed, each time he raised anchor, that he wouldn't return in one piece, and as he was now getting on in years, having lived considerably longer than most folk thought he had any right, he left these sundry items in the charge of his cousin for safekeeping.

Or possibly for a good bonfire, as John commented dryly to his mother.

Reading down the list again, they were unsure as to the meaning of a Friday winch. No doubt it would be revealed in good time.

* * * *

Captain Downing had set sail the night before and she was supposed to have risen early to make a dawn exit before the landlord came for the rent. Sadly, she woke late and to the heralding barks of his bloodthirsty dogs in the hall.

Pounding his great stick so hard on the door of their lodgings that the boards rattled beneath her bare feet, the landlord paid no heed to her pleas for patience. The past-due rent might have been any amount more or less than a penny. It made no difference as she had no coin left whatsoever. Her jewelry was all pawned, except for a bracelet that once belonged to her mother, a pretty silver comb Lance gave her on her birthday and one half of an exquisite pair of pearl earbobs. These things were all she had left now of her family and she refused to give them up, however dire her circumstances.

"I come anon," she yelled, hurriedly seeking her shoes under the bed, while the ill-tempered landlord thundered away at the door.

It wouldn't hold much longer.

As well as her shoes, she grabbed the small wooden box in which she kept her remaining possessions, and then ran to the window, hitched herself up, swung her feet around and searched for a place to land.

Curious fortune was on her side, it seemed, for the dung-shoveler's cart waited below. Had she been in any position to choose, she might have preferred soft hay or woolsacks, but dung would have to do in this desperate situation. At least it would be a soft landing. With one deep breath, she leapt.

A scant few seconds later, the cart pulled out of the inn yard, carrying Lucy, slightly bruised, breathless and homeless, but with limbs, neck and spirit quite unbroken. She asked the startled dung-shoveller to drop her at the Pig and Whistle Tavern in the High Street, for this was where the next stage of her life awaited. Hopefully she was not too late.

As it turned out, *he* was late.

* * * *

For half an hour, she waited among Captain Nathaniel Downing's abandoned articles, left in the courtyard of the Pig and Whistle, slowly getting wetter, her temper piqued. Now, at last, here he came, the country cousin Nathaniel had promised would come for her.

He rode bareback astride a massive carthorse. His rolled-up shirtsleeves revealed two arms as thick as the hind quarters of the beast upon which he sat. His hair was dampened by the fine drizzle. The pace of his journey having rendered his skin much warmer than the air itself, a slight mist rose from his head and shoulders.

Trotting up to where she sat, her long-awaited rescuer squinted at her through the rain and said, "I'm John Carver. Who the devil are you? My cousin didn't say anything about a wretched woman."

His puzzled gaze inched over her in a methodical fashion, while she glared back at him.

And gleeful anticipation of rescue quickly turned to shock.

They'd met before.

Not that he would know it, thankfully.

Recently she'd dyed her hair with henna and indigo powders, but she'd already discovered a tendency for the color to run if she was caught out too long in the rain. Today she wore a linen cap over her bound hair and, because of the weather, she'd also raised the hood of her woolen mantle. She felt quite safe from any chance this man might recognize her. Nevertheless, her heart was beating too fast. Had Captain Downing known? He did have a slightly mischievous sense of humor and had been adamant she stay and wait for his cousin.

Her lips, formerly pressed tight, now snapped open in a gasp. "Do you know how long I've waited for you?"

His eyes narrowed. "No. Neither do I care." He'd already formed an opinion of her, evidently. That flamboyant gown, low-cut bodice and frilly petticoats must have told him all he needed to know. Nathaniel's taste in fashion ran to gaudy. Anything bright and lacy caught his eye and he would bring it home for his "ward."

Panicking, fearing he might leave her there, she snatched Nathaniel's letter from his hand, scanned it quickly and jabbed a gloved finger at the pertinent item on the list.

"Friday winch?" he read slowly.

"That's me."

His discerning gaze slowly swept upward again.

"He meant 'wench,'" she explained wearily. "His penmanship leaves much to be desired."

"Friday...wench?"

She nodded. "I'm Lucy Friday." Nathaniel called her that because he found her on a Friday. Rather than elaborate further, she'd let him draw his own conclusions.

"What happened to the other days of the week? Or was it only Friday he had the strength?"

She remembered that impudent mouth all too well. "Why not ask your cousin?"

"He's not here, is he?"

"Are we going to sit in the rain arguing? Or are you going to take me home?"

Still mounted, he eyed her stormily, one hand on his thigh. "Home? Where's that, then?" The rain had dampened his shirt so that it clung to his shoulders and chest. She tried not to look, but as she'd seen it all before it seemed petty to resist. He was built like a solid oak, no part of him soft or under-used.

"Your home, of course," she answered.

"Nah. You're not coming with me. I haven't time for all that jiggery pokery." Inferring, in a sly manner, that he was much busier than Captain Downing and couldn't be bothered with female company.

"He was once a merry rogue," Nathaniel had said, somewhat scathingly, "but now he binds himself up with responsibilities and thinks himself above me."

The memory flashed through her, startling, inconvenient and unpreventable as a chain of hiccups: the heat of her mystery man's skin, the perspiration on his back, the ale on his lips, the stiff bristles of his cheek against hers and the hard lines of his chest under her hands.

As he scratched his head, she noted the soft hairs on his arms, remembering too, how they'd felt against her naked body.

So he was once a rogue, but now reformed. Or he liked to pretend. She knew otherwise, of course. Interesting. Not that it should, or could, matter to her. He'd already gotten her into enough trouble, hadn't he?

Her heartbeat was uneven, too hard one moment, too faint the next.

If Captain Downing was this man's cousin, why had he sheltered her for two months without letting her know the truth? Perhaps he hadn't realized his cousin was the man she sought at Mistress Comfort's, or else there was something about John Carver the captain wanted to save her from knowing.

He was married too. That must be it. He was married with a half dozen noisy children and a put-upon wife.

Finally dismounted, he walked around the cart, checking over the other contents.

"Captain Downing promised you'd take me," she exclaimed. When he didn't look up from the list, she added, "Of course, if your conscience will allow you to leave me here alone, in the rain, a friendless woman with no food, no shelter and no coin, well...so be it." She turned away, chin high, blinking against the rain as it fell harder now, fat drops splashing in the puddles around the cart. "I daresay any villainy might be committed against me. But pray, don't feel guilty because you left me here. Alone."

"I don't need a wench," he muttered, still reading down the list, "not for Friday or any other day."

"But Captain Downing promised--"

"I'm certain he did. My cousin's notorious for promises he can't keep." He petted the goats until, after complaining steadily all morning, they fell quiet, soothed..

Lucy remembered that too, the skill in his hands. Realizing he might catch her staring somewhat wistfully, she snapped, "So you mean to leave me here, abandoned?"

"I very much doubt you'll be abandoned. You'll soon find some other man."

"But you must take me. I insist!"

He exhaled a quick snort, eyes wide. "Insist all you want. I can't take you. I've nowhere to put you. Everything on my farm serves a purpose." Folding the list, he tucked it away inside his jerkin. "I don't keep anything purely decorative."

Gesturing at her to climb out of the cart, he stood back, clearly expecting no further argument. Frustrated, needing a moment to compose herself, she covered her face with her hands, but he must have thought her reduced to tears, for he stopped tapping his foot impatiently and a series of gusty, exasperated sighs followed in quick succession. Peeking slyly through her fingers, she found him frowning and troubled, scratching his head.

"Have you nowhere else to take shelter?" he asked with a softened cadence. Once again he glanced at her crimson gown. His eyes were just a little too bright to be disinterested, no matter what came out of his mouth.

She lowered her hands. "I will be forced," she said slowly, "to beg in the street if you leave me here. But don't fret." With one shrug of her shoulders, she looked away over his head. "I'm sure my safety is of no consequence to you."

"You don't look destitute to me, madam, or friendless." He leaned his forearms on the cart, his restless perusal licking over her person and then her face. Again she worried he might recognize her. Surely one little leather mask wouldn't make such a difference. However, his expression showed no sign of recognition.

Typical man. He'd probably forgotten everything about their night together already.

"I'm a very poor fellow, you know. I could never keep a mistress in such frills and finery. You'd not be content with me for long."

"But I..."

"Until my cousin returns, you should stay here in Yarmouth. Find another gent with deep pockets and vanity to be preyed upon." This last was said with a slight harshness, his speech concluded in a sharper tone than it was begun, and he stepped aside again, waiting for her to climb out.

She remained seated, lips set firm, raindrops flicking from her eyelashes as she shook her head, determined. He took one step closer and she quickly grabbed hold of her wooden seat, gloved hands clinging tight.

When he saw she wouldn't be moved, he flexed his shoulders, complained softly, and then fetched his horse around to the front of the cart. Clearly he wouldn't put himself out to quarrel with her further, or waste his energy trying to eject her bodily from his cousin's pile of belongings. Instead, he calmly fastened his beast to the cart. She stayed quiet, but followed his movements warily with her gaze.

Leaping up beside her, gathering the reins in his callused hands, he warned, "Last chance to change your mind, Friday wench. If you come with me, I'll expect you to work for your keep." He shot her fine gown another questioning look from the corner of his eye. "Like I said, I've no place in my life for a purely decorative woman, even one on loan."

She protested. "I can be many things, as well as ornamental."

Snatching her hand, he tore off her glove and examined her palm. "As I thought." He sneered. "Soft hands."

"They may be soft, but they're quite capable, I assure you!"

"Soft as a babe's backside!" Even as he mocked her, he took up the reins again, urging the horse forward. "Don't say I didn't warn you, Friday wench." The cart wheels rolled over the bumpy yard and splashed through puddles, gaining speed.

Whatever perversity had made him decide to keep her that day, she was grateful for it.

* * * *

John Carver glanced sideways at the silent woman. She seemed far away in her thoughts. A daydreamer. Just what he didn't need. In fact, everything about her was inconvenient. He was a busy man with no time to waste keeping this fancy piece of petticoat fed and watered. Just as he'd told her, she'd earn her keep if she meant to stay with him.

Evidently this was one of his cousin's little jests. Nathaniel would think it all most amusing. Another trial for John's recent attempt at a celibate, reformed life. 'Attempt' being the operative word.

Again he considered the shapely woman at his side. Her lips were full and pursed. She was thoughtful or disgruntled, he wasn't sure which. Her eyes were a disturbingly bright shade of green, like a summer meadow. He counted five freckles across her nose. At least she didn't wear a ghostly white concoction on her face to hide them, the way some fine ladies did. He'd witnessed the oddities of fashion while visiting his exceedingly well-married sister at her husband's estate in Dorset, and in London, where she had a home beside the Thames. But John didn't visit her often. Surprisingly enough, he got on well with her husband, the Earl of Swafford, but John usually didn't mingle well with the nobility. He stubbornly refused to dress up in the fancy clothes his sister wanted to put him in every time she saw him, and since she was always matchmaking, trying to get him to pay attention to one of her ladylike friends, he found it easier on his temper if he stayed in the country. Where he wore what was comfortable and no one expected him to mind his manners.

Nathaniel's Friday wench was very clean, her skin fresh and dewy, daisy-white and lightly tinged with blush. Too clean. If she thought she could stay like that for long in his company, she had a nasty surprise in store.

He sniffed, stared ahead and flicked the reins. The horse picked up speed and the cart bumped over ridges in the lane, jostling her along the narrow seat, until she leaned against his arm, her leg touching his thigh. Ready to frighten her off, he stabbed a fierce scowl over his shoulder, but saw it wasn't her fault. She clung to the seat with great concentration, trying hard to keep a discreet distance between them.

A little hair was visible under the hood and cap she wore. It was very dark, contrasting almost too severely with her pale skin.

She turned her head to look at him, her lighter brows raised in a silent question. Had he met her before? No. He would've remembered those eyes, the strange coloring and the soft hands, the lips. And he would have remembered the little white scar under her right eye. It looked like a healed cut.

"What?" she demanded sharply.

"Have we ever...ever...?"

One brow tipped higher than the other. "Have we ever...what?" Did he detect a slight sauciness in her tone?

"Ever met?"

She shifted a few inches to her left and wrinkled her freckled nose. "Not likely!"

No, indeed. Just what he'd thought. As her cloak fell open, he looked at her white neck, then her bosom, which bore resemblance to a couple of well-fed, newborn piglets, nestling together, breathing excitedly. He quickly turned his head away. Not likely.

Two years ago might have been a different story, but since his father died he'd worked hard to reform his wild ways. He certainly didn't have time for women like this one. Not now. He didn't have much time for any woman, in fact, unless she made herself useful on the farm. Knowing he must marry one day, at thirty he was in no particular hurry. Alice Croft would surely wait for him. She wasn't going anywhere, was she? So he kept putting it off, this idea of settling down with one woman, of having babes, growing fat, losing his teeth and his hair, getting aches in his knee on damp days...

In that moment, his thoughts were even less inclined to settling down and growing old with Alice Croft, because the cart bumped over another rut and Nathaniel's Friday wench slid helplessly along the seat again, the side of her leg inadvertently pressed to his. He thought transiently of slowing the horse and giving her a chance to sit upright. Instead, betaken with a mischievous desire to watch her struggle, he drove the horse onward even faster, until she was obliged to grip his arm, just to stay in her seat.

He thought there was a quiet murmur of protest, but since he was whistling loudly he couldn't be sure and he didn't bother pausing his tune to find out.

Friday winch (on loan--handle at own risk)

The 'handle at risk' part he understood, but did that mean she was on loan to Nathaniel, or on loan to him?

* * * *

Curling her fingers slyly in the damp linen of his shirt sleeve, Lucy pressed her nose to it, briefly, just to inhale his scent. Her heart skipped a beat. At once she slid away again, putting a safer distance between them.

Lucy Collyer, she admonished herself briskly, *you're a very wicked, wanton woman to have used this poor man. It's a good thing he doesn't remember you!*

"Why don't you slow down?" she called out anxiously, teeth rattling.

"Can't," he bellowed back, quite inexplicably.

Another bump sent her several inches into the air and it was lucky he had quick reflexes. He grabbed her arm, jerking her back onto the seat, almost into his lap. "Hold onto me," he shouted. "You've no weight to you, that's your problem." And he clicked his tongue against his teeth, shaking his head.

There was nothing else for it but to hold his arm. He would make no gentlemanly allowances for his passenger, it seemed. She changed her tentative grip to a bruising hold, but he made no complaint, as if he barely felt it.

The rain stopped at last and the sun, finally recognizing it was summer, struggled to peer out through leaden clouds.

"Is it much further?" she asked.

"A fair distance."

Good. The further the better. Not having much knowledge of geography, when she first ran away she'd had the hazy idea of going to Scotland, but with Captain Downing's kind help, she'd managed to hide away without going too far among savages. She'd written to Lance in London, only to let him know she was safe, giving no clue as to her whereabouts.

"It is a farm then, where you live, John Carver?"

"Aye, Lucy Friday."

Good. No one would look for her on a farm. "Do you live alone?"

"With my mother."

Slight pause. Her heart thumped heavily. She felt it even in her fingertips as they pressed into his thick arm. "No wife then?"

"None."

She exhaled with relief.

"What are you smiling at?" he demanded curtly.

"My thoughts."

"And what are they?"

She shook her head. "A lady's thoughts are her own."

He disagreed, plainly, surveying her with a vexed, peevish countenance. "How long have you known my cousin?"

"Not long."

"Months, years, weeks....days?"

She sighed. "Does it matter?"

"Suppose not." And then he added gruffly, "But you're too young for Nate."

"Too young?"

"I'm surprised he has the will at his age, but then again he always was easily tempted and had eyes bigger than his belly, as my mother would say."

"And you're not easily tempted?"

He wouldn't look at her. "Better not get any ideas of tempting me, Friday wench. Leaning all over me..."

She realized how glad she was to see him again, no matter how dangerous it was. It had a dizzying effect, like leaning too far from a window, or spinning around with her eyes closed.

"I'm only holding your arm because otherwise I'd be killed at this pace," she pointed out. "If I had anything else to hold, I would much sooner cling to that, believe me."

He stared down at her again, full of suspicion, but he didn't say anything.

They rode in silence for the remainder of the journey and soon she was absorbed in the beauty of the countryside. The sun, fully out now, showed off with pride, drying John Carver's sleeve and warming her face.

Captain Downing had often talked about the place where he was raised by his aunt and uncle. He considered John Carver as much a little brother as a cousin and had spoken of him often, but his words had conjured a very different picture, far from the reality. The small, thatched farmhouse she'd expected was actually a large, somewhat cumbersome old building, coated with ivy and topped by a jumble of crooked chimneys rising up into the sky like dark, rooky elms. Surrounding the front yard there were stables and other smaller buildings, all captured within a flint and pebble wall, guarded by impressively ornate iron gates. It was no palace, but it was no humble dwelling, either, and with little beads of rain caught on the ivy, winking in the sunset, it seemed almost alive and breathing.

"Welcome to Souls Dryft," he said.

Already down from the cart, he raised his hands to help her out. Too overcome with nerves, she chose to make her own way, shoving his hands aside. "I can do it. Mind my gown. Your hands are dirty." She realized the redundancy of her caution almost immediately when she remembered her earlier escape on a dung cart, but it was too late to take it back. Out of habit, she'd brushed him aside, a woman who preferred folk to keep their distance. Sitting too close to him on that cart had already done enough damage, now at least she was in control again of her own body.

A deep frown darkening his face, he watched her clamber awkwardly to the cobbles without his help.

Giving her no time to look around or tidy her wind-blown dignity, he herded her onward, sweeping his arms at her as if she was a stray sow, driving her down the step and through the entrance, where ivy hung thickly, mingling with fragrant, twisty strands of honeysuckle. "Make haste, Friday wench," he declared. "I'm hungry for my supper." So she stepped down into the house for the first time, entering another new chapter in her life.

"I'm home, Mother," he yelled. "Hope you made a good supper. We've got a guest tonight and she needs a good feed to put some fat on her bones." And then he laughed, as she flung a scowl over her shoulder. "Looks like hunger puts her in an ill-temper too, but I'll soon spank that prissiness out of her with my filthy hands."

Chapter 8

Snoring loudly, a huge hound stretched out across the warm hearth, but hearing John's voice it woke, scrambled up and let out a deep, excitable bark. It galloped across the flagstone floor and John made a great fuss of the beast, rubbing its big head, kissing its nose, while it stood on a huge pair of back paws, thrusting its full weight into his chest.

"This is Vince," he introduced his dog proudly. "Short for Invincible. And this, Vince, is Lucy Friday, apparently a stray wench no one else wants and so falls to our care. Much as you did, fool beast." He grinned wryly. "Though she's more particular and remarkably proud for a mutt."

The dog turned its attention to her, sniffing the dung on her skirt and whimpering in excitement. Lucy inched away, sliding around the long trestle table, almost backing directly into an old woman who stood there, watching.

"What's all this then, John? What have you brought home this time?" The woman's eyes were very dark, but keen and sharp as a blade, cutting her up one side and down the other. Despite her evident age, those eyes were surprisingly youthful, holding the same spark of wit Lucy detected in John Carver. More than simple good humor, it was a lusty, mischievous curiosity in the unusual.

"This, Mother, is the Friday winch, of Nate's listed possessions," John explained. "He meant to write 'wench.'"

There was barely a glimmer of surprise to change her expression. "Friday wench indeed. He's never so organized with anything as he is the women in his life!"

"She claims to have nowhere else to go," said her son, still petting his dog, "I couldn't very well leave her there could I? If he ever returns to find her lost, he'd never forgive me. No, he left her to my care, so I suppose we must take her in and feed the wretch."

"I'll not be a burden," Lucy blurted. Hungry and overly tired, her manners were drawn very thin and brittle. "I shan't stay long..."

Abruptly his mother took hold of her chin, examined her face and, after a moment, duly proclaimed her a "well-favored" young woman with good color and very fine features. "Where did he find you, then?"

Lucy had no answer. How she came to be among Nathaniel Downing's shabby possessions was a tale she meant to keep secret, but the question raised many unpleasant memories, of Lord Winton's angry face leaning over her, his features strained tight, his hand raised to strike again, cameo ring gleaming in the candlelight.

"Who knows where he found the wench?" John exclaimed. "Nate spends his time and his coin in a lot o' whore houses."

"John!"

"'Tis true, Mother. You know how he is. Never passed up a pretty face and a firm set o' bubbies." He stretched his arms overhead. "No need to put on airs and graces for Nate's trollop, mother. I'm sure she's heard worse. Now where's my damned supper? Since I've now got two women in this house, perhaps I'll finally get fed when I'm hungry."

His mother ignored him, gently squeezing Lucy's hand. "My nephew Nathaniel is like me," she whispered. "He never would turn his back on a stray. No need to blush, my dear, I won't press you for answers. We're all entitled to our secrets. What would life be without them?"

She guided Lucy down into a chair, patting her shoulder in a kindly fashion, and thus she was accepted. Just like that. Lucy had never before met a woman so free of judgment.

Clutching her small wooden box of belongings, she looked around the large, open interior of the house and found it tidy, warm and well-kept, much like the old lady herself. The main fireplace dominated the room, an impressive carved mantle in very dark wood and stone that might have been too severe and overpowering, yet the multitude of windows around the house prevented any fear of stifling or any sensation of being closed in. The floor was simple flagged stone, covered with rushes and dried herbs to scent the air. There was a cushioned window seat with several embroidered pillows and Lucy thought how pleasant it would be to sit there on a sunny morning, looking out over the yard. Then she inwardly scorned herself for thinking she had any right to claim a seat in that house, among people who didn't know her, or the wicked things she'd done.

Mistress Carver was preparing supper in a large pot over the fire, exclaiming they were so late she hoped the stew wasn't burned. While tossing in a few more herbs from bunches hanging overhead, she turned to her son and bemoaned the fact he'd left that morning with neither coat nor hat. Now he had a wet shirt as a consequence and had probably sat in it all day. He was fortunate, she lectured him, never to catch cold.

"I'm famished, Mother," he declared, dismissing her concern with barely a thought. "At this rate I'll die of hunger and then you won't have to worry about me catching any cold, will you?"

Lucy, too, was ravenous, more so than she'd ever been, and when a bowl of rabbit stew was set before her she devoured it as greedily as good manners would allow. The dog took a liking to her, or perhaps to her foul-smelling skirt, and sat at her feet with his great head resting in her lap throughout the meal. Meanwhile, mother and son discussed the farm and various matters in which she had no part and no understanding. John spoke to his mother in an arrogant manner, often interrupting her sentences and snapping out sullen replies, as if he barely had time to answer her gentle questions. His mother didn't seem to notice. At least, she said nothing to correct his manner. Sometimes Lucy thought they'd both forgotten her completely; then one of them would glance her way, suddenly remembering her presence.

"If the Friday wench truly means to be of any use, she can milk the cows tomorrow morning," John muttered at one point, eyeing her across the table as she delicately tore little pieces of bread to mop up the last of her stew, careful not to spill any. "But I daresay she's not accustomed to rising early." There was challenge in the way he said it, even a little contempt in his blue eyes.

Taught never to speak with a mouth full of food, she chewed her bread and swallowed before she answered. "I'm glad to help."

He shrugged, stuffing a spoonful of stew into his own busy mouth. "We'll see."

Straightening her shoulders, she watched him eat like a pig at the trough.

"We'll see if you get up in time," he clarified. "We don't work on our backs around here."

She granted him one of her most disdainful looks, but he shoveled more food into his mouth, unperturbed. Apparently he thought he would talk to her in the same careless, uncivil manner he addressed his poor mother.

"What shall we do with all Nathaniel's belongings?" Mistress Carver asked, watching her son drain his second bowl of stew and another flagon of cider.

He burped with slow deliberation. "Suppose they can all go in the store shed. The Friday wench with them."

His mother laughed softly. "Lucy can have your sisters' chamber, now they no longer have need of it."

Elbows on the table, he tore into a hunk of bread with his greedy teeth. "Are you sure, Mother? Can we trust Nate's fancy trollop in the house? She might steal the silver spoons and the pewter."

This many rude comments in a row, aimed at their guest, was apparently the limit. His mother finally slapped him around the ear, warning him to be polite or he would be the one spending the night in the store shed. Ducking and laughing, he was not bothered by his mother's threats or her slaps. It was clear, Lucy thought sourly, he ran the roost and had done so for some time. She'd witnessed that flare of cockiness in him before and thought he merely did it to tease her, but now she saw he was accustomed to getting away with things. And why not, she mused, her mood darkening further. Even she, Lucy Collyer with ice in her veins and nothing but disdain for any man who came to court her, once had been unable to refuse this rogue anything he wanted.

No one had ever touched her the way he had. No other man would ever have dared do those things to her. Most were afraid of her haughty demeanor, her scornful tongue, and never got beyond it to find the real woman beneath.

But he had. Nothing, it seemed, stopped John Sydney Carver doing exactly what he wanted. Not even her intrinsic frostiness stood in his way.

"I suppose she can bed in the house then, as long as she gives us no trouble." He spared her a dismissive glance. "Best be up in time to milk the cows, wench. Or else."

He wasn't going to get away with it again. "Or else what?" She whipped out the words, sitting very straight in her chair, facing him fearlessly across the table.

John blinked. His eyes gleamed with sudden intensity above the fluttering drift of candlelight. Clearly he hadn't expected any questioning from her. "Or you can go back where I found you. I can't afford to keep another mouth unless the owner of it serves a purpose." Tearing another bite of bread with his strong teeth, he grinned slowly.

Watching his churning, smirking lips, she remembered how they'd once kissed her, how his busy tongue had lapped at her nipples and between her thighs with sublime dexterity. When he had feasted upon her as greedily as he devoured his supper.

Tonight he seemed determined to prick her temper with his brusque gestures and rude manners, challenging her like a naughty little boy, but she knew he could be gentle, seductive, a wonderfully persuasive lover. Raising her eyes a few inches to meet his gaze, she caught a sudden lick of heat, followed by a guilty flicker. She realized her own face was hot and his had turned a brilliant shade. A frisson of like ideas had passed between them, shocking and detailed.

He coughed, cleared his throat and changed the subject.

"Those goats are two strong specimens, healthy and biddable. At least Nate left me something of good use. I'll put them in the small barn, just until we see how they get on with ours."

A short while later, observing her yawning uncontrollably, his mother showed Lucy upstairs to a bedchamber. Both her daughters, she explained, were married and lived in the county of Dorset, leaving their old chamber unoccupied. It was a good-sized room with a window overlooking the yard and stables. The floorboards creaked, even when no foot walked over them, and between roof beams the low hanging plaster was thickly veined with cracks that seemed to spread and change shape as she watched. The chamber had little in the way of comforts, but it was a roof over her head and she would've been grateful then even for a store shed with the company of goats.

"Thank you, Mistress Carver, for your hospitality. I don't want to be in anyone's way."

"And you're not. Forgive my son, he has a tendency to let his tongue run away with him and be too sharp for its own good. He'll cut himself with it one day, and although I await the occasion with considerable impatience, it hasn't happened yet."

And it wouldn't happen, if no one ever stood up to the arrogant brat. "I'll not mind what he says then."

"See that you don't. I never do." The old lady used her candle to light another standing by the bed. "I'm very glad you've come, my dear." She stayed to untie the laces of Lucy's gown and corset, then she slipped away, closing the door with a rusty creak and a gentle thud.

Lucy sat on the bed, in her petticoats and shift, her mind too busy to rest now she was alone. Her earlier tiredness had vanished. If she lay down in bed, she knew she would toss and turn restlessly. Instead she mulled over her new predicament.

Hmm. John Sydney Carver.

He was extremely dismissive, because he assumed she was his cousin's mistress and therefore of less consequence to him than a pair of goats, from which he would at least get milk. But what a hypocrite he was, to be disdainful of his cousin's "trollop," when he was not above visits to a bawdy house and nights of unbridled lust with masked ladies he never expected to see again. There were two sides to him and she'd seen them both.

Low voices crept up through the floorboards and so, still too restless to lie down, she took the candle and tiptoed onto the landing. Creeping along barefoot, she made her way to the railings at the top of the staircase and knelt there. The door below was left ajar, or else knocked open slightly by a draft. A soft orange wedge of firelight slipped through the gap and lit the bottom few steps.

They spoke quietly, but she heard their words clearly now and, just as she suspected, they spoke of her.

"It'll be a welcome change for me, John, to have another pair of hands around the house."

His reply was curt. "She won't stay long, Mother. The moment she sees what real work is, she'll be off. You'll see. A woman like that isn't made for life on a farm."

"Mayhap you underestimate her."

"Seen her hands? Lily-white and soft as fallen rose petals. From the look of her, she's never done an honest day's work. Did you see her face when I told her how early she'd best be up for the milking? I'll wager she's never been out of bed before noon, nor had her hands on a cow's teat."

"I daresay her talents lie elsewhere."

Abruptly he laughed.

"Now get those thoughts out of your head, John. You know what I meant."

It spat out of him as if he'd tried, and failed, to hold it in. "I'm surprised my cousin still has the strength to handle a wench like her at his age."

"Strength is one thing Nathaniel never lacked. Restraint, yes. Good sense, yes. Strength of will, no."

"But why only on a Friday?" he mused. "If she was mine, I'd want her every day of the week."

Lucy almost dropped her candle. The slender flame rippled madly, pushed and pummeled by her breath.

"Variety?" His mother chuckled. "Nathaniel would never be content with one woman. He always feared he might miss something. Just like his father, your uncle."

"Or else she had other…commitments…on other days." She heard his chair scrape across the flagged floor. "I daresay he's not her only lover. He couldn't have kept her in all that finery," he added grumpily. "Nathaniel seldom has two coins to rub together."

"Well, she's a very lovely girl, to be sure."

He made some sort of peevish grunt in reply.

"And sweetly-mannered," his mother went on. "So there's no need for you to be coarse around her, John."

"I'll be the way I am," he replied, contentious. "And she can put up with it, same as anyone else. If she doesn't like it, she can leave can't she?"

His mother said nothing.

"She must have some well-heeled patrons in addition to my cousin," he added, "so why was she so eager to come here anyway?"

"Escape?"

She froze. Had his mother read it in her face when she'd examined her so thoroughly before?

"Whatever her reason, 'tis what Nathaniel wanted. I couldn't leave her there, could I?" Again he seemed to want reassurance and, at the same time, to absolve himself of any blame for her presence there.

"Of course, John. You wouldn't leave her behind." His mother's tone was quietly amused. "I suppose Nathaniel left her to you for a reason."

"Then she can stay for now…on a trial basis. But she won't stay long. Not when she has a taste of real work."

Those soft hands, of which he was so scornful, tightened around her candle. Thought she might be frightened away did he? Trial basis indeed!

* * * *

"No, no, no!" he lectured, shaking his head. "The cow decides when you're done milking. Keep going, Friday wench."

Shoulder pressed to the beast's warm flank, she continued the milking and when he heard the steady hiss of milk into the pail, he nodded sharply. "Ol' Buttercup must like those tender hands of yours, she's not usually so generous."

His mother had provided Lucy with an apron to wear over her gown, but even this didn't save that good scarlet damask from the stains of one morning in the farmyard. She'd been up since cockcrow and John put her to work at once. Breakfast, apparently, was not to be had until later, although he'd already taken a ladle of milk from her bucket and drunk it down thirstily, offering her none. When some dripped down his chin, he pulled his shirt over his head and used it to wipe his face. It was a swift, unconscious gesture, but with his finely-sculpted torso revealed so unexpectedly, Lucy forgot the task at hand and stared.

"I suppose you're thirsty," he remarked, noticing her peering up at him. "But you can wait for yours until you're done with your duties."

After the milking, there were eggs to gather and hens to feed, followed by mucking out the stable, the goat pen and the pig sty. Manure, gathered in a wheelbarrow, was taken to the pile beside the store shed and kept until it might be needed on the farm or garden. Lucy had never been so filthy in her life. She would now recommend the experience most heartily for rousing a goodly appetite. And a hot temper. By the time he found nothing more for her to do outside, the sun was high and her belly made as much disgruntled noise as the pigs. When the farm workers began to arrive at the gates, he hurriedly shooed her inside, out of sight.

"You can eat now," he muttered, as she stood before him, beaten and bespattered, but still having the strength to scowl. "Go on into the house. Mother will feed you." With his dog trotting at his side, he walked away, whistling and swinging his arms. Not a word of thanks.

After breakfast, Mistress Carver took her through the household chores, but she was not such a hard master as her son. That morning John had rarely spoken to her, except to give a command or chide her for being slow, but once he was gone to work on the farmland, which kept him absent for most of the day, the women of his house were left to work at their own pace and even, God forbid, to chatter. They shared a luncheon of cold meat, cheese and cider, which, for the first time in her life, Lucy thoroughly appreciated. In her previous world, food was brought to her and sometimes, if she was hungry and in the mood, she ate it. Seldom did she taste it, never had she considered all the work that went into bringing it to her.

Later, as they gathered herbs in the sun-drenched garden, Mistress Carver told her stories of John as a young boy. Apparently not always this hard working, disciplined farmer, he had been a wild, unruly youth. Her daughters, she told Lucy, were already grown up when she had John. A pleasant surprise, he was much beloved by her husband, whom she blamed for spoiling the boy.

"John was an incorrigible little monster for most of his childhood," she said,shaking her head at the memories.

He hadn't changed much then.

"Would never do a thing he was told and always might be found in scrapes of one kind or another. His father thought it all most amusing." Captain Carver, she explained, had been away at sea for most of John's youth. "Leaving me to the thankless task of raising the little devil," she added. "After my husband died, John made an abrupt change. Suddenly he was the man of the family. Since then he's thought of naught but this farm. I like to imagine he makes amends to me for all he made me suffer when he was a young lad. Oh, such a child he was, such a trial on my patience!"

She told Lucy how, when he was only thirteen, John stood on his pew in church one Sunday to call the parson a "scurvy, prattling knave." He accused the man of stealing from the collection to keep several "saucy harlots" and more than one local widow in new petticoats. His mother explained how John always kept a long list of people he disliked and to whom he would never, in his own words, "give time o' day". He thought nothing of expressing his opinions, however unwelcome, quite frankly and without the slightest fear. Anyone with whom he took offense, anyone who quarreled with him, usually ended up with a black eye. His visits to the local tavern had always ended with a stumble home across the common, while he loudly sang slanderous rhymes about any villagers who met with his wrath.

"Many a time I sat up into the small hours, waiting for that boy to find his way home," his mother said, shaking her head. "Wondering who he'd found to pick a fight with now and if, one day, his opponent would win. They never did. Perhaps if they had, once in a while, it might have taught him a lesson."

Lucy was amused to hear all this. Now, when he lectured her, turning up his nose, she would laugh inwardly, imagining him as a wild and wayward young savage, running naked around the yard as, according to his mother, he often had as a boy.

She thought of his hands. Despite those scarred knuckles, they were incredibly gentle and soothing, when they wanted to be.

"He tells me he's done with fighting now. Claims he's ready soon to settle down with a wife," his mother said. "Thankfully. I'm surprised he managed to keep all those fine teeth in his head." Then she paused, head on one side. "Just like his father. My Will always had very good, strong teeth."

Lucy nodded solemnly. Mistress Carver talked of her husband often that day. It seemed her son bore many resemblances to his father and Lucy supposed this was why the old lady let him get away with his cheek. It was no cause for her to do the same though, she reasoned.

At the end of the first long day, she asked if she might have a bath. The old lady looked surprised, but told her where to find the copper tub. "John can help you carry it in when he gets back from the fields. I'm afraid my back won't take the strain. But if you start heating the water by the fire now, it should be ready for you by then. There are two buckets in the store shed."

Perhaps a bath was not necessary after all. Stupidly, the work involved hadn't occurred to her, but there were no maids here to obey her every whim.

"Well, I suppose it is only a little dirt," she muttered. "It can wait."

Mistress Carver smiled kindly. "Light the candles then, will you, dear. If John sees them in the window he'll know it's time to come in for his supper, otherwise he'll stay out there all night."

She looked around and saw a few stumps on the mantle. "These are almost used up. Shall I get new ones out?"

"Gracious no, dear. There's a good few hours left on those."

Biting her lip, she quickly gathered up the stumps, lit them in the fire and then set them in holders by the windows. She felt stupid, lazy and naive, but Mistress Carver good-naturedly ignored her many stumbles.

Lucy had imagined on her first day that all the rising early and working hard was merely John Carver's plan to crush her spirit and prove a point, but as each subsequent day passed much like the first, she realized this was their life, no scheme for her undoing. It was their everyday routine, and now hers too.

Gathering her dogged strength, her courage and a considerable helping of competitive spirit, she got on with her new tasks.

Chapter 9

John reluctantly conceded that Nathaniel's trollop was not so useless after all. She threw herself whole-heartedly into the chores he gave her, no matter how demeaning and dirty. It wouldn't last, he reassured himself. But whenever he gave an order and she set her mouth in a determined line, eyes smoldering with defiance, like a sun-lapped forest soon to be consumed with flame, he knew she would prove him wrong if it killed her. He'd never known a woman so tenacious. On the outside she was small and delicate; on the inside she was strong as an ox.

She puzzled him, intrigued him, challenged him.

He didn't like the way she answered back with her quick tongue, as if she thought he was her servant. She criticized his manners, called him ungrateful and suggested he didn't appreciate his own mother. Even when she should be exhausted after a long day's work, she often still had breath to argue with him.

John was accustomed to women who did what they were told, thankful for his notice. It was true his mother had her moments of sauciness, especially after a cup or two of plum wine, but she generally understood it was best to keep him in a good temper. To have the table set for supper when he came in, to have his clothes clean and dry when he needed them, his boots brushed and set by the warm fire on cold mornings. His mother knew how to take care of him, and had done so for thirty years without feeling the need to question or raise her voice much. Even the occasional threat of a smack across the head with a ladle was never actually carried out.

Nathaniel's trollop appeared to take issue with this.

"Your mother is a sweet, loving woman. You should be ashamed of how you treat her. You take her for granted."

"Who asked your opinion?" he growled, at which she merely pursed her petulant, resolute lips and spun away in a flurry of muddied petticoat.

In his opinion, he treated his mother very well indeed. He worked hard, saved money, kept the house and farm maintained, even let her keep brewing plum wine, against his better judgment. So where this impertinent Friday wench came by the gumption to shout at him and tell him he was a "spoiled rotten little bugger," he could hardly guess.

She'd called him it twice now: once when he'd laughed because she fell in the dung heap and once when she'd caught and ripped her skirt in the stable door after he let it shut too quickly behind them. Both occasions had been in the midst of an argument. He couldn't even remember what started it, but it was probably one of her bossy remarks, or one of those imperious gestures she often used to send him on his way. A careless flick of her slender wrist, perhaps. That was always enough to spark his temper. So too was her coy ability to always be just out of his reach, avoiding his touch.

Lofty and obdurate, she was keen to repudiate anything he said, but it was obvious she had no grounding beneath, no proper education to back her up. For example, she insisted the sun revolved around the earth. Apparently she'd never heard of Copernicus. He wasn't surprised to learn she thought the world was flat, when everyone should know by now that it was round.

"Have you forgotten, wench?" he'd yelled at her, "I'm the son of a sailor. I think he'd know more about the world than you would."

"Why don't we fall off, then if the world is a big ball?" she'd yelled back.

"Sometimes people do. Skinny, light-headed creatures like you, for instance."

"Don't talk nonsense." And there went the irreverent flick of her fingertips, the toss of her cynical head.

The Friday wench possessed an oddly scattered stream of ideas, as if she'd been schooled by someone with their own beliefs to promote and no real intent of teaching her anything important or useful. He'd never bothered arguing his point to any woman before now, yet he took the trouble to set her straight. Not that she appreciated the time and effort on his part. He was convinced she frequently fell asleep by the fire in the evenings on purpose. Unless it was sheer coincidence that she began to snore in the midst of his lectures.

"See mother, I was right. She'll soon give up when the novelty wears off," he whispered smugly one night, while Lucy slept by the fire, curled up in the old rocking chair, knees drawn up to her chest, bare toes peeking out beneath the hem of her gown. "She'll soon start missing her wealthy gentlemen patrons."

"I think she likes it here." His mother bent over her sewing. "She never speaks of any other life left behind." She swept a fleeting glance at her son. "Or any other man."

He fidgeted in his seat, sliding down to stretch his long legs. "Perhaps there were so many she doesn't remember any one in particular, even my cousin." He clicked his fingers at Vince, who lay by Lucy's chair, sprawled over her discarded shoes, keeping them warm for her. The dog opened one eye, flopped his tail lazily and remained exactly where he was.

"She talks of you a great deal," his mother said nonchalantly, searching in her sewing basket for more thread. "Never stops asking me questions about you."

"What the devil for?" he demanded. "She likes askin' 'em but she doesn't answer any herself, does she? I told you, she can't be trusted." He knew nothing about this woman living under his roof and she adamantly refused to tell him anything. It was a great thorn under his skin, but he couldn't very well whip it out of her. He might jokingly suggest it, just to enjoy her outraged expression, but he'd never lay a violent hand on any woman.

"I daresay she'll share her past with us eventually." His mother was distressingly calm, refusing to bide his warnings.

"Damned wench will run off one day with the plate from the mantle, or steal one of the horses. Mark my words, Mother."

"Oh hush! She'll soon settle in, if you stop badgering the poor girl. A few words of kindness wouldn't go amiss."

He folded his arms, then tried to rest his elbow on the arm of his chair, then shifted position completely, sitting upright and looking for his ale tankard. "Hmph! Settle in?" He looked at her again, where she slept curled up in her chair. "Looks settled in to me."

She did, in fact, look as if she belonged there by his fire.

His mother kept her gaze on her sewing. "Lucy certainly has a very fine, neat stitch. Much better than mine ever was, even before my eyesight began to fail. She's quick, too. Finished the mending on your shirts for me this afternoon and then asked what else she might do before I'd even threaded my needle."

"At least she can do something, then."

Once more he tried to get his dog's attention, but the beast was too content, and beat his tail only once on the flagstones. Clearly decided he was needed where he was, Vince didn't bother to crack an eye in response to his master's summons.

"She's good company for me, John. I miss having your sisters around and since you won't bring a wife home..." She let her words trail off, concentrating on her sewing. He'd never seen his mother this enthralled by a row of stitches, he thought wryly.

There was a long pause. He studied his grimy fingernails. "I suppose she can stay if she's some use to you, Mother."

"No more trial, then?"

Again he eyed the sleeping girl before resuming perusal of his fingers, picking out a bothersome splinter. "As long as she behaves herself and stops quarreling with me she can stay."

"Thank you, John. You are kind to your old mother. I can see what an inconvenience it must be for you, having a young woman like Lucy around, but you make this noble sacrifice for my comfort."

When he slid his mother a sideways glance, she hid her smile, bent over her sewing again. He let it pass, not particularly eager to discuss his reasons for keeping Nathaniel's hussy in his house.

The young woman curled up in the chair now snored gently, hands twitching in her lap.

"Should be in bed, poor thing," his mother exclaimed, setting her sewing aside. "I'll wake her and tell her to go up."

"No." John stood quickly. "Don't wake her. I'll take her up."

"Oh...well...if you think that's best."

He did. The Friday wench was always moving nervously and usually away from him. To have her comparatively yielding and pliant in his arms was a rare opportunity. He worked his fingers to the bone every day, why not have a little reward at the end of it?

Slowly and carefully, he lifted her out of the rocking chair, one arm under her knees, the other under her shoulders. Vince scrambled to his feet with a low, questioning woof.

"Hush, fool beast!"

Might have been a warning to himself, as well as Vince.

She was very slight, needed feeding up. Her body shifted in his embrace, her head rolling against his shoulder. When she murmured his name, it was so soft he couldn't be sure it was even his, but he didn't want her dreaming of anyone else. Instinctively he nestled her tighter against his body. In response she threw one arm around his neck and her breath warmed his skin. His heartbeat quickened.

He daren't look again at his mother. She'd been acting oddly ever since he'd brought Nathaniel's Friday wench home, more oddly than usual and she'd always been a trifle eccentric. His mother liked the girl already, it seemed, but then Nathaniel's Friday wench was another stray in need of a home, and in his mother's opinion there was always room for such in that house. He sincerely hoped the hussy's rebellious quarrelling wouldn't stir his mother to similar mouthiness. One had to be careful with women in groups, so his father had always said.

Vince followed only to the foot of the stairs and then sat, his duties relinquished. He entrusted her to the care of John's arms.

Carrying his warm bundle up the narrow stairs, he moved slowly, fearing she'd wake and wonder what on earth he was doing with her, but he needn't have worried. She was deeply asleep, too tired to feel any jostling. With one foot he nudged open the door to his sisters' chamber, took her inside and laid her gently on the bed, almost afraid to breathe. The sky was bright with moon and stars that night, lighting the chamber even without candles. She liked the shutters open, he'd noticed.

Suddenly the house, usually full of creaks and groans, was quiet, watchful and waiting. The little white cap she always wore was nudged slightly askew, exposing the side of her smooth cheek and a little of that midnight hair.

Fighting the sudden urge to kiss her, he compromised by reaching down, touching her hair. Strange texture. He frowned. She dyed her hair? Of course, women in her profession used all manner of artifice.

She squirmed and stretched, sighing in her sleep. One word slid from her lips and into the hushed stillness of the chamber.

"Lance."

John straightened up, hands limp and heavy at his sides. He would not be tempted from his new path by this Friday wench. No indeed.

Battling the demon jealousy, he struggled for several minutes and then walked out, closing the door quietly behind him, leaving her to those passionate dreams of some other man. As he suspected, Cousin Nathaniel was not her only lover.

But although his doubts were proven, it did nothing to subdue his strange torment.

* * * *

Busy with her tasks each day, Lucy had no chance to explore far beyond the gates. They were generally kept shut to discourage wandering in any case, but from her chamber window she could see a quarter mile up the slight hill, to the rugged outline of an ancient flint tower. She learned this was once home to the Barons Sydney, the old feudal overlords and a family from which Mistress Carver was descended.

"My uncle, God rest his soul, was the last Baron Sydney, the last male of his line," she told Lucy one day as they cleaned the windows together. "He had no sons to inherit and when he died the property reverted to the crown."

"No one lives there now?" There were no lights visible at night and it was a dark, cheerless monolith.

"At present it belongs to Lord Oakham, but he makes his home at the much more comfortable Bollingbrooke Hall, when he's here. He's most often away in London, at court."

The name Oakham sounded vaguely familiar, but there were many folk she'd met under her father's roof. Titled fellows he'd wanted to impress, men who would help him advance in consequence.

Lucy rinsed her rag in the bucket, taking a moment to put her scrambled thoughts in order. It had never occurred to her she might meet someone in this place who had any connection to London and the life she'd left behind. Summoning every shred of calm, she inquired further about Lord Oakham and learned that John had purchased land from him on several occasions to expand the farm. He'd recently furthered their property with the freehold on ten more acres. In the few years since he'd taken charge of the farm, his mother explained proudly, John had also increased the livestock and hired farmhands. Through his planning and hard work, they now prospered more than ever before and Lord Oakham envied John's success.

"But we purchased the land outright and he can't raise the rents on us, as he can to his leaseholders." She rubbed hard at a greasy mark on the crooked window. "When he sold that land to my son, Oakham needed the money and quickly. Never seems to have enough to keep him in all his finery, and the queen planned to visit his manor on summer progress with the court. He required a great deal of coin to prepare the place. Then, after all his efforts, the queen changed her mind and traveled elsewhere." She chuckled at Lord Oakham's misfortunes. "I daresay, if John looked to buy more land in the future, he wouldn't turn down the money."

Lucy was surprised John had enough coin to purchase acres of land directly. He and his mother always dressed plainly and there was no obvious luxury in the house, apart from its many windows and chimneys, which seemed almost over-indulgent.

"John's never been one for boasting," his mother explained genially, reading Lucy's expression. "But he does well for himself, believes in earning his money. Like his father, he's never had much time for the nobility, those who inherited their wealth and never worked a day for it."

"But he's descended from barons," she said, gesturing through the window toward the rugged tower on the hill.

His mother chuckled. "Best not mention it to him. He'd rather not be reminded."

"Why not?"

The old lady considered for a moment. "I suppose it's because they lost it all, spent it all, wagered it away and never had the foresight to make more for themselves. They sat back and rested on what they were given. He can't respect them for that." She sighed heavily. "He has no time for spendthrifts."

What would John think of her, she mused sadly, if he knew the easy, wasteful, sheltered life she'd led in London? No wonder he'd been so scornful of her soft hands.

Looking through the newly-cleaned window, she watched him cross the yard with Vince trotting amiably at his side. John's clothes were stained and worn, his boots muddy again, after she'd spent an hour last night scrubbing them clean. But the sun seemed especially bright where it touched him, lighting him up like an angel. The wretched man might claim to have no time for something beautiful, like sunset over the distant ruins, or a jug full of wildflowers that she'd picked beside the gate and arranged for the supper table, but the sight of him certainly gave her pleasure. It swelled inside her more each day, buoying her spirits whenever she saw him. Sweeping the house with his busy gaze just then, he caught her looking and scowled hard to discourage it.

Her breath formed a slow mist on the glass, until he was obscured from view. He was quite right, of course. She shouldn't be looking at him, or nursing these wistful thoughts.

* * * *

Rather than answer questions regarding Nathaniel's harlot, John kept her out of sight, making certain his mother confined her to the house and yard. When Lucy asked him one day if she was a prisoner, he assured her she was free to leave any time she wished, but as long as she stayed under his roof he would protect her. For Nathaniel's sake.

"Protect me from what?" she exclaimed, her voice sounding odd, as she stopped shoveling dirt and swung around to look at him.

He was watching her clean out the pigsty, still not yet trusting her to do a thorough job without his oversight.

"Protect me from what?" she repeated.

"Just to keep an eye on you, that's all," he replied sharply. "Why?" Eyes narrowed, he studied her rigid form. She was holding the wooden handle of that shovel as if it was made of gold and he might try to steal it from her. "Is there something I ought to know, wench? Are you in some sort of trouble?"

Immediately she turned back to her work, throwing all her strength into it. "Your mother said the sow will have her piglets any day now," she said brightly, changing the conversation.

"That's right. We'll soon have a new litter. More work for you, Friday wench."

Rather than depress her, this news appeared to lighten her spirits further, much to his amusement. He saw her lips turn up. Not that she shared her smile with him. He had to walk around the fence post to catch a glimpse of it.

"If you like, you can be head swine-herd," he said, holding back the laughter.

"Can I? Really?" Last shovel of dirt deposited in the wheelbarrow, she wiped one sleeve across her brow. "Head swine-herd? Are you sure?" Her cheeks were flushed with the honor, eyes too bright. Anyone would think she'd never been given any responsibility.

She was disheveled today, a smudge of mud on her cheek, wisps of hair escaping her white cap, the sleeve of her gown torn, hem trailing stitches. But she was beautiful, possibly the most sorely beautiful woman he'd ever laid eyes on. It struck him, a sharp-set pain. Perhaps, while she stood there surrounded by the filth of the pig-sty, it only highlighted her unearthly beauty. He gripped the fence post to keep his balance.

"You didn't mean it," she said, shoulders falling, lips trembling. "I suppose you were teasing me."

He waited a beat, trying to assure himself she was no different than any other pretty wench. He'd seen a lot of women in his thirty years, many of them very attractive, all of them willing for a tumble. Back before he'd turned his new leaf, of course.

"I mean it," he said finally. "I can't think of anyone better for the job."

Her teeth came down on her lower lip and she wiped one hand across her cheek, smoothing back a stray tendril of dark hair. "Head swine-herd," she said softly.

John didn't have the heart to tell her she would be the only swine-herd he kept, not just the most important one. "Don't get excited," he warned. "There's no more pay involved."

"Pay?" She signaled for him to open the gate, so she could wheel the barrow through. "I didn't think I earned anything but food and shelter. Do you mean to give me a wage now, too?" He saw the little dimple deepen, her smile quirk.

As he held the gate and she passed close, not waiting for him to move aside, her skirt grazed his legs and the knuckles of his free hand. That slight touch from a woman who generally resisted physical contact caused a tremor all the way up into his throat. "You look after these pigs well enough," he muttered, hoarse, "and I'll give you something for it."

"I wouldn't dream of asking for more, Master Carver." She bobbed a shallow curtsey. "I'm in your debt already, sir."

He closed the gate after her and leaned against it, arms folded, watching her wheel her barrow across to the dung heap. She was being facetious, of course. Slowly he smiled. He had the mouthiest, best-looking swine-herd in all of England.

And yes, whatever trouble she was in, he would protect her from it. He'd seen those stunning green eyes widen in fear, her hands clasp tightly around that shovel. Nathaniel's Friday wench brought out his tender side, he realized somewhat resentfully, wondering why it wasn't some other woman, a good, pure, honest wench, who drew his attention like this. Her step was lively now. Was she humming as she worked? Yes, her feet were tapping, her head bobbing.

Naturally, he reminded himself briskly, she wasn't expecting this hardship to last long. Once Nathaniel returned from sea, she would go back to her pampered life and put all this behind her. Yet there was always a chance his cousin might not return. He felt a stab of guilt for thinking it, but Nathaniel might not come back to reclaim his wench.

Glancing over her shoulder, she smiled at him, granting him the full pleasure at last, and the pinches in his gut were soothed away. The ground pitched under his boots again.

Maybe he'd keep her.

As long as she made good use of herself.

* * * *

Later that day he returned home along the lane with the carthorses, and by some lucky providence, caught his longtime sweetheart Alice Croft and her friend Bridget Frye, just as they arrived at his gate. He bid them a hasty good evening while he scrambled for reasons not to let them in. Under no circumstances could they meet his swine-herd, he thought grimly. She required far too much explanation.

Had he not been so nervous, he might simply have let them in and introduced them to her. After all, there was nothing untoward going on, was there?

Instead he made up a hasty lie about his mother being sick, not wanting visitors. The two young women expressed concern, asking if there was anything she might need.

"She'll be all right," he muttered,

ashamed of himself. "She's just tired out lately and needs rest."

"Poor Mistress Carver," Alice exclaimed. "She needs help around the house." And her eyelashes lowered, as if he might think her too bold and putting herself up for the job.

Meanwhile, Bridget's watchful eyes ripped into his face like vulture's talons. "That house is too large for one woman to manage. It needs a wife in it."

He rested one hand on the bars of the gate. "I'll pass your kind thoughts on to my mother, Alice. Bridget."

He watched them go, guilt writhing alongside hunger in his belly. There were folk who thought he led Alice Croft on a chase. Sometimes he thought it too. She was a good girl and it was unfair to keep her waiting. He should've married her by now, even if it was just to help his mother out around the house. Yet, for all her teasing, his mother wouldn't hear of him marrying for such a reason. Once, when he'd suggested it, she lost her temper, shrieking that she'd hang herself before she let him marry just to get her a nursemaid.

So he'd put it off. He'd waited, but for what he had no idea.

Slowly he unlatched the gate and led the horses inside for their well-earned feed and a good rub down. The windows of the house were not yet lit with candles. He was home earlier than usual tonight, eager to leave work behind for once.

Because of the Friday wench. The thought vaulted in, over his protests; it was fluid, fast-flowing, unstoppable.

He'd promised himself he wouldn't touch Nathaniel's woman. Even if she was on loan to him and his cousin willing to share, John knew he couldn't accept those terms. He'd want her all to himself.

In any case, she was the very last sort of distraction he needed in his life, so he'd better stop imagining it. She couldn't cook, hadn't even known how to draw well water until he showed her. A bee sting on her hand yesterday caused such an unholy ruckus one would have thought someone stabbed her through the heart with a knife. When he'd carefully spread his mother's salve on the sting for her, she'd thanked him profusely, as if he'd saved her life. She spent a great deal of time daydreaming out of the window and playing with his dog. Even gave the animal a bath one morning, without his permission. Cleaning floors, however, was plainly something she'd never done before in her life; always forgetting to roll up her sleeves, she then seemed unduly surprised when finding them wet or dirty.

She argued with him too much, called him rude, arrogant, even thoughtless. There was, it seemed, much about him she disliked.

At night, while he lay in bed, staring up at the ceiling, making pictures out of the moonlit cracks, he thought of her across the narrow hall, mere steps away and remembered his mother's words. *I daresay her talents lie elsewhere.*

Lucy Friday was more tempting than a tree full of ripened chestnuts to a boy with a stick. The sooner Nathaniel returned from fighting Spaniards the better.

He paused a moment, breathed deeply and opened the door.

"You're home early tonight, John," his mother exclaimed. "Supper's not even ready yet!"

Vince lollopped over to greet him in the usual way, and he took a moment to pet the beast before glancing shiftily at the young woman setting bowls on the table. She was humming a quiet, blithesome tune, not even looking at him. Already, it seemed, she was part of the household, part of his life. "Finished with work sooner than expected," he mumbled, shrugging off his leather jerkin. "The next few weeks will be busy so I sent the men home early for a rest. It'll do the horses good too. Let them play in the paddock a bit."

Ah yes, all work and no play was bad for man or beast. That was his excuse tonight.

Moody, he slunk over to a chair, fell into it and stretched out his legs, forcing their house guest to step over them as she walked around the table. He wouldn't move aside for her, even when she stopped and looked, waiting politely. Finally she lifted her skirt and stepped over, resuming her soft humming.

Fingers tapping against the arms of his chair, he stared at her slender waist as she bent over to reach across the table. Her skirt stroked his legs and that caress, however unintentional, sent a quicksilver flame up through his limbs. He ceased tapping with his fingers and drew them tight around the chair arms. The wench turned, still humming, and stepped back over his legs again, skirts lifted to show off a pair of shapely ankles and a lace trimmed petticoat, certainly more costly than anything his mother owned. He hoped the pigs appreciated a well-dressed swine-herd.

"Was that Alice Croft I saw at the gate just now?" his mother called out.

Vince sat at his side with a grunt and began to scratch. "Aye." He watched Lucy walk to the sideboard for knives, cups and spoons.

"Why didn't she come in?"

Distantly he replied, "She was

just passing, Mother."

"That's not like Alice. She always calls in if she passes. Any excuse to see you, John."

At the sideboard, Lucy's attention was clearly caught. She turned her head slightly, listening. When she realized he followed her with his gaze, she got on with her work, clutching the cups to her bosom, bringing them back to the table, not looking at him.

"When are you going to put the poor girl out of her misery?" his mother teased, wiping her hands on her apron. "Are you going to ask her to marry you or not? This village has waited two years at least for a wedding."

He watched Lucy banging the cups down, biting her lip.

"Why should it be of any concern to the village?" he replied placidly. "It's no one else's business who I marry. Or when."

"Poor Alice." His mother was grave. "She's certainly been more patient with you than any other girl would be. This time last year I thought you were all but decided and then, this spring, after you came back from Norwich market, suddenly you wanted to put it off again. Suddenly you weren't sure anymore."

He caught Lucy's eye, saw a blush color her face before she speedily returned her attention to the table, fussing unduly over the placement of cups and plates.

"I haven't asked Alice yet," he grumbled, "but I will. Soon. Depend upon it."

Lucy's lips drooped and when she resumed her quiet humming, the notes were a little off. Either she had no ear for a tune or she was agitated.

"Alice Croft is the right woman for me," he added, fidgeting in his chair, cracking his knuckles. "Solid, honest, dependable." He stopped when he saw the sly arch of Lucy's brow and heard his mother snort with laughter. "What now?"

"I never heard a man count 'solid' as a female attribute."

He would have snapped at his mother, but thought better of it, catching Lucy's eye a second time. The Friday wench was probably marking down every time he swore in her hearing or spoke sharply to his mother. She would, no doubt, use the evidence next time they quarreled. So he bit down on the urge to quiet his mother's teasing.

He shifted in his seat. "'Tis best to chose a wife for practical reasons. Alice was raised on a farm and she's accustomed to a hard-working life."

"Like a cart horse," his mother agreed.

The Friday wench seemed amused by this. When she hummed with greater fervor, eyes smiling, he fell silent, watching her sulkily with a gaze fixed and stern, wanting her to feel it.

"I may as well wait to light the candles," she said, addressing his mother rather than the man of the house. "The sun is still setting and the light is so pretty."

Yes, indeed it was, especially the way it lit the high curve of Lucy's milky white breasts when she bent over again before the window, reaching for the bread she'd placed on the ledge to cool. He bit down on his tongue and resettled his long legs, switching one ankle over the other. Those damned teasing bubbies would shortly spill right out of her gown. She wore no ladylike lace partlet and apparently no corset today. Well, that would have to change if she stayed much longer in his house. He couldn't afford to have this sort of thing in his path tempting him intolerably. Just one more sway, one half inch further and that gown wouldn't hold her in. It couldn't take the strain any more than he could. It was ripened fruit ready for plucking, treasure left unguarded, risking plunder. He raised one hand to his mouth, fingers pressed on his lips as a hot surge of pure need spiraled through his body. New leaf be damned. He imagined grabbing Lucy by the waist, pulling her down into his lap.

He tasted the sweet warm skin on her neck....felt her squirm and laugh as he tickled her.

If she stepped over his legs once more...

* * * *

Realizing the bread was out of her reach, Lucy exhaled a short irritable breath and prepared to walk by him again, vaguely annoyed by his refusal to move his big feet, but not particularly bothered enough to give him the satisfaction of asking him to move.

She was poised to lift her skirt, when he leapt to his feet with such alacrity she almost stumbled into his arms. Without a word, he reached for the cooling bread.

Did he just growl at her or was he merely clearing his throat? His gaze was pinned to her bosom. The more she struggled to calm her breath, the faster it came and went, exaggerating the rise and fall.

"Thank you," she gasped, taking the bread from his hands. "I made it myself." She managed a smile, endowed with hope. "My first attempt. I'm not sure it's edible."

He was still not looking at the bread. "It will be," he muttered, the words rolling together, little more than a grunt forced out between his lips. "Edible."

Lucy drew a deep breath of honeysuckle blowing in at the window. "Perhaps I ought to light the candles after all."

"I thought you wanted them out."

Panic tightened around her heart. "What? Why...I never...it wasn't...Why?"

He looked at her face now. "You said the sunset was so pretty."

For one awful moment, when he mentioned her wanting the candles out, she'd thought he referred to their night at Mistress Comfort's. Perhaps because she'd been thinking of it herself, unable to shake off the memory.

She set the bread down and hurried to the fire, to the safety of his mother's side.

The next time she dared look at him, he was staring out through the open window, a gentle breeze blowing a dark curl from his forehead. And suddenly he snapped his head around and pinned her with those watchful eyes.

"Blow out the candles."

"No. I want to see."

She heard their voices clearly, the ghostly shadow of a conversation from two months ago.

"I'll keep the candles lit."

"Do as I say. At once! I'm paying you, remember? This is on my terms! Mine!"

Sudden understanding widened his eyes and then, almost immediately, his eyelids drifted downward, until there was only a sliver of color visible, but she knew he still watched her. His nostrils flared, his lips tightened.

Glad of any practical task, Lucy held the first bowl out for his mother's stew, her heart somewhere around her ankles.

Chapter 10

He didn't come home early from the fields again after that. For the next few days he was gone before she rose and back when she was abed. Lucy might have suspected he avoided her intentionally, if Mistress Carver hadn't assured her this was the busiest time of year.

"We won't see much of him for the next few weeks, until the harvest is over."

Hoping she might one day win his notice for something other than a scornful comment, Lucy asked his mother to teach her cooking and brewing. Her first efforts left much to be desired, but she persevered. One day she'd win a genuine smile from him, even if it killed her.

Determined to catch him before he left the house, Lucy rose extra early on the Saturday that marked the end of her first fortnight at Souls Dryft. As she made her way down, she heard him chastise his mother for wasting time with those cooking lessons.

"She rises late again," he protested, the low, rich timbre of his voice reaching her through the open door at the foot of the stairs. "Must have a pure conscience to sleep so deep and long."

It wasn't late at all, yet he was in the mood to criticize. As usual.

"What ails you?" his mother exclaimed. "Got out of bed on the wrong side? Or didn't you sleep well?"

"I never do of late. Some of us have too much to worry over. Some of us live by what we sow."

"What, pray tell, do you mean by that, John?"

"Well, she's just playin' at it, ain't she? As soon as she's had enough, she'll be off back to town and her fancy gentlemen. For some of us this is life, not a game to be played until we tire of it."

"Lucy works her fingers to the bone and she may not be the most efficient, but you can't fault her for trying. Time you stopped waging war on the poor girl. This is all new to her, but she's adapted very well, truth be told, with no praise from you. Would it harm you to be pleasant to the girl? I can't think what's got into you of late!"

Poised to speak again, he glanced over and saw Lucy emerging through the door. He blinked rapidly, cheeks reddening slightly under all the sun-browning. Grabbing his luncheon pail, he took off for the fields, not saying another word.

He left his mother in a very rattled mood. Angrily declaring the housework would wait for once, she announced a desire to stroll up the lane and show Lucy the fortress that was once home to the Barons Sydney. For the excursion she packed a small basket of bread, cheese and fruit, with a little jug of her special plum wine. It was a brew of considerable strength and something of which John disapproved, especially for women. His mother, apparently, was in the mood to defy his rules and orders.

Glad of the chance to get out and explore, Lucy followed her along the lane, hurrying to keep up, dodging puddles and tripping over muddy ruts. At such a furious pace it didn't take long to reach their destination.

Grass and weeds grew long between the ancient stones, and great tall thistles stood guard around the old gatehouse. No one had tended the place in a long time and the wildlife took over with relish. As they stood in the cobbled courtyard in the shadow of the great stone fortress, doves took startled flight from the battlements. It was a mad cacophony for a moment, the sky dark with fluttering wings, then all was still again, tranquil.

"Sometimes we forget where we came from," Mistress Carver said, hugging her basket of provisions. "I'm sorry to say it, Lucy, but my son is too much a Carver, with all his rough edges and hidebound ways. He's buried our noble Sydney pride under a hard skin and refuses to acknowledge my blood is just as much a part of him as that damned Carver insolence. He never appreciates the finer things in life, has no time for any of that. He deliberately drops his 'h's and 'g's, Lucy. He knows how it grinds on my spleen. I tried my best to instill a little of the gentleman in my boy, but now I see it was a lost cause!"

Lucy thought how strange it would be to see John acting like a fine gentleman. It would probably make her faint, or fall over laughing. But, seeing his mother upset, she kept a straight face. They walked further, into the shadow of a great apple tree.

"I hoped, having a young lady about the place, he might soften his ways and think of brushing his hair with something other than his fingers. I thought he might take an interest in his appearance and smarten his manners. But it seems he's more determined than ever to deny the noble strain in his blood." Mistress Carver shook her head. Looking up into the branches of the apple tree, she closed her eyes. "Of course, he idolizes his father's memory. I suppose that's why he acts that way, trying to be his father."

Sunlight trickled through the gently rustling branches and dappled her face with a veil of emerald and gilt lace. She looked girlish, dreamy.

"I used to sit up in this tree when I was young. Could hide in it for hours and no one would know where I was—especially amid the blossom in spring." She patted the thick, gnarled trunk, as if it was an old friend. "Well, time passes. We can't stay young forever."

"No," Lucy solemnly agreed.

"We shall never be younger than we are today. I try to tell my boy, try to make him see...but he's too busy with his head down, rushing forward like a bull. I'm afraid he pays no heed to an old woman like me." Then her mood changed, or else she forgot her train of thought. "Come, Lucy, I'll take you up the tower and we'll have our luncheon on the roof. You can see for miles."

They ascended the ancient tower steps, onto the walkway, skirting the battlements, and sat together looking down on the spread of villages, fields, lakes and a battalion of tall pines. The sloping roof and jumbled chimneys of Souls Dryft seemed closer than they did as they'd walked up the lane, and she watched birds bobbing in and out of the dovecote, Vince chasing their shadows across the yard.

When Lucy tentatively asked if Lord Oakham might think they trespassed on his property, Mistress Carver replied that this tower belonged to Sydneys long before any upstart Oakham trotted along to claim it and if he wanted some excuse to find her guilty of any crime, she'd damn well give him one.

"Oakham!" she snorted, passing Lucy the jug of plum wine. "Where were they at the Battle of Hastings? I daresay they weren't riding to victory like my ancestor, the great Norman knight Remy St. Denis."

Lucy agreed, sipping the wine cautiously and wincing as it burned her throat all the way down. Her father generally gave her watered-down wine and she'd never drunk anything like this. Mistress Carver's plum wine made her decidedly merry and also deeply thoughtful about everything, especially the shape of the clouds, which seemed close enough to touch.

Somewhere in one of those distant fields, glowing in the sun, John was hard at work. She wished she might work alongside, sharing his burden, but of course he would never let her. It was not her home and never could be. A hunted woman, she must soon be on her way again, for the longer she stayed, the more likely she'd be discovered, captured and taken back to face what she'd done.

She looked at the woman beside her and said warmly, "Thank you for making me at home here. I will always remember your kindness."

Mistress Carver smiled. "There is no need to thank me."

"But you've been so patient. It's almost as if you weren't surprised when I came, as if you expected me."

"I did."

"But how ?"

"Nathaniel wrote to me."

"Oh." This had never occurred to her.

"I decided not to tell John when he left to fetch his cousin's belongings. If he knew there was a woman involved, he might have refused to go, but I knew, once he saw you there, he wouldn't turn you away. Nathaniel wrote that you were a young lady in trouble, in need of friends."

Lucy took another drink from the wine jug before passing it back to Mistress Carver. Perhaps she'd had enough. It wouldn't do to lose her inhibitions and start telling the lady all her troubles. "Well, thank you," she said, meaning it with every fiber of her being. "I don't know what I would've done if he'd refused to bring me."

The old lady brushed crumbs from her skirt, brisk and no-nonsense. "John would never turn his back on a woman in need." She sipped her wine. "Whatever trouble you might be in, John will help. I know he seems a hard nut, but he's a good boy at heart, and loyal."

Still troubling over how much her hostess knew, she finished her luncheon quietly while Mistress Carver eventually continued her rambling lesson on family history and why Sydneys were, in fact, far superior to Carvers.

* * * *

John was not at all happy.

His mood grew steadily worse, as the truth became ever more inescapable. Why had he not seen it before? Perhaps because he daren't look at her too long, daren't let himself imagine...

For weeks she'd haunted him. He'd just begun to think she was fading out of his mind at last, and now she came back again, in the flesh, to torment him further.

Full of pent-up energy, he threw himself into the harvest. At night he was wakeful, couldn't settle and the summer heat gave little respite. All too well aware of the woman across the narrow hall, he tried innocent thoughts, of skipping lambs and such like, but in no time his mind returned to her, wondering whether she was awake too, and frantically counting sheep.

On this Saturday, when he stayed late haymaking in the fields, his mother sent the hussy to fetch him home to supper.

Hearing soft murmurs of surprise and appreciation from his hired laborers, he looked up, stretching out his back. There she was, venturing outside the boundaries he'd set. She picked her way through the field, holding her skirt out of the hay, eyes down. She still wore her hair up under a linen cap, which was looking decidedly worse for wear now, but a few strands trickled loose down her neck and the sunset caught on them as she came closer, revealing a deep luster under the patchy black dye. When she stumbled over her own two feet, the cap was dislodged briefly and, for just a moment, her hair was aflame.

"Hey ho! Who's this then?" someone said.

Fury leapt in his chest. He'd told his mother never to let her out into the fields, because he knew the other men would ask questions he'd rather not answer. And some he couldn't.

She stumbled again, falling forward. Every man, except John, stepped up to save her, but she saved herself, laughing. Another lock of hair fell loose down the side of her neck. Definitely copper.

"Are you coming to supper, John?" she asked, slightly breathless. "Your mother sent me to fetch you."

All eyes now turned to him in surprise, amusement and a fair spattering of envy. She waited for his answer, gently blowing a loose tendril of long hair from her lips, while the men looked from her to him and back again.

He turned away, not having decided what to do with her yet, and swung his scythe. "No," he muttered. He heard the rustle as she moved closer and so he stopped again. "Mind out o' the way."

"But it's late and your mother waits to eat. She said I'm not to come back without you."

He was painfully aware of the other workers standing around, gathering closer to get a better look at the beauty in the fancy scarlet frock.

"You must be hungry by now," she added.

When he made the mistake of looking over at her, he realized just how hungry he was. She stood framed by the sun's blush, hands behind her back, face turned up to the sky, her arching pose showing off her long, graceful neck and the plump curve of her bosom as she watched a flock of geese pass overhead.

"Aye...well..." All the pent up lust of a healthy, young red-blooded male soared through his veins and pumped life into his manhood. "I suppose I can stop...for now."

Her gaze still followed the geese for

a moment, while he greedily drank in the sight of her steeped in gold. Then she shaded her eyes with one hand, looking at him again. "Good." Her smile was a little too wide and relaxed, her body swaying. Something was amiss, but he didn't know what.

As he wiped his face on his sleeve, one of the workers closed in for an introduction. Martin Frye was an eager lad, whose callow boldness never concerned itself with stepping on another fellow's toes or territory. The boy almost fell over his own feet as he rushed forward. The Friday wench turned her gaze to Martin Frye, looked him up and down with interest, and smiled again in that lazy, sensual way.

John quickly stepped forward, took her elbow and steered her back across the field.

"Your friend seems a pleasant young fellow," she observed as he tightened his fingers around her arm.

"He's not my friend."

"Oh?"

He stared straight ahead, not yet trusting himself to look at her again. He smelled the plum wine on her breath, so now he knew the source of her odd smile and the stumbling. Churlish, he thought about finding every jug of that stuff and pouring it out in the yard. It was never wise to let a woman near something so potent, no matter how his mother protested she was allowed one vice in her life. At her age she ought to know better. Fancy giving this wench, who was plainly trouble enough, plum wine, just to add coal to the fire!

Once through the gate and out in the lane, he stopped abruptly, hand still around her arm. "It was you, wasn't it ?"

"What was?"

"In Norwich."

All amusement melted from her countenance. She tried to remove her arm, but he gripped her tightly. He would not let her get away again. She'd left him once before, left him to suffer.

"I don't know what you mean," she said, eyes flaring, shooting sparks of reflected sunset. "I've never been to Norwich. I...I don't even know where it is." Up went her eyebrows and the disdainful little nose.

"I met a woman there in a bawdy house, two months ago," he said slowly. "She wore a mask and wouldn't tell me her name."

"A house of ill-repute? How dare you suggest I ever visited such a place!"

Releasing her arm, he muttered, "Can't imagine where I might get the idea. Can you?"

"Certainly not." She fussed with those loose strands of hair, trying to put them back under her cap. "And frankly, Master John Carver, I wonder what business you had in such a place either!" She stormed off, head high, as if she had somewhere important to go without him. Oh no, the strumpet would not walk away, dismissive and haughty.

His long stride soon caught up with her. "Nathaniel put you up to it, did he, trollop? Was it another of his little jests to send you to seduce me at Mistress Comfort's?"

Even her freckles paled. "You stinking, wretched, hypocrite! Filthy, rotten...goatypig!"

"Goatypig?"

"Yes. That's what you are. A goat," she held up one hand and then the other, "and a pig." Clapping her hands smartly together, she just missed his nose. "But with none of the good, just the worst aspects of both rolled into one."

"You've been at my mother's plum wine haven't you?"

Hands on her waist, she stood her ground. "So what if I have?"

Glowering down at the bedraggled creature with the stubborn lips and prim, upturned nose, John once again suffered an undeniable jolt of need. At least once a day, since he'd brought her here, these feelings came to him and usually at a very inconvenient moment.

She could deny it all she liked.

But he knew her. Intimately. In every way.

Where had she been before then? How many other men had she known since him? Had she thought of him at all in the time between? Anger, jealousy and hurt battled for supremacy. No woman had ever done this to him. No woman would dare treat him this way.

She was leaving him again, her quick step already passing through the gates to the yard. He followed, grabbed a pitchfork from the hay cart and ran around in front of her, holding it like a weapon. She skidded to a halt, eyeing the pitchfork fearfully.

"Tell me the truth, Friday wench." She stepped back against the cart and he followed. "It was you, wasn't it? Confess!"

She regarded him sourly, lips pursed, head on one side. He resettled the pitchfork across his thighs, holding it with both hands.

"Well?"

"I've never seen you before in my life. Not before you found me waiting on the Captain's cart in Yarmouth."

The little scar under her eye was not familiar to him, but her lips were. So was the dimple and the hair, now its true color began to show. She had the sheer gall to feign ladylike, dainty manners when he knew exactly what she was and what she'd done to him, damn her.

She was the best birthday gift he'd ever had.

There was an odd break in the rhythm of his heartbeat.

"You're not a very good liar," he observed coolly, trying to remain calm. "Surprisingly enough, for a whore."

She was silent.

"Is that where Nathaniel found you? At Mistress Comfort's?"

"I don't know what you--"

"After you left my bed, did you go to his?"

"You speak nonsense." Now she put on a little display of exaggerated outrage, almost comical, waving her arms wildly. "I've never been in any bed with you. I'm shocked you would suggest it."

He stepped closer and she turned her face away. "Did he celebrate with you later?" he spat. "I'm surprised he didn't come to crow over me, once he proved I couldn't stay celibate until I married. He chose you, I suppose, because he knew I'd never resist you."

"How dare you mistake me for some sixpenny whore?"

"I've no doubt you charge more than sixpence." He remembered every sweet inch of her butter-soft skin. "I'm lucky Nathaniel paid your fee. It was my birthday, but I never expected him to remember me with such a generous gift. Since I'm covering your living expenses while he's away, I'm entitled to some arrangement surely. I realize your accommodation here in my humble abode is hardly luxury, but it must count for something toward the fee." The anger he'd sworn to restrain refused to oblige for the sake of his pride. It sputtered out of him, wild and tempestuous, too much even for him to handle. "What would you charge me, then? Just out of curiosity. Not that I've any intention of paying for it. How much for one night?"

* * * *

Lucy was too indignant to manage any reply. She certainly wasn't ready to tell him what sent her to Mistress Comfort's or how she came to be with Nathaniel. In many ways John Carver was still an unknown quantity to her, as much mystery as he'd been the night they'd met. Back then, the only two things concerning her had been his ability to perform the job and that she'd found him attractive. Now, he was an entire person with a life and family. She'd never wanted to make anyone like her before, never sought approval from anyone other than her father, and the Lord knew that was a thankless task. But she realized how much she wanted John to like her, respect her, not to have him think her a whore, shout at her with fire in his eyes, the veins standing out on his neck, his hands clenched into fists.

If he ever hit her he would do more damage than old Winton, she thought grimly.

But he wouldn't hit her. Or would he? How did she know?

She'd recently discovered she knew a great deal less about men and life in general than she'd thought she'd known when living under her father's strict governance. Sometimes, when more of this shocking self-pity welled up in her throat, she wished she'd never left her old world where all was familiar, even if it killed her slowly. Better that, perhaps, than to be out here, tired, sore and unappreciated, with this dreadful, uncouth, rough-handed, big, gorgeous man yelling at her. If her father were here, he'd have something to say. Yes he would. John Carver would be put in his place then and never dare raise his voice to her again.

Damn him! He was a country peasant who should be thanking her for the honor she once bestowed upon him, not accusing her of being a harlot who went from one bed to another. How dare he? How dare he? Had he taken no part in what had happened? It seemed he was just like every other man after all, another believer in the great double-standard. He would bed with a whore, then look down on her as a woman of loose morals, while thinking himself above reproach. He was ready to blame her, say she tempted him.

There was only one thing she could do when he questioned her so crudely: maintain her innocence. Deny everything.

"It wasn't me, you great stupid, country oaf!"

Still, even as her own fury mounted, the fire ignited by plum wine, she realized what she wanted from him most of all was a kiss. A long, hard, hot, wet one.

And he was staring at her mouth, as if the same ridiculous idea was on his own mind.

"You best tell me the truth, whore," he growled, "or I'll..."

She stuck out her chin. "Or what, plowman?"

"I'll send you back to Yarmouth, or Norwich, or wherever you came from. I won't keep a lying deceiver in my house."

"I told you, I've never been to Norwich."

"If I saw you naked, I'd know for sure."

"Well, you'll never see me naked, will you? So there!"

He gave her a dark, sinister look and she backed up another step against the hay cart, fearing he might actually try to rip the clothes off her there and then. He was arrogant enough to think he had the right. "You're on loan to me, wench, remember?"

"Nathaniel didn't mean it that way, fool!"

"Oh?" He leaned closer. "How did he mean it then? Am I supposed to look and not touch? You've teased me since I brought you here."

"I certainly have not!"

"Yes you have. And I've told you before, wench, don't argue with me! And don't leave these gates again without my permission."

"I thought I wasn't your prisoner?" she shouted.

"Now you are, since you've proven yourself untrustworthy. You'll do as I say and stay in the house."

"I'll do what I like and go where I like."

"Over my dead body," he yelled at her.

"Fine! Suits me!" He wasn't the first man she'd done away with, was he? With a flounce of her skirts, head tipped back proudly, she began to march around him, but he stopped her again with the pitchfork.

"Or over yours," he growled menacingly. "Confess, wench. It was you."

"If you're so sure, why do you need my confession?"

He considered briefly, eyelids lowered to hide the wicked gleam. "Until you confess your sins, you can't be forgiven and we can't get beyond it."

The plum wine sang in her veins, making her bold and considerably careless. "I'm weary of this conversation and I'm going in. Get out of my way."

"I'm in charge here, Friday wench, not you."

"If I wanted a master I would have stayed..." she stopped, recovered, and hissed through gritted teeth. "I told you...I'll do as I please."

"Not while you're under my roof and eating my food."

She said nothing. The sun had disappeared behind the chimneys of the house and all was still. The birds finally rested after a long day of song, but his mother's gentle humming drifted out through the open shutters.

"Whatever my cousin let you get away with," he said, every word succinct, loaded with menace, "you won't find me so tolerant."

"You don't frighten me...peasant!"

Throwing the pitchfork aside, he closed in the last little distance, one hand on each side of her as she leaned back against the cart. "Well, you ought to be afraid of me, Lucy. If that's your real name."

She wrinkled her nose and rolled her eyes, determined not to show an ounce of fear.

"You have no idea what I could do to you," he breathed against her cheek.

"Ha! I know exactly, don't I, since you've already done everything..." She froze.

He let out one sly, wicked chuckle. "Never been to Norwich, eh? Never been in any house of ill-repute or laid in any bed with me? Better not drink anymore plum wine or you might reveal all your secrets."

She cursed herself for the slip, but it was too late. John leaned over her, staring at her mouth and she was hot, melting like a pat of butter left on a sunny window ledge. Expecting a kiss, she parted her lips. Instead, he licked her cheek, slowly and carefully. She gasped, a quick, startled inhalation as his shirt brushed against her breasts and then she put her hands to his chest, pushing him back.

He licked his lips. "Just as I thought." He was hoarse. "I remember the taste."

"Don't you dare lay a finger on me again."

"It wasn't a finger." He grinned slowly.

Nose in the air, she swung her skirts to walk around him, but he caught her sleeve again and held it in his iron grip. "I know who you are, wench."

"You know nothing about me," she declared, half laughing. Oh, wouldn't he be surprised to know the truth?

"I know this," he whispered, his breath toying with a stray frond of hair as it tumbled down her neck. "You were mine first. Therefore you belong to me, not Nathaniel. And this changes everything."

Chapter 11

That evening, as the effects of the plum wine slowly wore off, she played solitaire by the fire, trying to ignore him, while he slumped in his chair, watching her as if she were a criminal under his guard. Vince sat beside her, his great head on her knee. Occasionally the dog's gaze flicked back and forth between them, is if he were unsure whose side he was on, but was definitely aware of a battle being waged. Knowing how much the dog's torn loyalties disturbed John, she patted his head, fondled his ears and told him how good he was, even occasionally planting kisses on his furry head.

Every angry little twitch, every muted ramble from across the hearth, counted as a small victory. He wouldn't talk to her again as he had today and get away with it. She was a lady, not a whore. Perhaps, just once, she had lapsed, but let he who is without sin cast the first stone, she thought angrily. As far as she recalled, he'd enjoyed himself as much as she had, probably even more, since he'd had no unhappy marriage hanging over his head at the time.

Mistress Carver didn't appear to notice the chill in the air, or at least, she was wise enough not to mention it. Tonight the old lady wrote letters to her daughters in Dorset. Lucy, searching for some conversation to take her mind off other matters, asked if they came home often to visit.

"Not so often as I might like," his mother replied. "But I'm glad to see them both happily wed, and they have families of their own now." She looked up from her letter. "Besides, I still have John to fuss over me."

Lucy glanced over at him. He'd just taken a sip from his pewter tankard and now, gaze trapping her in a fiercely possessive hold, he licked his lips. "I've no taste for cider tonight. I've a sudden hankering for something else."

"Do you want some ale, John?" his mother asked. "I'm sure Lucy will fetch the jug from the pantry."

"No Mother. 'Tis not ale I have the taste for either. Something sweeter."

"There's buttermilk, if you--"

"I can't think what it is I have a thirst for," he interrupted, nursing his tankard to his chest. "Can't think of the name. I had it once, a while since. Not sure if I ever knew the name of it in fact."

Clearing her throat loudly, Lucy slapped another card down. "You have many grandchildren, Mistress Carver?"

"Oh yes. My eldest daughter, Grace, has only one child, a dear little girl, but my younger daughter Maddie has eight children. Five girls and three boys."

"Eight?" Lucy felt the fire in her cheeks. "Gracious! So many!"

"And she acts as if each one was purely by accident." The old lady sniffed, returning to her letter. "I told her, by now she ought to know what's causing it, but she pretends not to hear and keeps making the same mistake. She always was a contrary girl."

"Always thought she knew what was best," John interrupted gruffly. "Always mouthy, eh Mother? Always telling fibs." He shot Lucy a dark, ominous look. "Always giving commands, trying to take charge. A woman is supposed to be yielding, obliging, and come when she's summoned, right Mother?"

Accustomed to this high-handed manner, his mother merely tut-tutted, not looking up from her letter. Lucy resumed her card game, keeping her expression bland.

"But I don't suppose my sister bosses her husband," he added. "He wouldn't stand for it. No sensible man would."

"Aye," his mother agreed this time. "She met her match with him. Thankfully. I don't know what we would have done with her otherwise."

"Women should know their place, stay where they're put and where they're needed," John added, his voice low, carefully measured. "They should be grateful to a man for his patience and generosity, not use him for trickery or take his forgiveness for granted."

Lucy flipped another card and her shoulders stooped when she realized she was losing her hand. She needed the ace of hearts, or there was no hope. It had to be there, one of the cards as yet unturned, unreachable. If she played by the rules. A veteran of many lonely games of solitaire, she thought nothing of making her own rules when necessary. She slyly slid a fingertip under each turned card, until she found the one she sought. Biting her lip, she fumbled the excess cards in her hand, dropped and retrieved them again, this time with the elusive ace of hearts safely shuffled into their midst.

"But my daughter Madolyn got her comeuppance," Mistress Carver continued. "Her eldest daughter, Catherine, is twice as bad as she ever was, so I hear. Quite a handful. It does my heart good to know she finally understands what a trial it is to raise a troublesome daughter."

Lucy smiled distantly, concentrating on her game.

"You have no nieces and nephews? No married sisters, dear?" Mistress   Carver   asked nonchalantly.

"A brother. Not married." Too caught up in her game, she'd answered the lady's questions without thinking and now John sat up, his interest captured.

"A brother? Where's he then?"

"I...don't know." It was true; she didn't know where he was exactly. Lance might be in London. He might be anywhere. As the Earl of Swafford's bodyguard, he was always traveling.

"Why aren't you with him then? Is your father still alive?"

In her peripheral vision, she caught Mistress Carver gesturing at her son to stop asking questions.

"If you were my sister," he exclaimed, "you wouldn't be living in sin with men old enough to be your father. Obviously he doesn't care about you."

"Not true," she replied heatedly. "He cares very much." A few months ago she would never have said it aloud. In her family showing one's feelings was not done and they certainly never spoke about them to others.

"Then he must not know what you've been up to. When was the last time you saw this brother of yours?"

"Enough, John," his mother intervened, blotting her letter with a sound thump. "Lucy is not required to answer your inquisition."

"Why?" He stood, throwing his bulky shadow across the hearth. Vince whimpered, raising his head from Lucy's knee. "She lives in my house. Why shouldn't I ask her questions?" Leaning over, he snatched the ace of hearts out of her hand. "Besides, she cheats!"

"I do not!"

"You do! I just saw you with my own two eyes. Will you lie about that now too?"

Lucy would gladly have gouged those blue eyes out with her fingernails. She gathered up the cards and shuffled them with dexterity, proving how many hours she'd spent doing it. After a pause, he let the disputed card flutter into her lap. "You wouldn't cheat if I played with you."

"Wouldn't I?"

"Nothing gets by me." He gestured to his eyes. "And these. I see everything"

Hubris, she thought scornfully. Pride comes before a fall.

Making a bored, weary face, she dealt her cards for another game of solitaire. "Unfortunate for whatsername...Alice Croft?" When she looked up, his sun-browned face was several shades darker, those supposedly all-seeing, all-knowing eyes narrowed beneath thick, black lashes.

"Why should it be? She's a pure, sweet, trustworthy girl. And faithful. If I play with her, I don't have to worry, do I? Alice Croft doesn't use men, doesn't whore herself out--"

"John!" his mother exclaimed.

"And she doesn't cheat," he finished firmly.

Lucy shrugged. "If you say so."

"I do."

"Good for you, then."

"Yes," he shouted, finger thrust into his chest, "good for me!"

"As I said, didn't I?"

After a quivering moment of silent rage, he dropped back in his chair and Vince trotted over to sit with him, panting.

"As long as you don't cheat, either," Lucy murmured, smiling at her cards, "I'm sure she'll be very happy. When you finally do decide to play with her and put aside your other games."

Victory. He petted his dog, sitting stiffly in his chair as if he might bolt out of it and strike her.

"But you're such an honest, pious fellow, now you're reformed and so very righteous. I'm sure you don't cheat either. Alice has no reason to suspect you play with anything but an honest hand, does she?"

She pushed her luck, she knew it, but simply couldn't stop herself.

"There's no truer man than my son," Mistress Carver interrupted from her corner, only partially listening to their quarrel. She sealed her letter with a drip of wax. "Any woman who gets John for a husband will be lucky indeed. Like his father--a rarity, a good husband." She sighed heavily. "It took Will Carver long enough to pin me down, but once he had me he never looked at another, nor did I."

Lucy smiled benignly at the old lady's fondness for her departed husband. John looked at her as if to say "see?" But she knew he wasn't faithful to his precious Alice. He certainly hadn't been two months ago, had he? Probably wasn't the first time he'd been distracted from his "pure, sweet, trustworthy" Alice either, or he would have married her by now.

Solid, he'd called the poor girl. The thought still made Lucy chuckle, but she swallowed it quickly, ashamed. It was hardly Alice's fault. The luckless girl wasn't to know what he'd been up to in Norwich, when he thought no one would find out. Like all men, he got away with whatever he could. Looking the way he did, a wicked devil in the guise of an angel, John Carver made more mischief than most.

"That reminds me, mother." He stretched languidly in his chair. "I must go to Norwich market next Wednesday. Forgot to mention it."

His mother did not, apparently, wonder why thoughts of a trip to Norwich should flow naturally out of a conversation regarding faithfulness to Alice Croft.

Lucy, however, felt her heart slow, her blood cool. He was going to Norwich again. To spread more wild oats at Mistress Comfort's? Faithful indeed!

"I won't be back 'til late," he said casually, one hand scratching his chest through the opened laces of his shirt.

"Perhaps you should stay the night and come back in the morning, like you did last time," his mother suggested. "I don't like you traveling in the dark so far."

He lurched forward, catching the cards as they slipped from Lucy's hands. "Yes. I suppose it would be best."

She snatched the cards out of his clutches. "Do you go to Norwich often?"

"Often enough."

"For the market?"

"For things I need and can't get here." Falling back again, he put his arms behind his head, stretching out his legs in a familiar pose. Smug. Watchful. It flashed through her mind: *"Take 'em off for me, wench."* Oh, he'd enjoyed himself, making her beg, making her say "please."

She tucked another loose lock of hair back under her cap. "Things for the farm?"

"Sometimes." He ran his tongue along his lower lip, as it curved in a thoughtful, distant smile. "There's not much to be had around here. Sometimes a man has to go all the way to Norwich to get what he needs. Find what he's looking for."

Clearly Alice didn't advance him any favors then. Smart girl.

Well, whatever he did whenever he went to Norwich, she knew he was not a regular at Mistress Comfort's. Unless, of course, the proprietress had lied to be discreet. More than likely.

Feeling sick now, she set down her cards. "I think I'll go up to bed."

"Why not take Lucy to Norwich with you?" his mother said. "She might like a day out. She's worked so hard."

There was a pause.

"No, thank you," she said. "I'd rather stay here." She never wanted to go back there again, never wanted to be anywhere near Lord Winton's house.

Stooping to light a candle in the fire, she was aware of John's gaze, raking over her with intense vigor. "Sure?" he asked silkily. "I'll take you with me, if you promise to behave and do as I say." He played the benevolent master now, deigning to grant her a day off, with conditions. He was also inequitably handsome in the burnished gold and bronze ripple of firelight.

"No," she said again.

"You might change your mind by then and want to ride with me. I thought you enjoyed yourself, the last time we rode together."

Passing his chair, stepping over his untidy legs again, she whispered, "I wouldn't go as far as the next village with you in that cart, unless I was laid out stiff as a board." She raised her voice then and smiled sweetly. "Good night." She took her candle up the stairs to bed.

* * * *

The next day he decreed Lucy would go with them to chapel in Sydney Dovedale. She balked, but he insisted.

"You live under my roof, you'll go to chapel like every other good soul in this village."

"It didn't worry you last Sunday when you and your mother went without me."

"Well, it bothers me now," he muttered.

There was no way around it. He was apparently ready to face the inevitable gossip at last.

Mistress Carver had not expected her son's sudden turnabout either and she fretted that there wasn't enough time to sew Lucy a plainer gown. She advised her to wear a cloak over her flamboyant frock and try not to pay heed to any of the looks they were bound to get. They seldom had strangers in the village, she explained, and John had given no explanation for her presence in his house. The village gossips, left to their imaginations, would doubtless let them run wild.

On this sunny day, sweltering under her cloak, Lucy quickly discovered John Sydney Carver was the most sought after bachelor in Sydney Dovedale and the surrounding villages. Not only hard-working and respectably prosperous, he was, of course, exceedingly pleasant to look upon. Being a supposedly reformed rogue made him doubly irresistible. Every woman, unmarried or not, eagerly watched him enter the church and subsequently took note of her trailing along behind.

Immediately she felt their suspicion and distrust. Surely, if she were in their shoes, she would react the same. But her empathy was wasted. It won her no points with them and, in fact, the more sorrowfully apologetic she made her expression, the deeper their frowns. To make matters worse, when she stumbled over a chipped floor tile, John put his hand on her arm and never let go again until she was safely seated at his side. The audible, anguished sighs drifting over the heads of the congregation raised the temperature to an uncomfortable degree.

Two women watched her closely. One was a brunette, lushly curvaceous and bordering on blousy. The other was fair, rather prim and very upright. Later she learned the fair-headed creature was Alice Croft, long considered the front runner in pursuit of John Carver. Her bosomy friend was Bridget Frye. Lucy attempted a friendly smile, only to be rebuffed at once by both young women. They turned their backs, their heads instantly bent together as they whispered.

John seemed oblivious to it all, his gaze on the parson, hands on his knees, tapping lightly with his fingers, no doubt impatient to be busy again. On his other side, his mother sat with her eyes closed, as if asleep. No one dared reprimand her. At her age, as she'd said to Lucy, she got away with a great deal more than most.

Sitting quietly, hands in her lap, Lucy paid only scant attention to the sermon, taking everything in: the dusty floor tiles, the damp, stately stonework and the bejeweled sunlight winking through the stained glass window above the pulpit. How many generations of Sydneys had sat their proud posteriors in that chapel, she wondered, remembering the man beside her was a direct descendent of Norman knights and barons. Her own family history was nothing compared to his, for her father, despite his wealth, was a mere parvenu, always striving to better his place in life, using his children to make alliances with old nobility.

John brushed the folds of her skirt and she knew his leg must have moved closer. Whether or not it was an involuntary motion, she wasn't sure. There was nowhere to move away--a stone pillar blocked her left side. And then his knuckle moved very slightly, stroking her thigh through layers of skirt and petticoat, but he kept his gaze fixed ahead, feigning innocence and dutiful attention to the parson.

Again his finger moved, slower this time, more definite so she couldn't possibly mistake it for any sort of accident.

Squeezing her legs together, she moved as far as possible against the stone pillar. Now his brows knotted, his jaw twitched. He slid just half an inch after her, pretending to stretch out a cramp in his knee, then his shoulder.

It was much too hot in that cloak. She might faint, and what would be worse? To faint in the chapel and possibly cause John Carver to carry her out in his strong arms, or be stared at with disdain, as she was already? Her choice made swiftly and in some desperation, she slid the cloak from her shoulders as carefully as she might to avoid any additional attention. John ceased tapping his knee. At least now he'd stopped touching her, but she cringed under the sharp, envious gaze of several young ladies, whose lips were quickly pursed in agreement about her. It was truly astounding how much trouble a little bosom might cause, even when doing nothing spectacular, only sitting precisely where God had put it. Even the parson momentarily lost his place, mopping his eyes with a kerchief before he found the use of them again.

In his raised pew at the front of the chapel, Lord Mortimer Oakham, recently returned from London, actually went so far as to open the little iron fretwork window separating his person from the unwashed mob, and peered out slyly. When he caught Lucy looking back at him, he quickly shut his window, only to re-open it a few moments later.

"Best steer clear of him," Mistress Carver whispered a warning from the corner of her lips, leaning across his son. "They say he has an eye for the ladies and an appetite for trouble."

Lucy caught John Carver's steely-eyed gaze fixed upon her, particularly on the parts of her revealed by the dropping of her cloak.

Apparently Lord Oakham wasn't the only soul with such an appetite.

* * * *

"Had to show off, did you?" John hurried her along toward the gate after church. Another angry gaze directed at her gown explained further, just in case she might have failed to understand his meaning.

"I was hot," she protested, heartily sick of his pious expression.

"Hot indeed! If you're looking for a new protector in Sydney Dovedale, you'd best think again. No one here has the coin to keep a strumpet like you, so you may as well put all that away."

They were interrupted by the arrival of Alice and her father, who approached the gate at the same time.

"Mistress Carver," Alice exclaimed with a note of forced cheerfulness, "I'm glad to see you recovered. I didn't think you'd be out today and I was on my way to bring you calves foot jelly, a great restorative for the blood."

John's mother looked surprised.

"You were? How sweet of you, my dear." Both she and Lucy glanced at John's unusually pale, angry face. Lucy frowned, but his mother swiftly hid her moment of confusion and covered for her son's lie. "I'm feeling much improved. Am I not, John?"

He nodded, fiercely examining his scarred knuckles.

"Thanks to our extra pair of hands," she added jauntily, dragging Lucy forward. "This is my nephew's ward, Lucy Friday. Lucy, this is Alice Croft and her father, Adolphus Croft of Bay Brook farm, just over the other side of the village."

Alice had a pinched face and close set eyes which, even as they tried to avoid looking, stared hard at Lucy's scarlet gown, particularly its low-cut bodice. Her mouth finally wedged itself far enough open to mumble a greeting, which Lucy returned with far more warmth, hoping the girl would see she had no design on John's affections.

Not far behind the Crofts came Bridget Frye and her brother, who Lucy had briefly met in the fields the day before. Martin Frye was evidently a forward young man and a fearless opportunist. Immediately he engaged her in conversation, asking how she liked the village, what she thought of the parson's sermon and whether she liked kittens, since his cat recently birthed a large litter. He completely ignored his sister's dark frowns and hard pinches, much to Lucy's amusement. John eventually pried her away.

"Best be going," he muttered, steering her into the shadow of the gate, cutting her conversation off mid-sentence.

"It was a pleasure to meet you, Mistress Friday," old farmer Croft exclaimed as she was whisked by, her feet barely allowed to touch the ground. "I hope you mean to stay a while, my dear. Your presence certainly brightened the chapel today. Such a change it is to see a pretty face in the village."

She thanked him for his kind comments, even as John gripped her around the waist, thrust her under the gate arch and out into the lane. Alice looked askance at her father, then at John, before she walked away toward the village, a slightly wilted slope to her shoulders. Instantly Lucy felt compassion for the girl, knowing all too well what it was like to be unappreciated by one's father.

Still pondering poor Alice's predicament, she was almost trampled into the grass by John following so closely on her heels. In the distance, she now heard a male voice calling out above the general clamor of villagers, "Mistress Carver! Mistress Carver!"

She twisted around to see who it was, but John tugged her along the lane with no further delay, clearly intent on ignoring those shouts. His mother hurried after them, chiding her son for making an unnecessary scene at the gate.

His haste was all for naught, in any case. Lord Oakham's horse soon caught up with them, clattering around in the dirt until they were forced to stop. Introductions were now inescapable, and since John kept his jaw stubbornly tight, his mother stepped up to the task.

Oakham was a slender fellow, with soft features and slumberous, pale blue eyes shot through with vivid red, but when they fixed upon Lucy they became more awake and attentive. He stayed mounted, obviously thinking himself above the Carvers in consequence. In the midst of aimless, stilted conversation he leaned down gallantly to kiss Lucy's hand, exclaiming she was a welcome addition to the village scenery. As he spoke, she knew, with a terrible pinch in her belly, that she'd heard his listless voice before. Those indolent, blood-shot eyes peering down at her were equally familiar.

She curtseyed, her mind scrambling, her gaze searching the ruts of dried mud at her feet.

"Have we met before, Mistress Friday?"

For a moment her world went black. An eclipse of the sun, of her new life.

They would come for her now. She would be discovered.

Her mouth was dry, her nerves stretched to snapping point after a morning subjected to hard stares, nasty whispers and surreptitious strokes of one roguish finger. "I think not, sir." Sobs stuck in her throat and she feared they made her voice sound strained, tense.

"Something about you seems familiar to me."

She felt John's stern scrutiny fixed upon her. His disapprobation was a palpable force.

"No, sir. I'm sure we've never met."

Lord Oakham's horse jibbed sideways. "Ah well, I shall look forward to furthering our acquaintance now, Mistress Friday. You mean to stay long in Sydney Dovedale?"

"She's only staying until my cousin comes back," John intervened, stepping between her and the horse's flank. "Now if you'll excuse us, we've work to do."

"On the Sabbath day, Master Carver?"

"A working farmer gets no day of rest, only an hour or two. We can't all be gentlemen of leisure."

Much to Lucy's relief, John's mother politely drew the conversation to a halt by inviting Lord Oakham to visit when he was next out for a ride. The man accepted, bowed his head and then rode back toward the chapel. Before the dust from the horse's hooves had settled, John took Lucy's arm and steered her onward.

"Oakham's eyes were nearly popping out of his skull," he complained, surly and cross. "Even old Croft...I'm not havin' any o' that. You're in my charge 'til Nathaniel comes back. He left you to me."

"I'm not a piece of property," she exclaimed. "Stop pulling me about!"

"I saw you fluttering your lashes for Oakham. Soon picked him out as your next quarry I suppose. Well, you're in for a surprise, wench, because he hasn't got a pot to pee in, no matter how fine and fancy he dresses."

"Let go of my arm! How dare you!"

He looked over his shoulder to where Alice remained in the lane with Bridget Frye, both of them watching the little tussle take place. Finally he released her.

"I daresay Alice will be one soul heartily pleased to see your cousin return from sea," his mother observed wryly.

"As will I," Lucy agreed under her breath.

She didn't expect John to hear, but he had. "What's the matter, wench? Tired of play-acting at last? Missing all the attention from your fine and fancy gentlemen who..."

She lost her temper then. It had been close to boiling over all day and she was in the mood for a scrap, so she stopped dead, swung around and screamed. Until then, she never knew she had it in her – so much passion and stifled frustration dying to be heard. But it came out now, every hurt and chafing resentment she'd never allowed herself to feel before.

Several pigeons took flight from the nearby hedgerows and somewhere in the distance hounds set up a rowdy howling.

His mother quietly laughed, shook her head and strolled onward, leaving them to do battle in the lane.

"What the devil was that for?" he blustered, glancing over his shoulder again to see who heard.

"All those wicked, derogatory comments, John Carver! I won't put up with it. I am not a trollop, I am not your cousin's mistress and I am not in need of another protector. Neither am I your responsibility!" She turned on her heel and followed his mother, who was already a good distance away.

He quickly caught up with her.

Prepared to scream again if necessary, she was shocked when he said nothing. Instead he awkwardly measured his steps to hers and they walked on for a long time in heavy silence.

* * * *

John knew he couldn't believe a word she said, but he hoped she was not Nathaniel's mistress. If that barrier might be removed, he could, perhaps, allow himself to regard her with less animosity. Finally, needing some way to hold her back, not daring to reach for her hand, he caught the pleats of her skirt. "If you're not his mistress, why were you with my cousin's possessions?"

"He was kind to me...fatherly."

"Fatherly?" he exploded scathingly. "I know my cousin and he's never been fatherly in his life."

"Well, he was to me. He was to me!"

John saw the damp beads caught on her lashes. "It was you in the bawdy house. Confess!" He wanted to hear her say it, needed her to admit what they'd had.

She blinked, one tear shaken loose to roll slowly down her cheek. "It was not me. It was another girl, a very different girl."

He wanted to lick the tear from her face. "She was a virgin who wanted me to take all, leave nothing behind." When she tried wrenching her skirt free, he held tight, determined and considerably stronger than her. "Where did she go when she left me?"

"She disappeared forever and she's not coming back again, so you'd best forget you ever saw her. She's forgotten it easily enough."

He leaned back, swaying slightly on his heels.

"You won't find her again." The words choked out of her. "It was for one night only, remember? She doesn't generally consort with knaves like you."

Finally he released her skirt. "So how much do you charge?" He straightened his shoulders, feeling the need for all his height.

She faced him boldy, chin up, eyes afire. "I thought you had no intention of paying for it?"

"I don't. Not in coin. But you've taken plenty from me in kind already. Time you paid me back."

"I've earned my keep since I came here. If anything, you," she pointed at his chest, "owe me!"

"That's a matter of opinion." Horn-mad, he grabbed her around the waist and pulled her hard against his body. "I'll write out a bill for what you owe me and you write out yours for what you charge for a few nights, then we'll see. Measure for measure."

"A few nights?" she gasped, winded. "I thought it was just one you wanted."

"I'll take as many as I can get. As many as I can afford, if you can deign to lift your skirts for me again so prettily as you did once before. Swine-herd."

He expected her to rail at him again, but now she was still, doe-eyed, very small in his great shadow. Hands pressed to his chest, making some space between them, when she spoke, it was barely audible. "All the coin in the world wouldn't tempt me to share a bed with you again. You're rude, obnoxious, arrogant and so full of yourself you need bursting with a pin, or one day you'll explode with all that hot air."

But he saw another emerald tear glowing in the corner of her eye and he almost relented, almost forgave her. Once again she brought out his masculine instincts to protect and cherish. He wanted to kiss her, let his tongue plunder as it did before.

"Besides," she whispered haltingly, watching his lips as they hovered above her, "you're a reformed rogue John Sydney Carver and sworn to celibacy, so I hear."

She was right, he shouldn't be doing this.

"So you'd best take your hands off me," she added, firmer this time, a slight tone of reprimand. "And let me go, before you do something we'll both regret."

"Ah yes, I forgot. My hands are too dirty for you." Slowly he ran those unclean hands down her back and grabbed her bottom. Knowing it was wrong didn't make it any easier to resist. As she squirmed, still pushing at his chest, he lowered his lips to the side of her neck and kissed her.

"John Sydney Carver," she exclaimed. "And on the Sabbath, too!" Somehow she got away from him and then she was off again, running away down the lane. He quickened his own pace, but out of pride didn't break into a run until the house was in sight. She got there first, slamming the gate, latching and bolting it from the inside, pronouncing breathlessly, "You will not come in until you apologize for calling me a harlot."

"This is my house!" He was incensed. "And you are a harlot."

She backed away from the gate, sticking out her tongue, actually laughing. Now, where formerly there were tears of pique, her eyes were warm with mischief.

He yelled for his mother to open the gate, but she'd disappeared. These women had formed a conspiracy against him, it seemed.

Flushed from the pace of her run down the lane, Lucy laughed so hard she could barely stand up.

Until she saw him climb the gate, agile as a tom cat, and then her mirth vanished.

He swung himself over the top bar, dropped down into the yard and stepped purposefully toward her, rolling up his sleeves.

"John...don't..."

"I'm glad I don't have your nerve in my tooth, woman."

"Stop...don't come any closer."

"You'd best not say another word, wench. Come here. Time for your punishment."

She dodged around the water trough. "Punishment?"

"You've been lying to me all this time."

"I didn't lie. I merely concealed the truth."

He shook his head, following her around the trough. "Have you known Oakham before?"

"Certainly not!"

"He seems to think so."

"Well, he's wrong."

He wanted to believe it.

Luckily for her, his mother trotted over from the pigsty, all excitement, to announce the imminent arrival of the sow's litter. There was no time now to fight. As the changeable, moody wench reminded him briskly, she had a job to do as head swine-herd and she took her duties with all solemnity.

* * * *

There were six healthy piglets, squirming happily around their mother's belly. A seventh, the runt of the litter, lay listless and very small, unable to fight for a teat.

"What can we do?" she cried.

"Naught," John replied with a shrug.

Her green eyes flashed. "You mean we just leave him to die?"

"It takes too much time to nurse a runt. Even then he might not survive. We're too busy. Time is valuable and stretched thin as it is. It's the way of things." He paused, angry and uncomfortable because she questioned his judgment. "Don't look at me like that," he snapped. He felt goosebumps on his arms from the blast of her cold fury. God help any man, he thought, who ever truly met with her full wrath. He had a sense he'd been lucky so far. He saw it in the quick shake of her head, the tight sigh expelled irritably. In her eyes, he was an insufferable, spoiled boy who needed a lesson, and she made no bones about telling him so.

He rubbed his arms, watching as she bundled the tiny creature in her cloak, lifting it carefully. "I don't care what you say, John Carver. I'll take care of him. You'll see! Heartless, unfeeling man."

"It'll take up too much of your time. He'll need feeding constantly, if he'll even suck from a bottle, and..."

She shoved him aside with her elbow, holding the runt protectively to her chest as if it was her own babe. "Am I or am I not head swineherd?"

"Yes, but..."

"Then I make the decision. I'll do all the work. I don't care. I'll sit up all night. All you need do is show me what to do, if it doesn't put you out too much, you rotten tyrant!"

He shouldn't let her get away with this insubordination. Fortunately no one else was around to see or hear them just then. It might be setting a dangerous precedent with her, but he had no other choice. He didn't like her calling him heartless, so she got her way and he let her keep the piglet.

After that she kept it nestled in her lap, or in a basket by the warmth of the fire, teaching it to sup milk from a bottle. She talked to the damn thing, he noted, as if it understood every word, lavishing the creature with love and affection, until he was quite sick of seeing it, especially since she now gave him the cold shoulder and barely paid attention to anything he said when they sat by the hearth in the evenings.

Just as he'd always suspected, he said to his mother, the Friday wench wasn't suited to life on a farm. What would she do when it was time to slaughter the animals? They weren't pets, were they?

"Oh, let her be," his mother replied, smiling. "Haven't you anything else to worry over today? Anyone would think you jealous of the piglet, John."

Chapter 12

In a matter of days Lord Oakham made his first parry, the gift of two pheasants in honor of Mistress Carver's new houseguest. John demanded they be returned at once, but Lucy insisted they were sent to her and therefore she would keep them. His mother agreed. Two plump, succulent birds were always welcome at her table, wherever they came from.

Mistress Carver teased her son for his sudden concern. "I don't recall such hesitancy about the providence of other birds you came upon by chance on Lord Oakham's land in the past, John, when you just happened to have a bow at hand."

He stormed out in a foul temper.

The next gift was a basket of fruit, prompting John to exclaim, "Doesn't he know mine are the finest orchards in all Norfolk? We don't need his blasted fruit."

Once again they kept it, Lucy thrusting a large strawberry between his pouting lips just to silence his complaints. His teeth very nearly caught her fingers too.

Finally, after this procession of gifts, Oakham himself appeared at their gate, making an impromptu visit with a large ham under one arm and a bottle of Gascony wine. He played the part of the concerned, interested neighbor very well, discussing the harvest yield expected and admiring the sheep flock he'd seen John driving down the lane recently. He asked after Mistress Carver's health, for he'd recently heard she was under the weather, and then he congratulated them on the fat, thriving new family in the sty.

"I'm the head swineherd," Lucy piped up proudly. It burst out of her before she remembered her vow to remain quiet and demure in Oakham's presence. She didn't want him getting any further ideas of having seen her somewhere before and she certainly didn't want John accusing her of flirting again.

"Is that so, dear lady? Then you do an excellent job." Oakham smiled broadly. "Perhaps I should hire you away from young Master Carver," he added with a sly wink.

John stood in such a hurry they all jumped a few inches. "She's staying here with me." He paused. "Until Nathaniel comes back," he added gruffly. "She was left in my charge." He strode to the fire and stood with his back to the room. Vince trotted over to sit beside him, always alert to any change in his master's mood.

Lucy sipped her wine, hoping to calm her nerves. It was never her intention to make such a tangled mess of things for John Carver, but she knew he was just as confused by it all as she was. He was a hard-working man with a life and a family. It made what she had done that night in May all the worse, all the more hurtful. He should be married to a good woman like Alice Croft, and for as long as she stayed in his house, she was in the way.

"I hear you made a good sale with your fleeces this spring," Lord Oakham ventured. "All sold to Winton in Norwich."

Lucy spilled her wine. It splashed across her skirt like a bloodstain, the mention of her husband's name as brutal as the fall of a headsman's axe.

"Aye, not that I've seen the full coin yet," John grumbled.

"I daresay he has other things on his mind, with the mystery of his disappearing bride still unresolved." Oakham's voice rattled around inside her mind, ruthlessly shattering all other thoughts. She set down her wine goblet and hid the stain with both hands clasped over it.

Mistress Carver asked what happened to Winton's bride and their visitor answered with surprising levity. "No one knows, madam. I wouldn't be surprised to find he ate her in his sleep."

She kept her gaze shuttered, attention on her lap. One sensible thought finally organized itself into being: Winton was not dead; she was not wanted for murder, then. This, at least, should be some consolation.

"There is a theory she was stolen by robbers. Winton insists he was attacked by a gang of ruffians in his own bed chamber, although no one was seen going in or out. 'Tis all most curious."

"Spirited away in the night, eh?" John chortled. "Probably by someone to whom he owes coin. Good for them. Time the crooked old bugger paid his bills."

"Good for the poor girl, too," his mother added. "Winton is notoriously hard on wives."

"Ah, but she will be found again soon, no doubt, madam. Winton has sworn to wreak vengeance on anyone connected with the kidnapping. The girl's father is scouring the countryside."

Complaining of the sun shining in her eyes, Lucy made a great fuss of moving her chair, scraping the legs along the flagstones, interrupting his story.

John's mother asked if Lord Oakham would like another slice of pie. He declined politely, his curiosity touching Lucy's face, prying like a blind man's fumbling, fleshy fingertips.

"And where is it you go, Lucy Friday, when the captain returns from sea?"

In a state of quandary, she said the first thing that came to her lips. "Scotland."

There was another awkward silence. She knew John and his mother exchanged glances across the room and then he strode to the door, whistling for Vince to follow.

"Scotland, indeed? A very great distance," Lord Oakham said.

"I believe it is, my lord." She kept her eyes downcast, the very picture of a meek country maid.

"And where did Captain Downing have the good fortune to find you?"

"In a whorehouse," John interrupted. "Where he finds all his women."

Silence fell, like a strike of lightning, rendering the conversation in two. No one moved until Vince trotted out through the door and John followed, slamming it behind him.

Every crease on Oakham's face straightened out and folded again. Mistress Carver was left to pick up the pieces left by her son and this she did ably, suggesting she'd had practice. "Well, Lord Oakham, what a lovely day it has turned out to be, when it was so overcast and dull this morning. I think you brought the sunshine with you!" As she spoke, she was already clearing away the plates and cups, subtly bringing an end to his visit.

* * * *

Lucy decided to say nothing to John about his comment in front of Lord Oakham. A childhood with her father had taught her how to deal with the thoughtless actions of men, mostly to ignore them, letting their comments, shot out in a flash of anger, roll off her back. If she had not learned how to defend herself, her skin would be pitted like a peach kernel.

But later, while she was out feeding the pigs, he came to find her, sent by his mother to make amends for his behavior.

"I opened my mouth, woman, and it just came out," he muttered glibly, the idea of apologizing for anything plainly an inconvenience.

"It doesn't matter, boy," she replied in a similar tone, waving her hand dismissively. "I don't care what you think of me." It was a lie; of course she did care what he thought. She cared for his approbation more than she should. On the other hand, what he said of her was true, there was no getting around it. Nathaniel did find her in a whore house.

"You're not going to Scotland, are you?" he said, leaning on the wall of the pigsty beside her.

"I might. Perhaps."

"Nate never told me he was going to Scotland."

"Did I say I'd go there with him?"

He frowned. "Who with, then?"

"I'll go alone," she replied with a great deal more bravery than she felt.

"You can't." He was all nonchalance. If not for the cracking of his knuckles, she might have thought he didn't care where she went. Which was, of course, what she was supposed to think. "Women can't travel anywhere alone."

She tossed her head. "Who'll stop me? You?"

"Mayhap."

Wary-eyed, she shot him a look. "A few weeks ago I was only here on a trial basis and you weren't sure you should keep me. Now you'll stop me leaving?"

He lifted one shoulder in a listless shrug. "I suppose I'm getting accustomed to having another woman about the place, as long as she's useful."

Before he turned his face away, she observed the hint of a slow, lazy grin creeping across his lips.

"So marry Alice Croft then."

"I'm not thinking of a wife, am I?"

"No, I'm quite sure you're not," she replied slowly. "You might fool your poor mother and those wide-eyed village girls into thinking you reformed, but I know differently. You got away with too much, for far too long, and I wish I never laid eyes on you."

Now he had the audacity to look wounded, as if he'd never said a hurtful word to her. "There's no need to take on like that."

"I'm not taking on like anything!" She was flustered, trying not to show how much his closeness affected her. "I'm advising you to get yourself a wife and then perhaps you won't need to go to Norwich to get what you need. Save the rest of the women in this county from your...your...wickedness. Unless, of course, marriage won't stop you looking elsewhere for the games you like to play. I daresay it won't."

* * * *

John looked at her. The sun was beginning to set, dripping down through the trees and over the roof of the dairy, dusting her profile and her eyelashes with a light layer of bronze. She was very still, watching the pigs, her arm almost touching his, her sleeves folded back today, leaving her soft skin exposed. The sight and nearness of her bare arm beside his was almost too much for his senses to take in and absorb. He'd tried to keep his distance. It wasn't working.

"I hope you don't plan to play games with Lord Oakham," he exclaimed, curbing his appetite with a terse reminder of what she was and the shallow, mercenary nature of a woman like her.

Her reply was instant. "Heaven's no! Why ever would I? I've no interest in his games."

He coughed, cleared his throat. "Good," he muttered. "I'm looking out for Nate's interests, o' course."

"Of course," she replied solemnly.

Feeling the prickle of goose-bumps, he rubbed his arm. "I thought you liked Oakham's fancy ways. I saw your eyes light up at his clean hands, lacy sleeves and ringed fingers. Impressed with frills and frippery, I suppose."

She swayed, moving an infinitesimal distance closer, as if it was suddenly windy out and no fault of her own. "It's not the clothes that make the man, it's what's under them."

She was very prettily flushed, although he put it down to the light of the wilting sun. Softly she added, "Your rough clothes and rude comments don't hide what you are, John, anymore than Lord Oakham's fine garments and high manners hide his true ungentlemanly intentions. Everybody wears a mask sometimes."

Sometimes he'd felt her looking at him, seeing through to a man he didn't even know he was yet. It made him want to live up to her expectations.

"Maybe you'd like to see under my clothes again, wench," he pressed, moving his forearm along the wall.

"Don't start that again."

He made a small frustrated sound. He'd never met a woman like her before. He usually got what he wanted as soon as he put any effort into it. This woman was different. She made the rules on where and when, as well as how much. It was all quite ridiculous. But he still had this fascination for her, forgiving every snappish comment, every insult.

Resting her chin in one upturned palm, she moved the last tiny distance until their elbows finally touched. It might have been accidental, but John didn't move away. It was pleasant to have her there with him.

More than pleasant. He was captivated.

"Kiss me," he whispered. "No one's looking."

She threw him an arch look. "You're awfully forward, John Carver."

"That's sweet coming from a woman who once put her hand on my cock and told me to get on with it."

"I never did! Will you stop saying that?"

He stared at her mouth. "Come with me to Norwich."

"No."

"Must you argue with me about everything?"

"I can't go back there."

"Why?" He squinted. "What are you afraid of?" Leaning closer, he whispered, "I'll be there with you. Just the two of us." He didn't quite mean it to sound the way it did, but once it was out, he let it sit there, a baited hook.

"You think I'm that sort of girl." She was haughty again now. "Well, I'm not. I know what it might seem like to you, but you're quite wrong."

He put his head on one side. "I thought you didn't care what I think?"

"I...I don't." Pressing herself away from the wall, she straightened up. "You ought to marry Alice and put her out of her misery. Then you'd have someone to kiss who couldn't say no."

"A wife can't say no?"

Moving out of the sunset, she paled a few shades and her fingers rose to the small white scar under her eye. "A wife is her husband's chattel. He can do what he likes with her."

"Hmmm." He tipped his head back, pretending to consider. "You're right. I will get myself a wife then." Sighing, he leaned on the wall. "Maybe it's time I stopped spreading all this about and gave it to just one woman instead."

She sniffed. "Won't she be honored?"

"Oh, yes. At least once a day."

"Full of yourself, aren't you?"

He laughed. "I don't recall hearing any complaint from your lips, only commands for more."

She scurried into the house, rushing to get away, almost tripping over the step. One of these days, she'd stop running away, he mused. She'd better, because he prided himself on not chasing after women, and he'd already broken that rule several times since she came to live in his house.

* * * *

On Wednesday he went to market in Norwich and since Lucy refused to go with him, he took Alice Croft.

They were home by supper.

Altering one of Mistress Carver's old gowns, Lucy was seated in the window seat, making the most of the lingering summer evening light, and when the cart rolled up through the gates, she saw Alice was still with him. Nudging the window open further with her elbow, she heard him ask the girl inside and Alice, smiling, agreed. Then he put up his arms to help her down.

"Ouch," Lucy pricked her finger and sucked on it quickly.

Mistress Carver peered over her shoulder. "Looks as if she's coming in."

Setting her sewing aside, Lucy hurried over to sit with the piglet, claiming her place in the shadows of the hearth. She supposed it was inevitable other young women would come to the house sometimes and she had no right to be bothered by it. Poor Alice deserved his attention. She, a married woman who would bring him nothing but harm, did not.

They came in chatting and his mother greeted Alice warmly, while John petted his dog, glanced over at Lucy, and asked how the runt faired today.

When she didn't answer, he came to her chair, rested both hands on the back of it and leaned over to look at the sleeping piglet in her lap. She stiffened, hardly daring to breath. He reached down to touch the piglet, but on their way back up again his fingertips strayed briefly over her shoulder, stroking back a lock of hair. It was over in seconds, noticed by no one but them, yet it left a deep pain in her heart.

"Don't," she whispered, fraught. Such a small word, but so full of heartache.

He withdrew his hands from the back of the chair as if the wood scalded him, or a spark flew up from the fire. He was angry with her, she knew, because she'd said "don't" and he felt he had a right to do exactly as he pleased, get whatever he wanted the moment he snapped his fingers. John Carver was unfamiliar with refusal. Apparently his day trip to Norwich without her had not helped matters.

"I'll only stay a few minutes," said Alice, somewhere behind them. "My father will be expecting me home."

Oh, why did he bring her into his house? It was too cruel. Lucy was undecided who would suffer the most out of the three of them, but each one would be wounded; it was inevitable.

Mistress Carver drew another chair up in front of the fire for Alice, and John took a seat between the two young women. Lucy would gladly have feigned a headache and gone to bed but Vince lollopped over to sit, as was now his usual custom, with his big head in her lap, and she hadn't the heart to move the silly beast. Somehow that dog knew, from the first day, he was more likely to receive a treat from her hands than from any other in the house and so he chose his spot wisely. Alice watched the dog with a nervous, skittish eye, much as she watched Lucy.

The conversation progressed slowly, most of it left to John and his mother.

"Did you get the rest of the money from the old villain Winton?"

"No. He wasn't in. Or so I was told. I suppose he was watching me from behind the shutters."

"Next time you'll know not to trade with the wretch."

"Aye. That old bugger's had his last fleece from me."

Whenever he spoke, Alice riveted her attention on John's face, ready to agree with any point he made, or to laugh, if he told anything with the slightest resemblance to a joke. During a lull in the conversation, she ventured to ask Lucy how long she planned to stay in Sydney Dovedale. Everyone, it seemed, wanted to know this, although they all had different reasons.

"Until Captain Downing returns," she said. Having heard it countless times from John's lips, it came out of hers now by rote, but as she spoke she heard him expel a labored sigh, tinted with acrimony.

Next Alice addressed John. "Your cousin sailed off to fight the Spaniards?"

Agreeing this was the case, his reply was informative mostly for its brevity. Alice directed her next question to his mother.

"Do you think we'll be invaded, Mistress Carver? They say beacons have been lit all along the coast. The Spanish galleons have been sighted and shall soon be upon us."

"I have the greatest of faith in our fine fleet, Alice, and in our fighting men, not to mention the tenacious spirit of the English. We shall never be invaded."

"You sound so confident, Mistress Carver, I am put at ease."

There was a short pause while John leaned forward to poke at the fire with considerable savagery.

Alice, watching the sparks fly, exclaimed with real feeling, "I do hope Captain Downing comes back safely. And soon. I shall pray for it."

Mistress Carver thanked her for the sentiment and said she had no doubt Nathaniel would turn up again, like the proverbial bad penny.

"And then Miss Lucy Friday will go back to Yarmouth with Captain Downing?" Alice quietly inquired.

"I might go to Scotland," Lucy chirped. "I haven't decided." Yes, she thought to herself, she should go soon, before she caused John Carver any further trouble.

They all looked at her. John sat back in his chair, muttering resentfully, "I don't know why you keep jabbering on about Scotland. You don't even know where Scotland is."

"I do. It's north."

He tapped his boots with the poker. "And what's in Scotland to fascinate you so much?"

She hesitated, for she didn't truly know what was there, but it always sounded like a most exotic, wild place and one had no need to cross the sea to get there, which was an advantage in her opinion. Surely it was far enough away.

"Many things," she replied.

"Have you traveled much, Mistress Friday?" Alice asked, unblinking, prim hands clasped in her lap. "I suppose you went many places with Captain Downing?"

"I've been...here and there."

"To London?"

Every eye turned to her. She patted Vince's warm head. "Yes."

"Is this another one of your fibs?" John demanded.

Alice looked at him, eyes narrowed, fingers tightening in a firmer knot.

"No," Lucy replied steadily. "It is true."

"Oh that's right." He stabbed at the fire again with the poker. "You don't lie. You conceal the truth. You're lucky you've got such a pretty face and all the rest of it, or you'd probably be in the stocks by now."

Alice flushed, her gaze darting side to side as if she didn't know where to look. Surely, Lucy thought, the girl ought to be familiar with his loud mouth ways by now, his bull-headed, opinionated announcements which paid no heed to feelings or propriety. Or was he usually on his best behavior around Alice? In any case he was not being discreet tonight, just his usual self. It was as if he didn't care who heard.

If she could do so without him letting everyone know, she would have kicked him, but she knew he'd make a squawking fuss over it.

"I lived in London for many years," she assured him.

"Tell us about it then." He stuck out his jaw, challenging her.

"What would you like to know? It's a large, dirty, stinking town and I was heartily glad to leave it."

Alice ventured sadly, "I've never been further than Norwich, but I should dearly like to see the great city of London one day."

"It's not so wonderful." Lucy thought of the street outside her father's tall gates, where gentlemen rode in litters, pushing poor, shoeless children into the gutter. She remembered the ceaseless clatter of hooves, the pitiful cries of desperate beggars and the shouts of those who fell victim to cutpurses on the streets. She could smell the stench of open sewers, the contents of chamber pots tossed lazily onto the uneven cobbles, and she saw the severed heads, dipped in tar, left on the gatehouse above the bridge. "The streets are filthy and crowded. You are much luckier to live here with..." She stopped abruptly and looked down at Vince, while she caressed his ears. "...the beauty of the country at your door."

"Of course, I love Sydney Dovedale," Alice eagerly reassured them all, as if any suggestion to the contrary was treasonous. "But I should like to visit London nonetheless. Perhaps I would catch a glimpse of the Queen."

"The Queen!" John sneered, swinging the poker again. "What makes her better than anyone else? She was born of a woman, same as you and I. She picks her nose, scratches her backside and sits on the privy same as we do."

"John!" his mother cried. "For pity's sake, must you speak so before guests?"

He did it on purpose of course, enjoying the shock value.

"Actually," Lucy advised him matter-of-factly, "she has someone to do all that for her, and to wipe her arse, too."

Alice Croft whimpered in alarm, but John laughed, almost choking.

"You two are as bad as each other," Mistress Carver exclaimed, trying not to laugh herself. "You must forgive the pair of them, Alice dear, I think they try to outdo one another."

Lucy smiled as she stroked his dog's head and wondered what Her Majesty would make of surly, opinionated John Sydney Carver, descended from a long line of noble barons and so eager to deny it.

Apparently, despite his new leaf, he still liked to point out other folks' failings, just as he did when he was a boy, the way his mother described it so colorfully, standing on the pew in chapel and mocking the other parishioners for their hypocrisy. One thing for sure, you knew where you were with him. He liked you or he hated you and he didn't care who knew it.

She dearly wished he would stop looking at her the way he did, making her feel guilt, making her fall a little more in love with every passing glance.

"You're a caution, you are, Lucy Friday," he muttered, still chuckling.

But Lucy caught the frown on Alice Croft's face and it was enough to wipe her own smile away.

Chapter 13

While he took Alice home, Lucy tried on her newly altered gown.

"It may be nothing fancy," said his mother, "but it looks a treat on you, my dear. Much better than it ever looked on me." Walking around to get the full effect, she said, "Why not let your hair down? It's such a lovely shade and it brightens this old, mousy gray gown. Here, take that silly cap off and let it down."

Before Lucy offered any protest, the pins holding her linen cap in place were removed and her long hair spilled free. Most of the dye was now completely faded, leaving her natural auburn to shine. It worried her, for the distinctive color made her far more recognizable.

"Perfect!" Mistress Carver proclaimed with a beaming smile. "You must wear it loose more often. I don't know why you would want to hide such bounty."

She should have pointed out that only unwed maidens wear their hair loose and since she was not one, she was not entitled. Instead she mumbled, "I never wear my hair down in the summer," and she fussed with it over one shoulder. "The back of my neck gets too hot."

So Mistress Carver braided it for her and Lucy allowed it, overcome again by the lady's kindness. John's mother was gentle and thoughtful toward her, as no one else had ever been. It was done quite naturally, loving, open and generous, expecting nothing in return. Was this what mothers did? She had no other experience of course, but it felt right, it felt...motherly. It brought a lump to her throat.

* * * *

He helped Alice down from the cart, taking care to warn her of the puddle in her way.

"Thank you, John," she purred softly, lashes lowered.

Although he knew she waited for a kiss, she didn't turn her face up for it. Alice would never be so forward. Not like his other hussy.

The moon was full tonight, the air warm and slightly damp from an afternoon of summer rain. It was the perfect evening for a sweetly romantic kiss with a pure maiden of good family. A kiss to go no further, demand nothing more from him. A kiss to leave her happy and him discontent. Alice didn't expect anything else before they were married and he must wait, be polite, civilized.

All day in Norwich he'd tried his best to give Alice his full attention, but failed miserably. Even without Lucy at his side, being there in

Norwich reminded him of her constantly. Why hadn't she wanted to go there with him? He'd thought she would enjoy the ride on his cart. They might have spent the day alone together, getting to know one another away from the daily chores. When she stoutly refused to go with him, he was angry, disappointed. He'd hoped, by taking Alice instead, he would make her jealous, but she'd showed no sign of it. The only thing he'd achieved that day was to prove his feelings for Lucy were beyond what they should be, beyond anything he'd ever felt before. He'd even come home early, cutting the day short to see her smile again and his first thought, upon entering the house, was to look for her, reassure himself she was still there.

She filled his mind when he should be thinking of other, worthier, sweeter young women. Women who answered his questions with no evasion and didn't cheat at cards.

In a sudden burst of resolve, he grasped Alice's hand and she went very still, holding her breath.

This was the moment. He closed his eyes. Get it over with. Propose. Now. Do it.

Reformed rogues didn't need Friday wenches complicating their lives. They needed good girls, pure girls, honest girls.

He brought her cool hand to his lips and kissed it gently.

"Good night, Alice."

He heard her exhale. "Good night, John."

Not looking at her, he leapt up into his cart, grabbed the reins and rode away, feeling like a cad, furious with himself for this indecision.

But mostly furious with Lucy for causing it.

* * * *

When he got home his mother had gone to bed, but Lucy was still up, sewing the hem of a gown, while keeping an eye on her piglet and alternately petting Vince, who occasionally reminded her of his presence with one paw on her foot and one lick of his tongue across the back of her hand.

She was too preoccupied to hear John come in and he was deliberately quiet, expecting them both to be upstairs. He stood a while, just inside the door, beholding the tranquil scene of a beautiful woman seated by his hearth, making herself useful. Waiting for him to come home. Again he felt incredible relief to see her there still, as if her disappearance would be his death and he was granted a stay of execution once more.

Ever since he'd turned fourteen and first looked at females as something other than a hindrance, he'd known one day he would marry. It was a sad inevitability that every capable man was expected to find a wife to bear his children. With his mother there at his side, however, he kept serious thoughts of marriage at bay. He had a woman in his house already, a woman who took care of him, saw to his meals, mended his clothes and occasionally reminded him about his manners. Very occasionally, since she knew him too well to expect miracles. Until now, it never occurred to him that his life lacked anything. But a myriad of previously unknown hopes and fears took hold as watched Lucy with her sewing. He'd never known this before, this ruthless determination to keep a woman in his life, to stop her from leaving.

Slowly he shook his head. Why couldn't he have felt like this a few minutes ago, when Alice stood waiting politely for his kiss?

Taking another step forward, he realized Lucy wore no cap this evening. Her hair was braided down her back, tied with ribbon, the true color richly evident in the firelight. To call it merely red was an injustice. It was every shade from amber to russet, entwined and gleaming like wet autumn leaves. It almost hurt to look at her.

He must have made a sound, for she turned her head and saw him there. Vince gave a low woof and dutifully lolloped over to greet him. Making a quick fuss of the dog, he strode to the fire, restless, his mind a whirl of nonsensical ideas and fancies.

"New gown?" he muttered, forcing the words out under duress.

"Your mother's. She gave it to me."

"Good." Walking across to the other side of the hearth, he leaned there, one arm propped up on the mantle. "You can wear it at the summer fête. Oakham holds one every year on his lawns at Bollingbrooke Hall."

She raised her warmly-questioning eyes to his.

"You'll go with me," he added, his voice firmer now, very much the master of his domain and all the creatures in it. He knew it would be polite to ask, but she'd only say no, wouldn't she?

"Perhaps," she said, her gaze drifting back to her sewing.

He pressed his lips tight, gritted his teeth. Was there any point about which the wench wouldn't argue? "I bought you something today," he spat out finally, sorely regretting the fact already.

Again her eyelashes lifted, a little smile tugging her lips crookedly upward. "Something for me?" Her joy was far too enthusiastic, not commensurate with what he offered. One would think she'd never been given anything in her life.

He walked over to a crate he'd brought in earlier and lifted the lid. It was filled with straw and had carried items for the pantry, gifts for his mother, but underneath, buried deep, was something he'd purchased for her in Norwich market, when his companion's back was turned.

John held it out to her, slightly embarrassed. "I thought you might have need…"

She leapt to her feet and almost ran to it, then stopped, hands a few inches from claiming the gift. "For me? You're sure?" Her face turned up to his. Like a fertile field lush with summer's abundance, her eyes were wide and clear.

"Should keep the sun off your face." He thrust the wide-brimmed straw bonnet at her. "Don't suppose you want any more freckles." He'd heard his sisters lamenting their own occasional "blemishes" enough to know how little freckles were appreciated by young ladies. And he'd seen Lucy constantly squinting, her hand over her eyes when she worked outside in the sunny yard.

Frugal with his coin, he'd never bought any young woman a gift before, not even Alice. A wise hussy like this one, he thought moodily, would run to whichever man had the most to spend on her, but he wanted a woman who shared her time with him out of genuine affection. This was the difference between him and Nathaniel. His cousin didn't care why a woman was with him, as long as he enjoyed himself. In the past, John hadn't cared much either, but that was before he met this stunning, sorrel-haired creature for whom every slight triumph was precious, every fresh accomplishment a discovery as great as that of a new world conquered.

She clutched the gift to her bosom. "It's lovely."

He looked at her, the need to speak almost burning a hole in his tongue. No, he'd let her do the talking tonight. He didn't trust himself, had a tendency to say the wrong thing to her, blurt things out. Like asking her to kiss him.

* * * *

"I don't know how to thank you," she added, his silence making her nervous. "It must have cost you…" she faltered. It wouldn't be delicate to mention money and how much things cost. Especially considering other conversations and quarrels recently had.

She put the bonnet on now, too excited to wait, dashing to look at her reflection in the window.

"Go on up to bed then," he said gruffly. "I'll put the fire out."

She turned, one hand on the crown of her bonnet. "I suppose Alice doesn't need a hat. She has no freckles."

He was bent over, checking the sleeping piglet. "Aye. Alice has none of those witch's marks on her face."

Lucy took one last look at her reflection before walking back across the room to where he stood. As he saw her coming, he straightened up, watching her warily, flinching in readiness.

When she should have come to a halt, she kept going, stumbling into him. He had to put his arms around her, just to keep from falling back and then she rose on tip toe, head flung back, and kissed him, full on the lips. The bonnet fell. His fingers spread between her shoulder blades, drawing her closer still, improperly close.

She'd meant it only as a quick, innocent thank-you, but should have known what would happen. Her arms went around his neck and he lifted her, holding her tightly, resetting his feet to steady them both. The unexpected kiss quickly turned greedy, a full-blown devouring, a sudden yielding, a wanton capitulation after too long holding it at bay. All the agony of those last few weeks in his house, the closeness and yet the distance, was too much to bear. Every casual glimpse of his well-honed body, the sound of his low, gruff voice waking her every morning through her open shutters, even the sight of his boots kicked off by the fire, made her heart pulse a little faster, made her long for his arms again. The idea of some other woman one day having him, when she could not, made her bitter, raging inside with self-pity.

John broke away first. His eyelids were half-lowered, lips still parted and wet. Sweeping his hands to her bottom, he moved her against his loins, her hips to his hard thighs.

"I need you," he managed, his voice like slow wheels over gravel. "I'm on fire, wench."

Lucy trembled, closing her eyelids all the way, leaning into his body, her cheek to his shirt. She needed him just as much, but it was treacherous ground for them both. If she went to his bed, she might want to stay there. She was in his way, preventing him from loving good girls like Alice. Unmarried girls.

"I didn't like it today," he said. "Too many hours without you in them. I need you to stay with me."

She opened her eyes again to find him watching her, his regard hot, heady with intent. Her body tightened, her breath stilled, strangled in her throat.

"No. It's impossible," she murmured.

With her braid twisted around his fist, he forced her head back, making her submit to another kiss, but this time, when his tongue began to press its way between her lips, she backed down, stepping out of his embrace. She suspected he would have struggled to keep her in his arms, but Vince growled a warning, a reminder, and so he thought better of it.

"Thank you for the bonnet," she said again, every word dripping with thwarted desire.

Retrieving the fallen hat, he passed it to her and she ran quickly up the stairs to her bed.

* * * *

The next day, while she was sweeping the yard, wearing her new straw bonnet, he crept into her bed chamber and searched until he found the wooden box she'd brought with her. Waiting for her to open up to him was no longer feasible. Despite promises to his mother, he wanted answers now. These thoughts and feelings she put inside him could no longer be dismissed as transient, a shallow, passing fancy. They were deep set, beyond the pale, and they demanded the truth.

There was no lock; the box opened easily, much to his surprise. Inside he found a small ivory and silver comb, a delicately wrought silver bracelet inlaid with mother-of-pearl and one pearl earring. He recognized it at once, the partner to one he found on the floor of a bawdy house chamber almost three months ago. For a moment he stared at it, then closed the box and put it back under her bed.

Prying into her possessions revealed little he didn't already know. She was clearly a light-fingered thief, however, and he ought to warn his mother to keep an eye on her own jewelry.

He went to her window and looked out on the yard, where she worked in her straw bonnet, humming a light tune. How had she done this to him and why? Surely there were a great many other men, richer, more powerful men, she might have trapped with her wiles. Sometimes he wondered if she was merely practicing on him, passing the time in a fashion to amuse herself. The kiss last night was lusty and willful, utterly unexpected. It was equal parts innocent and wanton, when he never before imagined it was possible to be both at once.

As if she felt him watching, she stopped and looked up. He ducked out of sight. Hunkered down under the window, he turned his head and saw the book of recipes his mother had lent her, set on the table beside her bed. There was something poking out of the pages. He reached for the book and opened it to find a small, torn square of linen and a pressed four-leaf clover.

He'd found that clover just a few days ago in the lane and given it to her, for luck. She'd claimed to have no belief in "silly superstitions," yet she kept it. Even more interesting was the square of linen, which he recognized from one of his own old shirts. There was a stain on it because he'd cut himself while wearing it.

Why would she keep that?

He shook his head slowly, concluding it must be part of this devious witch's spell she'd put upon him. What other explanation could there be for keeping an old, stained piece of shirt?

* * * *

When she went to her chamber later, Lucy knew immediately someone else had been there. The shift laying across her bed was moved. The wash jug and basin too had been pushed a few inches to the right by someone looking behind it, searching. On a sudden instinct, she crouched and drew out her box. She opened it.

There, beside her pearl earring, was its twin, once thought lost and now returned. The two fat pearls lay together, happily reunited.

Like she and John perhaps?

She slammed the box shut and closed her eyes, panic rippling through her, as well as something else. Something warmer and sweeter.

Last night, when he let her leave his arms after the kiss, she knew it was a reprieve. But those two earrings laid together sent her a message. He was waiting. This respite he granted was not infinite and neither was his patience.

Chapter 14

It was laundry day, a task she hated more than any other, apparently. It was a heavy, long, tedious job and she often burned her hands doing it. Now he watched her drawing water from the well. She'd been very quiet lately, ever since he returned her earring. She never mentioned it and he wondered whether she waited for him to say something.

He'd showed his mother the scrap of bloodied linen he found. "She's casting a spell. I knew it. I knew she was up to no good." It was the perfect excuse for all the odd things happening to him since she came.

"Why the devil would she want to do that?" his mother exclaimed. "You get yourself in enough of a pickle without interference from the supernatural. If you don't know what to do with yourself lately, it's your fault, not hers."

"What else would she want with an old bit o' shirt?" he demanded.

"Perhaps she was merely marking a page."

"Hmmph!"

"Or perhaps it's a keepsake."

"A keepsake? For what?"

"Oh, I don't know. Perhaps she's in love with you, John." His mother had walked away laughing, leaving her son in a state of confusion.

Until then it had never occurred to him that Lucy's motives in keeping the scrap of old shirt might be entirely guiltless, even in his favor. He'd instantly assumed the worst. He did it a lot with her, he realized, chagrined.

Was it possible she had feelings for him? Good feelings? Deeper feelings?

His mother was right: he didn't know what to do with himself. He was usually very self-assured when it came to women. He knew what he wanted and he always got it, but he didn't poach from other men, it wasn't sporting. She claimed not to be his cousin's mistress, but was it the truth? There was something in the way, something keeping her always in motion, running away, withdrawing whenever he advanced a step. He pondered her thoughtfully through the window. She was an intriguing blend of fear and boldness, tears and laughter.

Since John was her first lover, in his eyes she truly belonged to him, but what did she think? What rules did a concubine live by, if any? There was much to be resolved and straightened out, not the least of which was the cryptic comment on Nathaniel's note: *On loan, handle with care.*

"What are you still doing here?" his mother exclaimed, finding him by the window as she came out of the scullery, rolling down her sleeves.

He stared through the open window. "She'll spill half the water before she gets it inside," he muttered, watching Lucy struggle with a heavy bucket.

"Then go and help her. Is it so hard for you to be a gentleman? There's no one watching, fool boy!"

It was true, he thought, scanning the yard hastily. No one was out there today but her. Perhaps, he could...

On her way back to the house she stopped and set down her bucket a moment to greet the growing piglet she'd nursed with such dedication and against his wishes. Flourishing against all expectation, the piglet would soon be ready to join his litter mates, if she could be persuaded to give up her pet. Then she'd have nothing to distract from her duties to the man of the house.

"What are you grinning at, John Sydney?" his mother demanded, catching his reflection in the window.

"Naught, mother." He certainly wouldn't tell his mother about a night spent in a Norwich bawdy house with a masked whore his cousin purchased for him as a birthday gift. Or how gentlemanly he'd been then, taking care of her thoroughly, many times over.

Lucy gathered the bucket strap in both hands and made her way unsteadily across the yard, full lower lip puffed out, back bent with the effort. Her hair was loose down her back today, not yet braided. It was long enough for her to sit on. He felt the sudden urge to wrap himself in those silk and cinnamon locks while he took her again as before, making her moan so deeply with pleasure he felt the vibrations on the length of his thrusting cock.

"John, you'll break the window latch if you keep twisting it." His mother's voice interrupted the lurid daydream. He quickly dropped the latch.

Enough of this self-doubt. Enough of this unusual nervousness. She was only a woman and she should do as he commanded. The mystery he'd built around her was probably all in his head.

* * * *

Surprised to see him trotting over to help, she tipped the bucket, splashing water over his boots. He took it from her hands, mildly protesting her clumsiness. This morning he wore a clean shirt and it looked as if he'd shaved. If she   didn't know him better, she might even think he'd combed his hair and washed it.

Her heartbeat slowed. "Is Alice coming to visit?"

"No. Why?"

She smiled. "No reason."

They took a few steps together until he stopped, setting the bucket down again. "Where does this brother of yours live? If he truly exists, of course."

Goose-pimples pricked along the nape of her neck. "I don't know where he is. Why?"

"I'll write to him. If you're going to stay here with me, he ought to know. I'll do this properly."

She was confused. "Stay here with you?"

"That's right. You belong to me."

"I don't belong to you," she replied, wiping her sticky palms on her apron. She supposed, if she belonged to anyone, legally, it was to Lord Winton, although he would never own her heart, mind and soul. Some days she was able to forget completely, but the reality always returned to bite her on the nose and wipe the smile from her face.

On that day it hit her, just like her husband's hard, bony hand all those months ago. She'd stayed here too long already and now John Carver was looking at her as if he might not let her leave. He was a prideful, opinionated, hot-tempered young man. Who knew what fool idea he'd get inside his stubborn head? Since that volatile kiss by the fire, his bold declaration of how much he needed her, the air was so heavy between them she could bite it.

Now look what she'd done. Fallen in love.

She wound her hair over her shoulder, watching him lift the heavy bucket again, his forearms chorded with muscle.

Stop it. Stop it now, Lucy. There can be no happy ending, only tragedy in this play.

This was impossible. She simply mustn't.

Ah, but though a man can be chosen for one night of lust, one cannot choose where one loves, as she now knew to her cost.

When he reached toward her, she flinched on instinct, but he only meant to pluck a stray chicken feather from her hair. He showed it to her as evidence, his eyes hurt, quizzical.

She opened her mouth but no words would come out. The sadness piled in and, afraid she would burst into awkward tears, Lucy ran for the gate.

* * * *

Yet again she ran away from him. John would have followed, but his mother emerged from the house, urging him to let her go. "A gentle, patient hand achieves more than an angry, rushed one," she lectured. "Your father learned that, eventually, when he wooed me."

"I'm not wooing her," he replied curtly, confused and frustrated, fearful of these sensations dancing inside his chest. The damned woman didn't even want him touching her and yet he couldn't help himself. "I'm not wooing her," he repeated.

"Perhaps that, my dear boy, is the problem," his mother remarked dryly

* * * *

Lucy went for a long walk down the lane, breathing in the fresh, fragrant summer air. Sparrows and blackbirds chirped at her in greeting while shyer rabbits darted away into the long grasses of the verge, hiding. Sweetbriar and wild roses entwined with prickly bramble in the hedgerows and occasionally a sly rustle gave away the presence of more wildlife sheltered there. A fox, perhaps, or a mouse.

Absorbed by the beauty of nature, she didn't see the two women approach until they were almost upon her and it was too late to turn back. She straightened her spine, resolved to be friendly. As she'd told herself many times, they had every right to distrust her, considering the strange place she held in John's house. Now she would make amends for all her sinful lustings in regard to John Carver.

So she greeted them with a smile. Bridget would have walked on, but Alice stopped. "I was just on my way to see John. He wasn't in the fields this morning. Is he at home?"

Lucy agreed that he was.

Alice eyed her rival's straw sun bonnet and two scarlet spots appeared on her cheeks. There was a glimmer of recognition and Lucy suspected the purchase of her bonnet had not gone unnoticed, even if he thought he'd got away with it. "You're walking out all alone, Mistress Friday?"

"Yes." Her smile widened, for the pleasure she took in walking alone, no father to admonish her for wandering out of his sight, was something still shiny and new to her.

Bridget came back to stand at her friend's side. Usually she said nothing, merely glared disapprovingly. Today, however, finding Lucy alone and unguarded, she took no pains to swallow her dislike. "There's no need to look so pleased with yourself, slut."

Alice blushed, tossing her friend an anxious glance of reproof.

"I am not pleased with myself," Lucy replied, shaken by the suddenness of Bridget's insult. "I am merely pleased to be out walking on such a glorious summer day."

"Glorious day indeed! Well, aren't you miss dainty prim and proper. As if we don't all know exactly what you are."

"I beg your pardon…"

"Why did you come here, anyway?" Bridget stepped closer, her round face damp with perspiration. "This was a nice respectable village until you came here and moved your slut's petticoats in at Souls Dryft. You leave John Carver be! He doesn't need your sort hanging around."

"Bridget," Alice muttered in anguish, "you mustn't…"

"Someone must. Everyone thinks it; they just don't like to hurt Mistress Carver's feelings, and we all know her kindness to strays and poor folk, but she shouldn't harbor a filthy dirty slut who'll give her son the pox."

Horrified, Lucy simply stared at Bridget Frye, whose plump, shiny face loomed ever closer.

"Alice won't speak up for herself, so I'll do it for her! You ought to leave this village, whore. We don't want your sort here and you'll do John Carver no good whatsoever. He'd have chosen himself a wife by now if you hadn't come along."

Still Lucy was silent, knowing in her heart that much of this virulent accusation was justified, even if it was uttered in a purely mean spirit, with far less consideration for John's welfare than was claimed.

"Like my brother says, John Carver's got no need now for a wife while he's got you to warm his bed at night. My poor friend Alice has to stand by like a fool, waiting for him to be done with you and realize his mistake."

Finally Lucy found her voice again. "Do you speak for Alice, Bridget, or is it for yourself mostly, this concern about John's future bride? I've seen the way you look at him."

Bridget lunged forward, ripped the straw bonnet off her head, flung it to the ground and flattened it under her feet. Alice cried out in protest, but Bridget trampled the defenseless bonnet into the dust with relish. Lucy's emotions were already on edge. Now the floodgates opened.

She pulled on Bridget's long dark hair, hissing and spitting. "If John

Carver ever marries you, it'll be a cold day in Hell!"

Bridget grabbed her skirt, ripping a large hole. "You'd know about Hell, sinner!"

From a safe distance on the verge, Alice called for the two of them to stop fighting, but to no avail. Hands slapped hard at faces, fingers tangled in hair, clawing in desperation. Feet kicked out and knees buckled. "Please stop!" Alice cried again as the two women rolled in the dirt, swearing up a storm.

Thankfully, at this moment Lord Oakham rode up and put a stop to the fight. Swiftly dismounting, he clasped both women by the arms and drew them upright. "What is amiss here, then?" he demanded.

Lucy was too winded for speech, but Bridget still had enough spit left. "She's a whore, milord, and she ought to be pilloried!"

Whether he agreed was not immediately apparent. Lucy was lifted onto his horse with no further ado. He swung himself up behind her, and then they were off at a gallop.

* * * *

Bollingbrooke Hall was an impressive house of brick, sturdy and squat, in the midst of gently rolling green lawns with a small lake, a fountain and two lines of cypress hedge leading up to the front entrance. If she were in a better mood, she might have enjoyed her impromptu visit, at least for the first half an hour, while Lord Oakham was kind and attentive, and before other ideas bloomed in his head.

It was quiet and cool inside, with dark, oak-paneled walls reminiscent of her father's house. This was something familiar to her, the steady structure of everything in its place, no one questioning, servants quietly obeying and eager to please. But, oddly enough, she felt more at home in the Carver's farmhouse than she did here. Probably looked more at home too, she realized, running fingers through her tangled hair. Her skirt was torn and stained with dirt. She'd even lost a shoe. And her hands! Looking down at them now she thought of John once mocking her "lily soft" hands. Well, the last few weeks had put paid to that, just as he'd promised.

Anger bubbled up again when she thought of Bridget Frye assaulting her straw bonnet. That insult was worse even than all the wicked names spurting from those fat, ignorant lips. The lovely straw bonnet, pounded into the road, flattened, killed. Lucy began to cry then, the tears she'd choked back earlier now falling without mercy.

"My dear lady, you have been much abused!" Lord Oakham poured a glass of wine and passed her a kerchief to wipe her tears, both accepted with gratitude. "You must tell me what happened."

She blew her nose soundly. "It was nothing, Lord Oakham. A silly argument, a trifling affair over a…a hat."

"Bridget Frye has a hot temper and should learn to tend it better."

She smiled crookedly through her tears. "I fear the same could be said of me, sir." Despite everything, including her decimated bonnet, she didn't want to get anyone in trouble over this absurdity. It was all her fault from the very beginning. Her long-suffering father, confused John, generous Nathaniel, the kindly Mistress Carver, poor, patient Alice and jealous Bridget. Somehow she'd got them all entangled in her sins, just because she once made the reckless decision to spend one night with a stranger. Then there was her own poor mother, a death for which she might also be blamed. Was no one safe who came in contact with her?

She once thought leaving her family would be best for everyone, but now it seemed there was nowhere she could go without causing further chaos.

"My beautiful straw bonnet," she sobbed, her mind spinning. In her confusion over John, she sought one symbol to focus on, unleashing all her emotions upon it. "It's ruined! My beautiful new bonnet."

"Never mind, my dear. I shall get you another."

He didn't understand, of course. It was impossible to replace that particular bonnet, her first proof John had more than lust in mind when he thought of her. She'd meant to keep it with her forever, no matter what happened, no matter where she traveled.

A servant brought in a silver tray of cherries, freshly picked, and Lord Oakham insisted she taste them, holding them out by the stalks with his own slender fingers, until she accepted them between her lips. Very broken and unhappy, she took the cherries in her mouth and felt more tears trickle down her cheeks.

She had wounded them all. And John, John worst of all.

He would surely never forgive her when he knew the truth. She should never have walked into that Norwich bawdy house.

* * * *

Bridget's broad face was crimson, her hair strewn over her shoulders. He saw her first as she marched through the gate toward him, fists clenched. Alice walked quickly behind her friend and appeared in some distress.

He was on his way out to find Lucy, but stopped when he saw the two women on his property.

"John Carver," Bridget exclaimed with a brisk nod. "Is your mother in?"

"Yes, she's..."

"Good, I've much to say to her and it can't wait. By the by, your whore's been taken to the stocks on the common. "

While he stared after the irate woman in some bewilderment, Alice scurried across the yard and handed him a shoe. "There was a fight. Lucy went with Lord Oakham on his horse."

He stared.

"I'm sorry, John. I tried to stop Bridget. It's none of our business what you do, but you know how Bridget is, with her temper."

"Oakham?" He tried to understand.

"He rode up and stopped the fight. Lucy went with him."

Enraged, he snatched the shoe from her hand. "Did she indeed?" Of course she did. She'd been waiting for just such an opportunity to move on to greener pastures, no doubt. Leaving Alice behind and knowing his mother was well capable of handling the likes of Bridget Frye, he mounted one of the farm horses, not bothering to fetch a saddle, and rode full-tilt for Bollingbrooke Hall.

* * * *

She began to feel a little sick of cherries.

"Perhaps a sugared nut or some marchpane?" he asked, showing her one of the other trays his servants had brought.

Laughing uneasily, she teased, "Lord Oakham, are you trying to fatten me up for slaughter?"

"Food, so I find, is a great soother of the nerves."

Suddenly conscious of his chair moving subtly closer to her own, Lucy got up and limped to the window in her one shoe. "It is very kind of you, my lord, but I'd best be going."

"Where?"

"Back to the farm, of course."

There was a slight pause. "Not to Lord Winton?"

All those half-chewed cherries now piled up in the back of her throat. She stared at him, the tear-soggy kerchief clutched tightly in her fingers.

"Or to your family in London, my dear?" He smiled. "You should never have removed your linen cap, Lucasta Collyer Winton. Your red hair is all too recognizable."

And the sun came crashing down.

"Don't be alarmed. I will help you. It is not my intention to cause you further harm." His eyes were very pale, his expression placid. Lord Oakham was probably a very good card player.

"What can you mean?" she demanded.

Watching her thoughtfully, he caressed his pointy beard. "I knew from your manners at table, your posture, your refined voice, even your ladylike gestures of hand...."

The cherries turned sour, panic squeezing and grinding in her belly.

"Clearly you were accustomed to grander surroundings than Souls Dryft."

"Lord Oakham, I..."

"Young lady, your secret is out." He smiled, playfully waggling a finger. "You were not born to a life of drudgery with a yeoman farmer. I saw at once. And when I heard about Lord Winton's runaway bride..."

"You are mistaken, sir." She tried to force out a laugh, but her throat was too tight.

"I do not yet know how it happened that you came to be here, I cannot conclude whether it was John Carver or Captain Downing who stole you away from Winton, but I am aware of the debt your husband owes Carver. I also have some familiarity with John Carver's vengeful temper. Supposedly reformed, he has never fooled me. They are a family of reprobates who would not know how to treat a lady of your exquisite charms."

"I assure you, my lord," she snapped, the words frostbitten, "I am not that woman."

"No. I see you are quite changed."

Not knowing what to say, she blew her nose again, loudly.

"My dear lady, there is nothing to fear. You are quite safe here with me. I would never mistreat you as they have done." He crossed the room to clasp her hands, turning them over, tut-tutting. "Making you work until those silken hands are sore and chapped. Hush, hush." He held a finger to his lips. "There is no need to thank me now for this rescue. I'm sure you will have ways to show me your gratitude later, my dear. Now let me order you a bath."

Rescue from what? Oh, but a bath, that would be lovely, she mused.

"And we'll see what we can find for you to wear," he stood back to survey her gown. "We can do much better than this! And you need shoes, stockings, something for your hair."

It occurred to her that she was not about to be arrested. What he had in mind was something else entirely. "Lord Oakham, I must..."

"No one need know you are here." Long fingers wrapped around hers, he raised her knuckles to his lips and peppered them with kisses while she gently struggled to pull away. "Lucy, my sweet, your reluctance only increases my amour. I am in the grip of a very powerful emotion..."

She was amazed, watching this fine fellow cover her clenched hands with wet kisses, sink to his knees and declare himself her slave. "Please, my lord, you really must try to control yourself. My brother would say a man is only as strong as his stiff upper lip."

But he persisted, following her across the Turkish carpet on his knees, trying to kiss the muddied hem of her gown. "I will give you anything, Lucy, anything your little heart desires!"

She'd never known any man to make such a display, especially not for her, but in the past she'd never been alone with her suitors. The night with John, at Mistress Comfort's, was the first time she'd spoken to a man without her father present, listening to every word.

"My lord, please, stop! I thank you for the offer, but I'm quite happy where I am." She'd said it aloud at last. Yes, she was happy on that farm. Even when John was angry with her, she would rather be there with him than anywhere else. How odd it was she now knew happiness, while her entire life was turned upside down and inside out, while she didn't know if she was coming or going.

Whipping his head back, Lord Oakham observed her warily, as if fearing she'd come unhinged. "But how can you be happy there?"

"I can't explain it. I feel as if I belong there." So many times she'd warned herself it was time to leave, to get out of his way before she brought more trouble down on John's head. Yet she stayed, insensate to reason, too engrossed by this man she might never have met, if not for one chance encounter in a Norwich brothel.

His eyes hardened. "You mean to stay with John Carver? You choose him over all that I could give you?"

"Yes," she whispered, the sound of his name warming her through to the very bones. She would never be his wife, of course, could never make love to him again, but simply being near must suffice. Somehow she'd manage. He needed her to look after him.

And in the next moment she cursed inwardly at this madness, knowing it wasn't feasible to stay, under any circumstances.

Oakham made another grab for her hands. "Madam you will oblige me to tell what I know, if you go back to his farmhouse. I cannot keep your secret if you deny me the pleasure of your company, Lucy."

She tried to think, desperately searching for escape.

"Stay with me, my sweet. I'll keep you safe, buy you the finest gowns."

With what, she wondered dubiously. She knew he'd sold land to John Carver just to keep himself solvent.

"Beside me, you'll lay your head on the thickest of goosedown pillows..."

"But I cannot stay with you."

"Then you force me to turn you in."

"My lord, you rush to hasty conclusion. I said only that I could not stay with you today. Perhaps you will give me time to consider...."

"How much time?"

Eyes scanning the room, they landed finally on the table centerpiece, a horn of plenty. "Till the harvest fête, my lord. 'Tis not long." She'd be gone the day after, she decided, gone for good. "If you can be so kind as to keep my secret until then, I shall know I can place my trust in your noble hands." Pausing, she gave what she hoped was her most flirtatious smile. "And likewise, the rest of me. But you must promise to not tell anyone I am here."

He was consoled, content to wait. Reaching for her bare foot, he drew it up onto his thigh, exclaiming over the delicacy of her toes and the slender curve of her ankle. She laughed because his fingers tickled and also because she was quite hysterical by then.

Chapter 15

The door burst open. John Carver marched in with a whip in his hand and a frown on his face. Her avid suitor dropped her foot, scrambling upright.

"This woman belongs to me, Oakham, whether she likes it or not!"

"To you, Carver?" Lord Oakham exclaimed in outrage. "Perhaps for now, but only temporarily."

"Outside then, if you please, and we'll discuss this further."

"Oh John!" Lucy cried. "Such a fuss you make. Lord Oakham was just..."

"Aye! So I see." He stormed across the room, but she met him halfway, blocking his path. She saw the determination in the set of his jaw, the readiness in his braced shoulders and clenched fists.

"John! Behave yourself, for pity's sake," she hissed, fearing he might strike out at Lord Oakham and forget the vow he'd made to his mother. "No more brawling, remember? New leaf?"

"You're coming home with me."

"Well, of course I am."

"Because I ..." he stopped, his frown lopsided, blue eyes quizzical. "Oh. You are?"

She sighed, shaking her head. "I was simply returning a neighborly visit to his lordship, who very kindly gave me some cherries." With one bob curtsey for Lord Oakham, she dragged John back out again. For once she was the one doing the dragging.

"Cherries?" he growled, booted heels kicking up dust, bicep flexing under her hand. "Why would you eat his cherries, when you have ours at home?"

"Is that all you care about? Damn the cherries!"

"Don't say damn to me! Watch your language!"

His hypocrisy made her laugh out loud. "He offered me a bath, too," she said, living dangerously, unable to stop herself.

"A bath?" he choked out.

"He clearly knows how to treat a lady."

"You want a bath, you can have one at home."

"So you can spy on me, I suppose," she threw over her shoulder.

He spun her around to face him and leaned down. "I've seen it all before. I don't need to spy. I've got it up here." He tapped his temple with clenched knuckles. "Where I can look at it anytime I want."

"Do keep your voice down," she muttered wearily.

"Why should I? 'Tis the truth. I made you mine that night. You're mine to look at, no one else's."

She turned her face up to his, eyes narrowed, and then said, very deliberately, "Damn you. Damn. Damn. Damn...." She lifted on tiptoe for the last breath. "Damn."

They had stopped by his horse, which waited placidly, drinking out of Lord Oakham's fountain.

He ground his jaw, sheer vexation oozing from every twitching muscle. "Do you want a bath or not?"

"I'll wait," she replied, smiling sweetly, "until the next time you go to Norwich market. For your needs."

Slowly he nodded, tongue pressed into his cheek. Reaching inside his jerkin, he brought out her missing shoe. "No one looks at your bare feet except me. Put this on."

"No." Still irritated by the way he burst into Lord Oakham's house, swinging his whip as if she were an escaped cow or pig, she wasn't about to follow his orders. He was a possessive ogre with no manners and he'd embarrassed her once too often. John Carver needed a lesson, if he thought he could treat her like cattle.

"Put it on," he repeated.

"Who was the whip for, John? For Lord Oakham, or me, if I refused to go with you?"

He inhaled sharply. "Have I ever hurt you?"

"No, but I suppose you will, sooner or later. You're a man aren't you?"

"Put the blessed shoe on, Lucy."

Instead she took off her other shoe and threw it at him. It hit his shoulder because he was too slow, too astonished to duck in time. Hands on her waist, she waited for his reaction. His shoulders tensed; his jaw moved in another slow grind while he tapped his whip against the palm of one hand. A moment passed. Then another.

Finally he stepped forward, swept her up in one fluid motion and sat her on his horse. Before she spoke another word, he mounted behind her and turned the horse for home, her shoes in his hand, along with the whip.

"Never go off alone like that again."

She'd tried his patience as far as she could and now he simply put his arms around her and took her home. Whatever reaction she'd expected, this was not it. Apparently he wasn't willing to fight with her today, but he would've fought for her, she knew it.

John Carver would never hurt her physically. Her first instincts were true.

Comforted, she nestled further into his chest, her head against his shoulder, her own anger abated by his steady, calm strength. How might any woman stay cross with him for long? She'd tried it and failed miserably each time. And it wasn't always anger making her quarrel with him, she knew that now. She'd never had much patience with men before and they'd had little for her. This was all so new and strange, it took a while to settle within.

"I suppose he plied you with the same treats and promises he gives every beautiful woman, to win her over." He tossed her shoes into her lap. "Fell for it, did you? Like a fish on a hook." He teased her now. "I would've thought you'd know all the tricks employed by men."

She was silent. He rode very slowly, holding the reins and his whip loosely in his left hand. The right hand rested on his thigh, until it moved to her hip, holding her lightly in a caress that might be excused as accidental.

Just in case it wasn't accidental, she let her own hand rest on his thigh, her fingers spread timidly over the broad muscle.

He thought her beautiful.

Somehow, when he said it, she believed it.

Her lips were smiling, but since he they were hidden from him, she felt safe.

"The blacksmith's wife in Sydney Pines just started the pains for her first child. My mother's gone to tend her. Don't know when she'll return."

That secretive smile faltered.

"So she's leaving you in charge of me for tonight." He cleared his throat and she thought she felt the rumble of a stifled chuckle traveling through his chest. "Hope you've been studying your cooking lessons, Lucy."

Her heart was racing. They would be alone tonight in the house? This was bad, very bad.

"Why else would I ride all that way to bring you back?" he added slyly. "Someone has to cook me my supper, don't they?"

* * * *

Once the shock subsided, she was quite excited by the challenge of preparing a meal alone, looking after him, fussing over him. She might never have another chance. While he sprawled by the fire, playing with Vince and lecturing her about losing her bonnet, she tied his mother's apron over her grass-stained gown and set to the task with determination. She'd never had a man to take care of before.

He only had one complaint, when he found a long, red hair in his fish pie, but otherwise he appeared satisfied with her efforts, even a little surprised she managed not to poison him.

"I think you're improving, Lucy Friday. One day you might almost be as good a cook as my mother. Almost."

Later, he sat with his tankard of ale, his feet up on the table despite her admonishment, and talked of his sisters who hadn't lived in the house since he was a boy. She sensed he missed them, although he wouldn't admit it.

"I grew up in a house full o' women," he muttered. "It was a blessed relief when they went off to be married."

"Now you have a house full of women again."

"Aye." He winked at her over his tankard. "But this time it's different."

Ignoring the comment, she went into the pantry to tidy the shelves. "I wonder how long your mother will be gone."

"All night perhaps," he replied. "A woman's first babe always takes longest."

Looking at the neat rows of pickle jars, she had a mischievous idea. Bringing out two pots of jam, she set them down on the table before him with a spoon. "Your mother made one and I made the other," she said proudly. "You see if you can tell which is which."

He was eager enough for something sweet to finish his meal. "I'm an expert at jam tasting, you know."

"Hmm." She chuckled. "Just like you're an expert at everything, John Carver."

"Can't help that, can I?" He grinned.

"Pick up the spoon and get on with it."

His eyes narrowed. "If I get it right, what prize do I win?"

"There is no prize."

Leaning back, he folded his arms high over his chest. "Then I'll not play."

"Very well then, what do you want?"

"A kiss. If I guess correctly."

He was, of course, taking advantage of his mother's absence.

Anxious, she looked at the two pots of jam. He might be able to tell just from the writing on the labels, she thought. If this was to be a true test of her cooking, there was only one thing to do. Taking a black wool scarf from its hook by the door, she tied it firmly around his eyes, while he laughed at her excessive caution.

She guided his hand to the spoon, but he wanted her to hold it and feed him, so she did. What did it matter? In another few days she'd be gone. Lord Oakham's threat had made certain of it, so she may as well make the most of the time left.

He tasted the first mouthful of jam slowly, making a great deal of show, relishing his performance, his hand closed over hers holding the spoon. Lucy waited impatiently, wishing she never thought of this game. She might have known it could only lead to trouble. Perhaps, she mused grimly, that was why she did it. Around him she seemed to have a disgraceful lack of restraint.

He licked the spoon clean. "Very good," was the eventual assessment.

"Now the other." She took the spoon to the second pot and he kept his hand around hers, drawing her subtly closer, until he had an excuse to slide his other arm around her waist.

He opened his mouth wide for the second tasting and she thought he would swallow the bowl of the spoon.

* * * *

With the scarf tight around his eyes, John enjoyed her closeness with all his other senses heightened. It did nothing for his new leaf; everything for his roguish desires. He urged her down into his lap, but she resisted. The spoon dropped to the flagstones with a small clang and amid all the tussling her bosom brushed the side of his face.

"Which one is mine, then?" she demanded breathlessly as he finally got her into his lap, closing his arm around her waist.

"This one," he whispered hoarsely, one hand clutching her warm hair, easing her face down to his. She made a soft, whimpering mewl of annoyance, quickly quenched by his lips moving over hers. He felt her hands on his shoulders, firm at first, then softening their grip, her fingers spreading, sliding around his neck, touching the curls at his nape. Her warm, full lips opened timidly, succumbing under his, and he hungrily, greedily claimed what she so shyly offered.

The fire crackled gently behind him and Vince, somewhere nearby, snored contentedly. John slid one hand to her breast, stroking her through the old gown, longing to get her out of it. "Come to bed," he murmured thickly, adjusting her in his lap.

Her hands moved back to his shoulders now and she sat up straighter, ready to leave his knee. "You're incorrigible, John Carver."

"You started the game," he whispered. "And the first jam I tasted was yours, was it not?"

He heard her startled inhale, felt her fingers digging into his arms. He closed his hand over her breast.

"Am I right?"

"Yes," she sulked.

He celebrated by kissing her again, any part of her reachable with his lips —and felt her pulse skipping giddily. "See? I told you, I'm an expert."

"Must you always win?"

"Yes." He laughed, licking his sticky tongue along her rigid, stubborn little jaw. "And at the harvest fête, you'll see for yourself."

"Will I indeed?"

"I'll win every game for you, Lucy."

"Don't bother on my account."

"I must. My mother says…"

"Says what?" she muttered scornfully, wriggling in his lap.

His arms were immovable, holding her across his thighs. Already he felt his arousal vigorously straining under her. "She says I'm to court you. Properly."

The woman refused to be still. "Court me? What the devil for?"

"She says it's time you were properly wooed."

"Let me up, damned knave. I know what you have in mind. I can feel it already. Woo me indeed! And you're getting me all sticky."

With one hand he cupped her chin, firm but gentle. "Lucy Friday, I hereby give you notice: I intend to court you and win you. There now, 'tis said and done. Can't be any plainer."

"No," she managed.

"Yes," was the calm retort. He was never so sure of anything in his life. When he went after her that day, he did so to bring her back and keep her there. Didn't even think twice about it. Whatever it took, he was willing to do it, anything to keep her. Anything. He was ready.

"Please don't," she groaned, his hand still around her jaw, fingers lightly caressing the warmth of her cheek.

His hand drifted slowly down her throat, across her shoulder and down to her breast again, slyly measuring the reckless, scattered beat of her heart. "If I win every game at the fête, you must promise to be mine."

"I'll promise no such thing."

He began to tickle her again while his mouth sought her breast, kissing her sloppily through the gown until her nipple was evident, a soft prick against his tongue. She hadn't worn a corset after her first day in his house, finding it too difficult to work in such a binding garment and being too stiff and tired at the end of the day to fuss with all those tight laces. He'd often remarked to his mother that Lucy should wear a corset, but tonight he was certainly glad of the absence.

She was laughing too hard now, too winded to make him stop, so he licked that little prize and teased it with his lips until she was finally still in his arms.

"John...your mother could be home any minute."

He stopped and raised his head, staring into the blindfold, feeling for her in the darkness. She was struggling, he sensed, with something more she daren't tell him. Damned woman kept too many secrets.

"Promise me," he coaxed, his hands around her narrow waist. "After the harvest fête...if I win every game..."

He didn't finish.

"We shouldn't," she groaned, her brow falling to his shoulder, as if her will to resist him was crumbling away to dust. His own will had gone that way long since.

"Well." He stroked her hair with one trembling hand. "I might not win every game."

He felt her smiling, her lips moving his collar, briefly touching his neck. "I thought you always win."

"You'll have to take that chance, won't you?" As he would, too.

* * * *

After a moment, during which Lucy battled with every denial in her head, every protest against her heart's demands, he suddenly began to sing to her. Shocked, she sat very still, her head pressed to his shoulder, his fingers combing through her long, loose hair. He sang of a bird on a briar, an old song she'd heard before, but one that had never been sung to her. Solely for her.

Not knowing what to say or do, she sat very still and let him sing on.

Later they went to their separate chambers, but only just. He had now drawn a line across this flirtation and set a date for her thorough and complete undoing. For tonight he was content with the promise she gave in a rash moment, when it seemed as if she had no choice.

He'd sung to her. He meant to woo her. He'd brazenly announced it. What was a woman supposed to do?

Chapter 16

His mother, it turned out, had given Bridget a hearty slap when she learned of the fight, and when John was teased by Martin Frye and the other farm laborers, he told them all that Lucy Friday was a young lady who should be treated with respect from now on and if he caught anyone doing otherwise he'd set them straight with his own fists.

This, to many villagers, was a declaration of sorts. It angered some of the young ladies who'd hoped one day to catch his wandering eye, but Alice kept her head up and put on a brave face. Bridget, so they heard along the grapevine, assured everyone that his fascination for the "bold tart" wouldn't last long. The village, she said, would soon be rid of the scourge. But with the threat of John's vengeance hanging over them, no one else spoke out against Lucy.

The day of Lord Oakham's summer fête dawned bright and warm with a high violet sky kissed by fluffy clouds. While John readied their transport to Oakham's manor, his mother went into the pantry and brought out a circular posy of wild, plum red roses, picked from the thorny bushes covering parts of the old flint wall.

"I made this for you," she said to Lucy, pinning it in her hair. "For today. Since you lost your bonnet."

With her foolish promise to John hanging over her, not to mention Lord Oakham's threat to turn her in, Mistress Carver's thoughtfulness was all too much to bear. Lucy threw her arms around the lady, kissed her and thanked her.

"It's only flowers, Lucy," the woman exclaimed, bemused.

Apologizing for her impulsive actions, which lately surprised her just as much as they did these kind people, Lucy wished for the ground to swallow her whole and put her out of this misery. But Mistress Carver smiled and soothed her gently. "You can't help it, Lucy dear. I've seen how every sadness and every joy is so deeply felt in you. It must make your life very hard. Never mind. I daresay you'll toughen up."

Poor lady, thought Lucy miserably, she had no idea how many years had been spent "toughening up." But underneath, as she now discovered, she was weak, lonely and afraid, her façade prone to cracks worn away by constant disappointment. Now, under the slightest display of kindness, she shattered like glass.

"Women have it harder than men," Mistress Carver went on. "We are sensitive to the tides of the moon. Men are too thickheaded to sense anything unless it strikes hard against their skull."

Lucy swallowed her mournful thoughts. It was a beautiful day, her last at Souls Dryft, and she wouldn't spoil it. Vince put his front paws on the seat beside her and licked her cheeks, tail wagging. Outside the window John whistled as he harnessed the horses to the cart. He'd been looking forward to this, she knew. He prided himself on winning most of the games at the fête. A natural-born show-off, he liked any chance to flex his muscles. Today, of course, he had additional incentive to win.

Had it rained, or the sky been overcast, it would've been much easier to think of leaving soon. The sun being out only threw salt in her wounds, reminding her she would never have another such day of happiness. But she shouldn't have stayed here as long as she had already, and each day brought her closer to discovery, closer to calamity.

* * * *

John noticed her peevish silence but didn't comment on it. She sat behind him in the cart, clinging to the sides, a little posy of roses bobbing in her long hair. Today she looked more beautiful than ever and he felt a warm, different sense of pride because she rode with him to the fête. At the end of this day, she would be his at last. She'd promised and he knew, instinctively, she kept her promises. Why else would she be looking at him so fearfully? He grinned back at her and winked.

Lord Oakham always laid on a fine feast and the day was filled with competition: horse racing, throwing the hammer, wrestling and a particularly savage sport of shin-kicking. Later in the evening there would be a bonfire and dancing. It was John's intent to impress her with his skill in every competition and then sweep her off her feet at the dancing. No woman could resist dancing. After that…well…he didn't want to get too far ahead of himself, but he felt something in the air, a change coming.

When they arrived, he helped his mother out of the cart and then raised his arms for Lucy. For once she let him lift her down, but kept her face somber.

"Smile, Lucy," he teased softly, more pleased than he should be when she let him help her out with his unworthy hands. "You'll see me hurled around in the wrestling. You'll like that."

Her gaze shyly swept his chin and then his lips, but no higher. "Don't get hurt." She hesitated. "Your mother wouldn't like it."

"Hurt? Me? Nothing hurts me!" He chuckled, running his thumb over her lower lip as he did once before, readying it for a kiss, but she ducked away, hurrying to join his mother.

So she was going to make him work for it. Fine. He'd never shied away from hard work.

* * * *

He'd won three wrestling bouts in quick succession when Martin Frye ran up to take his turn. Shielding her eyes from the sun, Lucy watched with her heart in her mouth. His mother observed wryly that she hadn't seen him act this way in years. There was a little blood on his lip, but Lucy barely noticed since he'd stripped off his shirt some time ago, revealing a bronzed, rippling torso with careless, shoulder-shrugging arrogance. He claimed not to be vain, but he must know the effect it had.

The village girls crowded around to watch, having far less interest in the outcome than they had in the handsome young men who competed.

She was shocked when Alice Croft approached, battling with the semblance of a smile. "I hope you're enjoying the day, Lucy."

"Yes. And you too, Alice."

They stood a moment in awkward silence, both wanting to speak, but having little to say and only one thing in common. Eventually, Alice managed a tight apology. "I don't agree with Bridget's behavior. She shouldn't have picked a fight with you."

Lucy assured her it was all forgotten, but Alice had more to get off her chest. "Nor do I agree with her reasons for saying what she did." She paused. "I do agree with her, however, that you will cause John trouble and hurt."

Lips clamped shut, Lucy watched as John celebrated another win, beaming over at them, careless of his bloodied lip.

"I've loved John since we were young together in this village," Alice went on quietly. "I never thought of marrying any other man but him. I've saved myself, waited all these years." She made an odd sound, almost a laugh, or a low scream of frustration. "And now here you are and I see how he looks at you. He never, ever looked at me that way."

What could she say? Could she try to deny it, when the man stood over there, preening like a peacock for her?

"I'm not a fool to try fighting against it. I shall try to overcome my pain. If he loves you, then he should be with you. I want him to be happy."

"Alice, you don't have to say all this." She was wretched when she thought of this quiet girl struggling for his notice all those years, finally seeing it slip through her fingers for a worthless hussy.

"But I must." Alice drew a quick breath and looked over at the wrestling again. "I must let you know where I stand and I must know where you stand. I love John. Do you?"

Her tongue was thick, her pulse racing. The sun on her head was too hot.

"Because I don't want to see him hurt, Lucy. Don't lead him along and then break his heart."

"I...I would never do that. I don't want him hurt, either."

The tall, slender woman nodded. "Then stay and love him forever. If you can't, then leave now, before the damage is more severe."

Her piece said, Alice returned to her father's side, head bowed, long, honey-gold hair, dripping down her back.

Stay and love him forever. She wished she could. He was coming over now, filling his face with a pasty, two more in his hand for the women of his house.

"Did you see, Lucy?" he demanded, spitting crumbs. "I won four bouts."

Like a little boy, she thought. "Oh yes. I saw."

He grinned, handing her the other pasties. "Where's my mother?"

"Talking to Farmer Croft about milk-yield." Holding the warm pasties in one hand, she lifted the corner of her apron to wipe his mouth. "You don't need to fight every man in these three villages, I hope."

"Why? Worried for me?"

She was trying not to look at his chest, gleaming with sweat under the bright yellow sun. "Not really," she muttered. "But Alice worries."

He took another ravenous bite of his pasty.

"Why don't you go over and talk to her?" she asked, keeping her voice light.

"What about?"

"She loves you."

He stopped chewing, glanced over at the young woman and then back at Lucy. "Aye." His eyes were very clear blue today. He sniffed, wiping the back of his hand across his mouth. "I'm sorry for it, but what can I do?"

Swallowing her unhappiness, she smiled. "Love her back, of course."

He looked down at the grass around their feet. "You can't choose where you love, Lucy. It just happens. Like it did to me, the very first moment I laid a finger on you." This lethal statement laid at her feet, he returned to the games, trotting back across the lawn and into the rowdy fray.

Later, as the heat of the day wound down, a log was placed across the widest bend of the stream bordering Lord Oakham's property. Two at a time, the men approached one another from opposing sides, armed only with a stick and a horsehair pillow, each man's aim to dislodge the other into the water. It looked dangerous and the men took it extremely seriously, despite the copious amounts of ale and cider already consumed. Thrashing and swinging at one another with violent glee, they very often ended up in the water at the same moment, receiving a sobering ducking and immediate rescue by their anxious womenfolk.

Only men, Lucy mused to herself, would think up such a sport. John Carver, naturally, was one of the first to volunteer, while she and his mother were obliged to watch on tenterhooks, cringing and wincing at every blow he took. Lucy's fingers dug a little deeper into his mother's arm each time he wavered on the log, but he balanced well and somehow escaped a ducking, sending each reckless opponent to the water below, suffering only a handful of beatings and swipes in the process.

She didn't know whether to be glad he won, or wish he might take a tumble and have some of the boundless arrogance knocked out of him.

Looking over the crowd she caught sight of Lord Oakham making a slow approach, stopping on his way to talk to other villagers, smiling benevolently. Lucy's pulse raced, throbbing in her temple until she felt certain it must be visible to the eye.

He reached her side in due course. "I hope you enjoy your sojourn in the country, Lucasta." Clouds swept in to cover the sun, the day grew dark, the air thick with the promise of thunder.

"Indeed, Lord Oakham, very much." Her dream was almost over.

He smiled thinly. "You will recall our recent conversation."

"Yes."

"You have made your decision?"

She was watching John, who saw them talking together on the bank side and subsequently swung his weapons harder, swifter, his eyes turning savage with more than a hint of verdigris seething in those blue depths.

One hand shielding her face from the sun, she looked up at Lord Oakham. "I have, sir."

He waited, brows arched high, self-confident.

"I cannot live with you and must decline your kind offer. If you cannot find it in you heart to let me be free of the past, then by all means turn me in. It does you no harm to let me go, but you must do as you think best, my lord."

He blanched. "You are making a grave mistake, young woman."

"Am I? There was another man who wanted me against my will, once before," she added softly, "which is how this all began and how I came to be here. I never understood why any man would want a woman who did not truly want him." She studied his face from the shadow of her palm. "Would you not rather have a woman who loved you and stayed with you out of choice? Or would you be satisfied with a woman who might one day crack you across the skull with a pan of coals?"

Behind him another man landed with a splash in the stream and John yelled over at them, "Mayhap you'd like a try against the champion, your lordship."

Several other villagers joined in the hue and cry, but Lord Oakham blustered awkwardly. "One does not generally participate." With slender hands he checked the stitching of his gold embroidered silk doublet.

"Aw. Go on, yer lordship," Martin Frye bellowed drunkenly from the other side of the stream. "Show us 'ow it's done."

"Aye," shouted his sister spitefully. "Someone should put John Carver in the water and wipe the smug grin orf 'is face."

Of course, Lucy thought acidly, there were some who wanted to see John's pride brought down a peg or two. She'd thought that herself just a few minutes ago, but they would also laugh at his lordship taking a ducking. In their eyes, there would be no bad side to either man losing.

"Well sir. I gave you my answer. Now you must do what you believe to be right." She forced her fear down, her chin up. As always, when anxiety threatened to beat her into submission, she rose to the challenge, haughty temper taking over. "Will you fight John Carver for me, Lord Oakham? The water, I am told, is not cold today."

Still he hesitated, showing his cowardly colors, blaming it all on not wanting to get his finery wet, or step down from his exalted place.

"Do you mean to turn me in?" she asked, straightforward.

No answer.

She swept a lock of hair aside, showing the scar under her eye. "Lord Winton gave me this gift on my wedding night."

There was a very slight fluttering of his eyelids, no more.

"That's why I ran," she added steadily. "I was not kidnapped. The Carvers are not to blame for any of this."

Lips pursed, he regarded her face in a methodical fashion, giving nothing away.

Behind her John Carver called out for an opponent, scorning them all for cowards.

Well, she couldn't let John Carver win again, could she? If he did, he would soon come to her to collect his winnings and she would have no choice but to keep her promise. Grabbing the stick and pillow being offered to his lordship, she kicked off her shoes and made her way down the bank to the stream.

Restless silence fell over the watching crowd, not knowing what to make of this.

Seeing her standing there, weapons at the ready, John's shoulders sagged. "Don't be daft. It's not for women."

But there was no stopping her now with everything tumbling down around her ears, the truth soon to be out. "Who says?"

"I do."

"Well, we'll see about that, won't we?" She stepped gingerly along the log.

For a few more shocked moments, everyone held their breath.

"Stop and go back," John shouted. "You're being foolish, woman. You can't fight me."

"Really?" She swung her pillow and it hit him in the thigh. He wobbled, cursing, but kept his footing.

A solitary shout of encouragement rang out from the crowd and then came two more.

"Do that again and you'll be sorry," he growled, eyes wide.

"This game doesn't seem so hard to me," she exclaimed cheerily. "Prepare to be vanquished, John Carver."

"You're mad, woman. You'll be hurt."

"I'm sure I can stand it. Only men make a fuss over aches and pains, and they never have to withstand the agonies we do."

Someone laughed and cheered her on, followed by a small chorus of female voices now taking her side.

"Give up, wench," he exclaimed, crouching, eyeing her in some bemusement as she stepped closer along the log. "You can't beat me. Don't make a fool of yourself trying. I don't want to have to teach you a lesson and humiliate you before the entire ...."

She swung again, hitting him harder this time with her stick across his legs. He grunted and spat, fighting to keep his balance.

On the bank side support grew for her cause, female voices mostly, among them Alice Croft. A steady rumble of laughter broke from the men, who were ready to enjoy the novelty of seeing a woman pushed in the water. Naturally, they expected John to win, but they admired her bravery.

She saw his jaw set, his eyes darken, fist gripping that stick. "I warned you, woman."

They swung at the same time. The log bounced and rolled. She scrambled but stayed upright. As did he.

The crowd grew louder, shouting for their favourite in this unusual battle.

John shrugged, tossed his weapons into the water and declared he didn't need them in any case. "I can take you down barehanded, wench."

The men cheered, the women booed.

Head down she ran at him, swinging the pillow at his head. He ducked, caught her round the legs, and they fell together into the stream, much to the delight of the crowd, for whom it was a fitting resolution.

Submerged in the sun-warmed water, all was silent but for the gentle froth of bubbles around them. Her heart was still beating, but distant and wistful. If only she could stay there forever, under the water with him.

They couldn't, of course. Soon they needed air and he dragged her up into reality.

"Why did you do that?" he gasped, shaking his head like a wet dog.

"Because you should lose once in a while, John Carver." But she did it for herself, too, she realized. She wanted to prove her bravery, her worthiness, for in his world actions mattered more than words and intentions.

He smoothed the wet hair back from her face and when she blinked up at him, drops glittered in the corner of her eye, as if her lashes were decorated with tiny diamond chips. "Don't even think of kissing me," she gasped, breathless. "Not in front of everyone, like this."

"Why not? Why shouldn't I kiss my woman?"

But several folk waded into the water to help her out, saving her from his clutches. She was now something of a heroine. Farmer Croft brought her a cup of cider and Alice lent her a shawl to dry her hair. Martin Frye came over to shake her hand, although he held it longer than necessary and was soon sent on his way by a stormy-faced John. She felt giddy with her victory, if it might be called that. John, naturally, insisted he only fell in to save her pride.

"And we fell together," he reminded her slyly. "I still won every game today."

"'Tis a matter of opinion. It might be said you forfeited the last game."

"To save your pride."

She shook her head, laughing. Incorrigible, she decided, wasn't even a big enough word for what he was. Indefatigable, splendidly passionate, mad as a March hare, might suit him better.

Finally she remembered Lord Oakham and looked for him. To her surprise he was exactly where she last left him, still watching her. His countenance was stoic, unreadable again, but he bowed his head a half inch in her direction before walking away into the crowd.

Her heart would not come down to a steadier canter, for she had no idea what it meant. She'd challenged him brazenly to turn her in and he might very well do so. There was no reason for him to keep her secret, unless he should be struck with sudden kindness and charity.

"Lucy!" John was at her side, taking her hand. "Day-dreamer!"

They danced by the light of the bonfire and the yellow harvest moon. He was not her only partner. Almost every fellow with two working feet sought her out and she refused no one. Throwing herself into the fun, she laughed at every jest, even told a few of her own, and drank too much cider until, complaining he'd watched her dancing with other men long enough, John lifted her over his shoulder and carried her to the cart. She protested loudly at this manhandling. "What would your noble Sydney ancestors say if they saw you treat a lady this way?"

"They'd no doubt cheer me on." He checked on his mother, who was asleep in the back of the cart, wrapped in a fleece blanket, the long day having worn her out. "I don't know what she told you about our fine Sydney ancestors, but every one of 'em was a scoundrel. A bunch of cheaters, liars, schemers and bride stealers. So there you have it." He smiled as he leapt up beside her and took the reins. "That's the noble line I come from. That's the Barons Sydney for you."

Tonight, since his mother took the back of the cart, Lucy sat up front, at his side. The moonlight cooling her face, she looked up at him, suddenly solemn. "Bride stealers?"

"Oh yes. They didn't care who a woman belonged to, if they wanted her."

She snuggled up to his sleeve and rested her head against his wide shoulder. "Would you ever steal me away?"

"I don't have to. You're here with me now."

"But if I wasn't..." Something selfish squeezed hard around her heart, forcing her to ask. "....if I was married to another man."

"Well you're not are you? Look at the moon, Lucy. It will fall on us at any minute."

She closed her eyes, feeling as if the moon had already fallen and crushed her flat.

Chapter 17

His mother was roused from the back of the cart and she trundled into the house, yawning , Vince trotting at her side, leaving them to put the horses away and lock the gate.

Lucy checked on her pigs first and then returned to find him. Busy with the horses, rubbing them down, he was aware of Lucy watching, leaning against a wooden beam, hands behind her back. Her presence had become so important to him, he couldn't imagine what he'd do if she left.

She was turning slowly now, leaving the stables. He followed her, his step quicker, catching up before she reached the door. He captured her in his arms, the breath hard in his lungs, the need to claim and keep her as sharp and painful as the prick of a blade in his gut. "I'll have my winnings now then, if you please. As you promised me."

"John...stop, you fool..."

"You've made me wait long enough, but we're alone now and I want my prize. Give it to me!"

"You truly are a spoiled only son..."

"Say you love me, Lucy," he groaned into her hair, the sweet fragrance of those roses filling his nostrils, making him dizzy. "Say it."

"I can't." But her face turned, so he nuzzled her soft cheek, slightly colored now by her weeks in the country.

"Why?" He drew her back, away from the open door. "Is it Nathaniel? Are you worried about him? Don't be." He turned her around, his hands on her waist as he stepped back into an empty stall, bringing her with him. "I'll talk to him. I'll explain everything..."

"It's not Nathaniel," she mewled.

"Then what? Who?" His heart thumped so hard in his chest, he thought it would break a rib. "There's another man?"

"No," she gasped. "There's only you, John. Only you."

He kissed her then, unable to wait longer, ready to take this pleasure he'd known before and never forgotten. "I've dreamed of you since May," he muttered gruffly into her lips and her cheek. "I think I've dreamed of you all my life."

She kissed him back the same way, her fingers in his hair, her body falling against his, bringing back every stinging, delicious sensation he'd enjoyed in her company on that rainy night, not so long ago.

Then she pulled away. "But I can't. I can't do this."

This time he wouldn't let her go and, struggling together, they tipped into the piled straw. "Why can't you love me?" he demanded, holding her under him, his hands around her wrists.

He felt her breathing as if every breath was her last. Her eyes gleamed bright with unshed tears. "It's not that I can't love you," she cried out, helpless, frustrated. "I can't not love you."

John stared down at her, at this beautiful, beguiling creature who brought out the rogue in him, just when he thought he had it vanquished. And he knew he would never let her go again. This was what he'd waited for every day of his adult life. He'd known she was out there, somewhere, his to claim, just as soon as he found her.

"You said yourself, John," she whimpered, writhing under him, "we can't choose who we love. If I could choose, my life would be so much easier." She was still trying to get free, arching her back, heaving with her hips, when she must know the futility of fighting him. He was much stronger than she and she wasn't going anywhere without him ever again.

Laughing softly, he leaned down and kissed her nose, then her chin, then let his tongue travel slowly up along her smooth jaw to her ear. "Thank God I found you again," he whispered, banking the desire to take her too quickly.

"Damn you," she whined.

"Do you like saying 'damn,' Lucy?" He'd noticed her saying it a lot lately.

"Yes."

It amused him, the way she cursed, spitting it out in a rush of breath, trying to sound fierce, as if she meant it, when he sensed she really wanted to say something quite different. She struggled with her emotions, just as he struggled with his. They were both out of their depth, he suspected.

The few dampened, bedraggled flowers still left in her hair now tumbled down the thick tresses, some petals laying in the straw already, standing out like bright drops of blood in the lantern light. Her sleeves were down over her shoulders, the pulse in her neck throbbing visibly with a passionate temper.

"I've waited months for you, Lucy, since the last time. I'm ready to burst with wanting."

Her eyes flashed. "You've had no other in all this time?" She didn't believe him, of course. Who knew what Nathaniel told her. Probably nothing good.

"I'm a reformed man," he protested, sitting astride her hips, shedding his shirt and flinging it to the straw.

"And you were once a rogue. Your cousin told me."

She was very solemn now, her hair a ruffled cloud of cinnamon and nutmeg, her eyelids lowered, as if she daren't look at him. He reached down with his thumb and forefinger, pinching her chin gently, lifting it.

"There might be a little of the rogue left in me, but only you know where to find him, Lucy." He brushed a hair back from her cheek, dislodging another rose. "I know why you're worried, but I don't care about your past. I don't care what you were before. None of that matters now."

Her lashes fluttered wide open in surprise and he saw his face reflected in her wide black pupils. Liquid passion bubbled over inside him, his pulse quickened, his arousal too exultant, irrepressible.

He began pulling on her bodice and her sleeves, forgetting the purpose of hooks and laces. They rolled together, straw sticking to hair and skin.

* * * *

He kissed her fervently, as if he needed her for sustenance. In the beginning she almost feared it, this passion he had for her, but her own desires soon kept apace and she let her doubts fall away like the rose petals from her hair. All the facts of how she came to be there, the things he didn't know that she should have told him, all the warnings, they were insignificant when measured with this yearning that had dwelled inside her since the first time they had met. Here she was, living her heavenly dream. Let it last a while yet.

Nuzzling her breasts, he gasped her name, his thighs hard between hers, sliding them apart quickly. In the next stall, a horse whinnied, wondering what they were doing on the other side of the wooden barrier. And then he entered her, slick and hot, her skirt and petticoat up around her waist, since he was in too much hurry to remove it. She felt him inside her, filling her, stretching her sheath, plowing forward and upward. He found the rhythm quickly, his expression strained, the light in his eyes purely carnal, covetous.

They rolled again until she was astride him and he lifted his hips, grunting, thrusting upward. She cried out, her head flung back, his hands on her breasts. Her body was his now and his belonged to her. They couldn't stop, there was no end in sight. There were no words, only sensations, pleasure, pain and ecstasy.

* * * *

Pounding into her, strange sounds spat out over his lips and then he drowned inside her, rapidly emptying his seed into her warm haven. It came so quickly, he didn't even try to hold back. She would have moved off him when she felt the peak begin--he felt her shift--but his hands came down on her hips and held her there, his singular intent being the ultimate sharing, the most potent sign of his love, and his declaration to her, a commitment to their future.

He lay still, spent, relaxed in the straw. They'd have twenty babes, a mix of redheads and dark, boys or girls, he didn't care as long as they were healthy. He already saw them all, mischievous little creatures, running around the yard, avoiding their chores, laughing and happy. His heart sang wildly at the thought of it, at the picture of an idyllic family life. Children, a wife, all things he didn't give much more than a cursory, skeptical thought to before this.

She curled against his chest and kissed his nipple. "Is that it?" she whispered.

"Is that it?" he repeated, shaking his head so the straw crackled. "I forgot how demanding you are."

"It was very....quick. For all your insufferable boasting..."

One hand to the back of her head, he drew her lips to his and kissed her hard. "I've only just begun, wench."

So had she. She reached down to hold his sac in her hands, stroking. "I remember how easily you're roused again after the first."

Yes, he thought happily, they were both starved for one another. It wouldn't be long before he was ready again. Slowly she kissed her way down his chest and he, blissfully supine in the straw, gazed up at the beams as he felt her warm, silken mouth descend, making love to that part of him no one ever lavished with so much adoration as she did. Her tongue wrapped his crest in velvet and he moaned, a slow shuddering breath of delight. She lapped at him, kissed and sucked. He clenched his muscles, lifted his hips, his hands feeling for her hair as it spilled around his thighs and stroked his groin.

He wondered then about his cousin, but when he thought of her with any other man he felt a sharp pain in his heart, bile rising in his throat, so he quickly emptied his mind again, promising himself never to think of her past. Whatever had come since May, it was now August, and he would erase those other months between. Tonight she would know for sure where she belonged and with whom.

* * * *

She felt his fingers in her hair, pulling her up. His manhood was marble-hard again now, lifting and pulsing, thanks to her steady ministrations. Blushing from all the attention, it stretched almost to his navel, making her womanly core melt with joyous and greedy anticipation. Lucy gave the very tip one last lick, tasting his salt and the musk of her own body, and then he whispered at her to turn around. Straddling his chest, she did as he asked. He pressed his flat hand to the small of her back, bending her gently. She took him in her mouth again, only seconds before she felt his lips and then his tongue repaying the favor eagerly between her own thighs. She paused a moment as the quicksilver delight shot through her. Her eyelids were heavy, her heartbeat galloped, warm lust flooding through her veins, bursting forth in all directions. He stroked her thighs with his strong, firm hands, but his tongue between them never stopped, never broke its rhythm. Drawing a sharp breath, she let out a soft moan and arched.

Already it started, the rapturous surging swell. Not wanting to get there before he did, she hastily continued as she began, pleasuring her lover, while he did the same to her.

* * * *

She woke in his bed, not even sure how she made it there. In the fever of their passion, somehow, they must have put out the lantern, locked the gate, bolted the door and found their way upstairs. All she remembered were his kisses and his hands on every part of her, his body over her, under her, inside her.

Little quakes, even now, could be felt deep inside where he started the waves hours ago.

Through his open shutters, the big moon spread a wide arc and lined his profile with silver. He was asleep on his back, arms and legs flung out with carefree abandon, hair ruffled and messy. The little cut on his lip had started to bleed again in the stables, but now it dried. Tomorrow she would put a salve on it for him.

But tomorrow…tomorrow she must leave. The thought broke in abruptly, destroying her peaceful, loving perusal of his face.

Stretching, she sat up, the sheet falling away to her hips. She was naked. Presumably he got her that way, although she seemed to recall it was a struggle since he tried to do everything at once. Her most vivid memories of those last few hours were not of practical acts done by rote, but of sensations, soaring heights of ecstasy, frenzied demands scratching in her throat, slippery skin on skin, the prickle of straw in her hair, the scent of him inhaled in great, greedy gusts and the taste of his kisses, far more potent than his mother's infamous plum wine.

Now there he lay, innocent as an angel, one arm under his head, the other stretched out toward her, palm up, thick, square fingers curled in a claw. She should go back to her bed across the hall and try to get some sleep or she'd be in no fit state for her journey tomorrow. But when she moved to slide off his bed, his hand was suddenly around her wrist, eyes observing her sleepily.

"Stay with me," he purred, drawing her hand to his chest. "I've never had the pleasure of tumbling you in the morning."

She shook her head. "I can't stay with you."

"Yes you can." He was watching her through drooping lashes, fingers stroking her arm.

"I should never have come here, John," she murmured. "If I'd known...I would never have waited on Nathaniel's cart for you."

"You know what my father used to say?"

She sighed. "No. Do tell."

"Could've, would've, should've. Won't help us now, will it?" Slipping his arm around her waist, he drew her down into the bed and she went limp, helpless.

"What about your mother? She'll know."

"Let me worry about mother. In the morning. Now sleep."

Snuggled against his side, his arm under her, she laid her head on his shoulder and eventually closed her eyes again, too comfortable and replete to argue.

Tomorrow she'd tell him. Tomorrow she'd say goodbye. She could hardly do it now.

Tomorrow.

* * * *

In the morning he woke her with a kiss, ready to resume their games. He had a long day ahead of him, he said, couldn't lay abed with her all day, much as she might want him to.

"So I'll take some comfort now," he said, "in case I'm weary later."

They both knew he'd never be too tired, but she willingly complied, charmed by the warm blue light in his eyes, the mischievous gleam of a little boy getting away with his naughtiness. The seasons might change, but he never would, not completely, no matter how he tried, because perpetual summer lived there in his luminous gaze. Today she was heart-achingly reflective, dwelling on every touch, every glance.

He made love to her slowly this morning, entering her from behind, careful, deliberate, anchoring her hips in his hands as he plowed her furrow, inch by inch, until his loins were flush with her buttocks and there he stayed a moment, evidently delighting in the possession. He ground into her and she muffled her cries in the bolster, her hair an untidy, tangled sprawl over her shoulders and his bed. Then, just as slowly, he withdrew until he was almost all the way out, but not quite. He stopped again, reaching around to clasp her breasts in his hands, before he re-entered, thrusting deeper still.

She felt his chest arching over her back, the power of his thighs braced against the back of her legs and, as he gently squeezed her nipples, she clamped her teeth down on the luckless bolster. To be on her hands and knees before him was the ultimate submission and before she met him she would never have imagined allowing this. Ever. But then there were many things she'd never imagined before John.

She sheathed him eagerly each time, pressing back against his groin, trying to hold him inside longer, the desperate craving building with every lingering, torturous retreat. Her breasts hung into his hands like ripe fruit and when he plumbed her again, harder this time, losing a little of his self-control, the bed trembled, shaking his juicy prizes so he closed his fingers around them, gripping tighter. His breath scorched her neck as he covered her like a stallion to a mare, nibbling her skin, working his hips against her.

The tide came in faster waves as she, unable to hold still any longer, pushed back against the tumultuous pressure, squeezing, her orgasm fluttering around his cock as it swelled inside her sheath. And they both felt it, like a thousand tiny kisses lavished on his thick shaft, a decadent sensation comparable to none other. Then he came. The cry rolled out of him like thunder as he emptied wildly, his hips slapping against her bottom, finally pushing her down to the bed.

He slumped over her, breathing hard, still holding her hot breasts, his heart pounding madly where his chest pressed to her back, her own orgasm still coursing through her body, leaving her limp and careless, glad to die under his weight if need be. There were no words. None at all.

And she knew she wasn't leaving that day.

Perhaps tomorrow would be soon enough.

Perhaps tomorrow she could give him up.

Chapter 18

When John tripped downstairs an hour later, whistling merrily and pulling a leather jerkin over his shirt, his mother had just come in from the hen house holding a basket of eggs under her arm. They exchanged the usual greetings, but he always knew when something troubled her.

She stood by the fire with her back to him, complaining of a chill in the air this morning. He walked up behind her, laid his palms on her shoulders.

"It's all right, mother. You don't have to be angry with me."

Immediately she turned around, the poker in her hands. "You shouldn't have done it, John. The poor girl…couldn't you resist your base urges?"

"It's all right, mother," he repeated calmly, planting his feet firm, hands on his hips. "I'm going to marry her. Of course. What did you think I planned to do?" And then he laughed easily, clapping his hands together while she turned pale and wan.

"You might have told me!"

"I just did, didn't I?" He eyed the poker in her hands. "Do put that down, mother. I thought you were going to take a swipe at me for despoiling your precious Lucy."

"Hush!" She put the poker on its hook, scrutinizing the low ceiling. "Is she still asleep?"

"No, she's up," he replied loudly, "and fiddling around with her hair. She'll be down shortly. Where's breakfast? I'm famished." Resuming his jaunty whistle, he began juggling three eggs from the basket, until his mother took them off him, one by one.

"When will you be married then? Let it be soon. There's been enough gossip in this village."

"As soon as the parson will take us," he replied with a grin, bursting at the seams with it this morning, exhilarated. She was his now. She was staying and he would make her his wife.

He quite liked this wooing business after all.

His mother looked relieved, putting the eggs gently back in their basket. "Best tell Alice first. Wouldn't want her to hear it from another."

"I will, I will." He groaned, not looking forward to it. Taking an apple from the dresser, he bit into it, complaining he thought breakfast would be ready by now.

"And when you tell Alice, be a gentleman for once and remember where you come from and don't…"

"Oh, mother," he rolled his eyes, taking a second, bigger bite of apple.

"…roll your eyes at me," she continued, not even looking up from the pot over the fire. "If you're going to be a married man with a wife, you can start remembering your manners, because you'll soon have your own sons to be an example to." She paused then as the reality hit her. "My John, a married man at last! I began to think I'd never see the day."

He was glad he'd pleased his mother. She may not be the sort to let her emotions overrun these days, but he knew the signs of her excitement. His father used to say she had a temper when she was younger, but she'd mellowed over the years and now, when she felt life getting the better of her, she would sip her plum wine and soon get over it.

His merry mood uncontainable, he surprised his mother again, wrapping an arm around her shoulders and planting a kiss on the top of her head. "I'm sorry, mother, if I haven't always been good to you."

"Good to me? For pity's sake, what brought this on?"

"I've spoken harshly sometimes, not been respectful as I should be."

Her dark eyes twinkled. "That much is true." She reached up, slapping a playful hand against his sun-tanned stubble. "I see Lucy's been a positive influence on you already."

He chuckled. "She has that."

"The girl has a wise head on her young shoulders. Sees through you right enough. She'll handle you as I never could, for all my years on this earth."

His mother claimed not to know her age, but his father used to say she was sixty-five. Unfortunately he said she was sixty-five every year, sometimes changing it to a hundred and twenty, whenever she'd pricked his temper for some reason. At other times, when his father wanted to make up for some quarrel, he would say she was one and twenty. Since no one knew exactly how old she was, she seemed to think she could live as long as she liked, but often she'd remarked to John that even she couldn't live forever to see his children born.

He thought of his first born child, still marveling at the idea of fatherhood. It was a good thing, he decided, to be done with boyish games, to grow up, settle down. Someone had to continue the Carver name, since his sisters, of course, took their husbands' names. Perhaps he'd name his first son Sydney. His mother would be overjoyed.

"I'll go and see the parson

today," he said through a mouthful of apple, thinking practically.

"Aye. You'll need the banns read." She paused, finger to her lips. "I wonder if there's time to get some silk and lace from your sister for a wedding gown? She might send us some from London since she'll be there next month. I'd like to make Lucy something pretty, something to do her justice for once."

"Lucy doesn't need a wedding gown, mother. I'd marry her stark naked. That's the way to do her beauty full justice."

She grabbed her ladle and batted him round the shoulders while he laughed and dodged away.

* * * *

By the time Lucy made her way downstairs, John was already gone out with his dog. Worried they'd made too much noise last night, Lucy was surprised and grateful when Mistress Carver hurried over to embrace her, exclaiming she couldn't be happier and she'd known it from the first moment she saw her.

"I've wanted John to be happy and find the right woman, but I began to despair of it, I admit." She held Lucy's face in her hands, brought it down to her level and kissed her brow. "No woman was ever quite right for him. They were all too in awe of my son and would let him get away with anything. Not you, though. When I saw you and the way he looked at you...you made him nervous, Lucy." She chuckled. "And that's always a good sign." She trundled off to the pantry and Lucy took the bucket of scraps out to her pigs, as she did every morning.

It wasn't until later, as she and his mother collected the last of the apples from the orchard to make cider, that Lucy learned they were all at cross purposes.

"I shall write to my daughter and see if she might spare us some cloth for the bridal gown. Her own wedding was such an extravagant affair." The old lady stooped to gather some wind-fallen apples from the grass at her feet. "I'm afraid we can't put on anything quite so grand, but it should be a memorable day. After all, my son is a Sydney, as well as a Carver!" She tossed the apples in Lucy's basket. "There'll be no rushing about, no scandals. It'll all be done properly."

Lucy gripped the basket in her arms, watching his mother's lips as they moved, but not quite certain she'd heard correctly. "A wedding?"

"You didn't think I'd let him dash you off to the parson for hasty vows, without all the feasting, dancing and bridal lace, did you? The day my son finally gets himself a wife? This will be a very special day and we'll celebrate accordingly."

A drowsy wasp passed her line of sight, but with her hands holding the basket she couldn't bat it away. She stared as Mistress Carver shook her apron at it, knocked it to the grass and then ground the insect under her foot.

"Don't you worry, Lucy. We'll have the finest wedding Sydney Dovedale has ever seen."

Sunlight dripped between the branches like melting copper. Playful fingers of a gentle breeze lifted the leaves, rustling them idly, and birds, swooping and darting, performed their last songs of summer.

"What is it Lucy? You've gone white as snow."

I'm a ghost, she mused, ghosts are meant to be pale. Surely she'd died. She couldn't feel the grass around her feet, or the sun on her face. "Who told you we are to be married, Mistress Carver?"

"Why, John of course. He did ask you, didn't he?" One hand slapped to her brow, the old lady moaned under her breath. "Fool boy, he would rush on ahead and not think to ask!"

"No." She bit her lip. "He didn't ask."

"Then he just assumed! For pity's sake." His mother shook her head, but then carried on with the apple picking. "I'll make certain he asks you properly, Lucy, and on bended knee! Fancy taking you for granted. I do apologize for my son's clumsy manners, but how like him."

Not wanting to upset the lady, Lucy merely smiled as best she could and followed along with her basket. This was it then, now the truth must come out. She'd known this day would come. She should have been prepared.

But even if she were, nothing would have prepared him.

* * * *

"What do you mean, you can't marry me?"

She'd walked out to the fields to tell him, so his mother needn't hear. They'd just passed over a stile and into the lane, when she told him she was very sorry but marriage was out of the question.

"Had I known that's what you were thinking, I would have said sooner," she exclaimed nervously, "but I never expected you to marry me, John."

He halted, glaring at her, flicking sweat-dampened hair out of his eyes. "Of course that's what I was thinking. After last night, what else is there to be done but to marry?"

"You don't need to feel guilty," she assured him. "I was quite content just to share your bed."

His eyes kept growing wider, but at the same time darker, when it was usually the reverse. "You'll marry me and that's all there is to it. I'll not be accused of misusing you."

"Who would accuse you of that?"

"I would! In my heart I would."

"Oh, John…"

"I want you for my wife, Lucy. I want you to bear my children and live with me side by side, every day of my life."

She covered her face with her hands, frustration and sorrow fermenting within, making a potent, volatile brew when mixed with anger at herself for not having the gumption to explain. "I can't marry you, John. Please don't speak of it again."

He took hold of her wrists, pulling her hands from her face. "Why? Tell me! Because of my cousin? I told you, I don't care about your past and he won't stand in our way."

She gritted her teeth, shaking her head, nauseous. "You and I can never marry. Would you get it through your thick, stubborn, mulish head? We can't have everything we want John Carver, not even you!"

He released her wrists and stood looking at her for a few moments. His chest, bare under his sleeveless jerkin, moved rapidly in and out with the strain of holding his temper. His broad shoulders heaved, those thick, tanned arms lifted in supplication. "But you won't tell me why?"

"I can't. What do the reasons matter?" she cried, hating herself more with every word.

"I see." He stepped back, face taut, knuckles cracking. "If that's the way you want it. I must've been mad to think of marrying my cousin's whore in any case."

After this he gave her the silent, brooding treatment. Love was a cruel torment, she decided, if this is what it did to them, especially what it did to him, when none of it was his fault. She took all the culpability for this on her own shoulders. No one should be in pain, or bear the punishment, but her.

* * * *

He couldn't understand it. She was willing to share his bed, yet she wouldn't be his wife, neither could she tell him why marriage was impossible for her. They'd had word of English victory over the Spanish Armada and soon they should receive a letter from Nathaniel with some date for his return. John wondered if this was what kept her from making a commitment to him. Perhaps she waited for his cousin's return, biding her time until Nathaniel came to fetch her.

He kept thinking of what she'd said. "We can't have everything we want, John Carver, not even you!" It surely meant she wanted to stay with him, but something prevented it.

Although he pretended to ignore her all evening, he slyly followed her in any polished surface: the window, the blade of his knife, the plate over the mantle. In the corner of his eye he saw his mother exchanging glances with Lucy. The two women were of like willfulness, thick as thieves almost the moment he brought the hussy home from Yarmouth on his cart. He shook his head, slumped his shoulders, rested his forearms on the table and shoveled stew into his mouth, as if it might be his last meal.

Well, he wasn't going to beg the wench to marry him. He'd offered to make her an honest, respectable woman, but apparently she didn't care to be one. Really, he mused darkly, he should have realized. She was a creature who gave her virginity to a complete stranger in a bawdy house, why would he think she wanted to marry him and become a decent wife and mother? Clearly that was never her object in life, or else she would never have done what she did.

So many unanswered questions. They tore at him, chewed at his anger until it became subdued, a mellow heat instead of a raging inferno, but one just as dangerous as it tickled away at his insides, stealthy and sly, threatening to burst out at any moment.

Lucy went to bed early. Noting the dark shadows under her eyes, the weariness in her usually proud posture, he thought he must have tired her out last night. She would sleep soundly then tonight, if her damned conscience would let her.

As soon as her last steps faded away on the stairs, his mother came over to his chair and kicked his feet until he sat up.

"You might have asked her," she hissed, "before you came down all full of yourself and told me you were going to marry the girl."

His reply was cool. He didn't bother lowering his voice. "I didn't think I needed to ask her...after last night. I made my intentions plain, I'd say!"

"Apparently not! Had the two of you spent a few moments talking sensibly last night, instead of acting like two beasts in heat, you might have discovered a difference of opinion on the matter of marriage."

"Don't lecture me, mother! I'm not in the mood for it tonight."

"Are you going to marry the girl or not?"

"She says not."

His mother's dark eyes burned with her own inner fires. "And you're going to give up that easily? Your father never would have." Before he answered, she swept away with her candle, muttering, "Well, that's it, then. I suppose I'm forced to stay alive another twenty years to look after you on earth, when I should be with your father again by now."

John watched the door at the foot of the stairs close behind her, listened to her footsteps slowly mounting the old crooked staircase. He looked over at Vince, who sprawled by the low, smoldering fire, dreaming of chasing coneys through the forest, blissfully ignorant of his master's unhappiness. He wished his father were there now. His father was a straightforward man, not formally educated, but a damn sight smarter about life than most other folk he ever knew. He'd always had an answer to John's questions, always a simple solution to his many boyhood dilemmas. No problem was insurmountable in his father's eyes.

"You can do anything, Johnny lad, if you put your mind to it, if you want it badly enough. Don't you let anyone tell you otherwise."

He sighed, rubbing his unshaven chin as he stared across the room at the old chair where his father used to sit. His mother was right, of course, his father wouldn't give up when he wanted something.

And John wanted Lucy. Plain and simple. Nothing else for it.

It happened when he walked across the dusty boards of that bed chamber in Norwich and placed his fingertips to her proud little jaw, forcing it up so she'd look into his eyes and stop staring so fearfully at his leather breeches. He'd known it then, when he felt her tremble and it rocked his body, sweeping from his fingertips to his toes, back up to his heart, bringing him to life when he thought he already was.

He finally went up to bed, pausing outside her chamber door to listen, wondering if she was still awake. All was silent. He tried the iron loop handle, expecting to find it bolted from the inside, but her door creaked open. Moonlight flooded the chamber.

The bed was empty.

He panicked. His first suspicions took him swiftly to the open window and he stared out, expecting to see her running across his yard. She must have climbed down the ivy; it wasn't a great distance. Somewhere in the trees, an owl let out a soft, soothing hoot, almost questioning.

Damn her! She'd left him. He should have known. Running into his own chamber for his riding boots and whip, he stopped dead.

She was naked in his bed, sitting up, waiting patiently, her arms around her knees, hair trickling over her bare shoulders.

"Thank goodness," she whispered. "I thought you were never coming to bed!"

* * * *

For what seemed to her a small lifetime, he stood with his hand on the door latch, staring, rapt. It reminded her of their very first night, when she'd feared he might not do what she wanted.

"I worried I'd made a mistake when I chose you that night," she said, the words slipping out into the stillness. "Did I?"

At last he closed the door and came toward her slowly. She looked up at him, her heart close to bursting.

"No," he replied huskily, reaching out to run a finger along her jaw, lifting it. "You chose well." One knee on the bed, he slid closer. "Never have any doubt."

She closed her eyes as he kissed her lips gently, little more than a flutter. The bed dipped as it took his weight and then his hands were on her shoulders, easing her down.

"So, my saucy swine-herd...what am I going to do with you?"

Her eyes opened. "I'm surprised you need ask. Surely, you know what to do, Master Carver. I've been a naughty girl again and I need guidance."

He kissed her harder this time, lips slanting to hers, hands under her head, fingers entwined in her hair. Before his breeches were even down to his knees, she wound her legs around his hips and he entered her in the same moment.

"Do you know what I love most about you?" he whispered, holding her tenderly.

"My welcoming availability?"

"Well, there is that," he grinned, moonlight flaring across his fine teeth. "But more importantly, your utter unpredictability." He kissed the tip of her nose very gently. "I never know what you'll do next."

"Really? I would have imagined that to be one of the things you disliked."

"Funnily enough, so would I. Until I met you." And he began to move slowly, making love to her with gentleness tonight, unhurried, controlled, anxious to please.

"I'll stay, John," she cried into the warm hollow between his neck and shoulder. "I'll stay as long as you need me. Just don't ask me to marry you."

"You're killing me," he groaned softly.

"Then we'll die together. Like this."

"Yes." He moved his hips, pressing ever deeper, his breath quickening. "Yes…"

And she hugged him tighter with her legs, her hands stroking his broad, flexing shoulders, whispering sweet promises in his ear, vows to love him forever, in sickness and in health, for richer or poorer, to worship and honor him with her body. To keep herself only unto him.

Forever.

And ever.

And ever.

Chapter 19

That halcyon "forever" lasted a mere nine days. The time was gilded with late summer gold, just as she'd imagined in her dream. Lucy helped around the house every day, cleaned out her pigs, and learned how to make cider, even succeeded in getting her petulant lover into a bath. There were no further visits from Lord Oakham, no warning of dark clouds on the horizon. She allowed herself to believe he granted them a reprieve, that he had some tenderness in his soul after all. She had to believe it, because she was desperate to dream on and never be woken.

She joined John's mother on visits to the sick, poor and elderly, soon becoming known for her kindness and gentle manners. Mostly the villagers accepted her, only a few still held any disdain for John Carver's woman. Rumor had it they'd be married just as soon as he persuaded her. Hearing how she resisted his persistent, inequitable charms for so long, other girls in the village looked at her with sheer admiration and wonder. But at night, unbeknownst to them, she didn't resist his charms at all.

His mother made no comment, although she was clearly annoyed and impatient with her son for allowing the bed-sharing to continue with no marriage date set.

John, it seemed, knew better than to argue with either woman in his life, for he loved them both, so he let the days and nights roll by, enjoying them to the fullest, never wasting a moment, declaring himself the luckiest man on earth. Almost.

"If I give you a child, Lucy, you'll have to marry me then," he whispered one night, as she fell, sated, across his body.

Rather than answer, she sighed sleepily and rolled over, hugging his arm, nestling her back into his side. However, she lay with her eyes open, thinking him a wily, amorous beast, one who apparently never balked at a challenge. Bull-necked John Carver would try to get her to the chapel door one way or another. He might employ all manner of trickery to get her there, but he was coy for now, knowing a good thing when he had it. Just to be on the safe side, she took all the precautions she knew to prevent her womb quickening. These included jumping up and down on the spot for the count of fifty each morning and making sure to eat a spoonful of honey mixed with salt, while turning in left-handed spins in the northern most corner of the yard. She also took a lock of his hair, while she had him in the bath, entwined it with a lock of her own and burned it in the fire, just to be sure there would be no unwise pregnancy.

Oh yes, she had it all under

control.

* * * *

It was a crisp Thursday morning when Mistress Carver asked Lucy to take some eggs and one of her restorative potions down the lane to a sick neighbor.

"I would go myself, but my joints plague me this morning. Must be the change of seasons to come. It was foggy this morning down in the valley."

Basket under one arm, Lucy crossed the yard to the gate, daydreaming. Her eyes slowly focused on a tall man standing there on the other side of the bars, looking in at her, his familiar face grim.

"Lucy!"

She stumbled, almost dropping her eggs. "Lance!" Her heart's blood was in her mouth. It had happened, then. They'd found her. She knew how a deer felt when it saw hunters emerge from the forest and heard the hounds at its heels.

He pushed open the gate and it creaked on rusty hinges. "You'd better come with me at once."

She glanced back over her shoulder to be sure Mistress Carver was still inside. "How did you find me?"

"Mortimer Oakham sent me word you were here."

He had betrayed her after all.

"We were at Cambridge together," Lance added. "He recognized you at once."

Her heart was bleeding. "Oh Lance, I can't leave. Please don't make me go back. Please!" How easily and desperately the word came out now, a word she'd never been accustomed to until she knew what she wanted in life. Until she'd met John Sydney Carver.

"It's over Lucy. You must come with me now. These people," he looked over her head at the house, "will be in great trouble if anyone else finds you here."

It was true. All this fuss she'd caused...

Lance frowned, impatient. "Come with me quickly, unless you want these poor folk to suffer. Haven't you caused enough trouble?"

Tears burned. She blinked them back, searching for courage. "Can I at least say goodbye?"

"There's no time. Father and Lord Winton are searching for you in Yarmouth now. I'm ahead of them by no more than half a day's ride."

"But I..." she looked around dizzily, thinking of her pigs, of Vince who'd grown so fond of her, of the cows waiting to be milked, hens to be fed. Of John. There was a ponderous, sob-choked silence. She would never see any of this again, never know this life again. Never see him again.

"Lucy!" Mistress Carver appeared in the entrance of the house, her small figure framed with ivy and honeysuckle. "Who is that? Bring them in, dear."

Despite her brother's insistence on haste, Lucy dragged him to the door. "She's been so good to me, Lance. I must say goodbye."

"Lucy!"

"Five minutes. No more."

* * * *

Staring through the window, only half-listening to Mistress Carver, Lucy said a mute prayer of thanks to whatever deity had granted her these wondrous few months with John. She might never have known him. She could have gone to her grave never having experienced this much happiness. So she shouldn't be ungrateful now, and bitter. Some folk never knew love like this.

"Lucy has told us very little about her past," Mistress Carver was saying, "but she did tell us about her brother. I'm so glad we had the chance to meet. We've all grown to love your sister, Master Collyer."

"Yes, well," Lance cleared his throat, sitting stiffly at their table, "I must thank you for giving her shelter all this time, but now I've come to take her home."

The old lady nodded, her lips working as if she would like to say something, but knew she couldn't.

"My father has been most anxious to find her," Lance added.

"Oh, to be sure, he must have worried. One's children are a precious gift."

Lucy looked at her brother, pleading silently, but he avoided her gaze. "And her husband, too, is keen to have her back."

Mistress Carver barely moved, nothing but the slightest paling under her naturally swarthy skin. Lance wouldn't notice it, but Lucy did.

"I see," the old lady muttered, hands clasped in her lap.

"If he should come here," said Lance carefully, "I advise you not to tell him she lived under your roof. Lord Winton is ready to claim kidnapping, coercion, any number of crimes. It would be best for all involved if he never knows exactly where she was all these months. She must come with me now. I'll take her to them, before they find her."

Mistress Carver arched one graying eyebrow, but said nothing.

Lucy explained in a quaking voice. "I ran away from him. I thought I might get far enough…but I was wrong. I never meant to cause you any trouble."

John's mother nodded slowly, wearily, her misty gaze swinging to the window and the gate beyond. Lucy knew she was thinking of John and what to tell him when he came home to find her gone.

"I'll never forget your many kindnesses," Lucy's voice faltered. "Those that you and your son have shown me. I hope you'll tell him."

"I'll try."

They both knew how hard he'd take the news and Lucy was sick with guilt at leaving the explanations to his poor mother but, as Lance warned, if her father and Lord Winton arrived there to find her, the Carvers would be blamed. Lord Winton could sue them for everything they owned, drag their names through the mud if he wanted. And her father--there would be no appeasing his wrath.

She collected her wooden box of belongings, kissed Mistress Carver goodbye and left on her brother's horse.

"Look after him for me," was the last thing she said, her heart too full and breaking under the unrelenting pressure.

Forlorn, the old lady nodded. "He'll miss you. You know he'll never forget you."

Lucy turned her face away, unable to reply. Of course she'd known this day must come. Why then did it rip into her heart like a bolt from the blue, never expected, striking her dead on the spot?

Chapter 20

October 1588

John watched Alice walking along the verge, a warm shawl wrapped tight around her, breath evaporating in a fine mist around her mouth. She stopped and waved.

On his way out of the threshing barn, he blinked up at the dull sky and sniffed. The autumn air was dank and thick, tinged with the acrid scent of burning leaves, mold and old, dead rotting things. But somehow it pleased him. He supposed it was another of his odd quirks, but he looked forward to winter. Perhaps it was because the summer and spring months were so busy for him, the days long and hard. In winter, as night drew in sooner and daylight came later, he enjoyed a sense of calm, the harvest accomplished for another year, the barns and storage shed full for the winter. His mother worried he'd have too much time on his hands, too much time to think, but he was unconcerned. As he said to her, he had nothing to be sorry for. Life went on. It had to.

"Alice!" he called out, trotting over to her. "Where are you off to?"

"I promised to help your mother salt the bacon and she's going to show me how she makes her smoked sausage."

They walked along together toward the farmhouse. "You're looking well, Alice." He was trying these days, trying hard.

"Thank you, John." She smiled hesitantly.

She was a good-looking woman, he thought, considering her profile again, as if he hadn't seen it before, many times. Alice was a little stern and solemn, took life too seriously at times, but he liked her. They wouldn't quarrel. She would never disobey and if she questioned, she'd keep it to herself. There were no extremes in her. Alice certainly wasn't brazen, neither did she hide any vulnerability. Even her unrequited love for him was something she faced and dealt with calmly. She was just Alice.

He ought to marry her. He'd always known it in the back of his mind.

That other woman was a distraction for a while...he abruptly brought the hammer down on that thought, because he kept the bronze-haired deceiver out of his mind as much as possible.

Again he looked at Alice, dear, worthy, patient, pure Alice. She did have a few unfortunate habits, such as chewing her fingernails and clicking her tongue against her teeth. She very seldom met him eye for eye and she didn't care much for his dog. But all these things might surely be overcome in time.

"I ought to tell you, John,' she said, looking ahead, "I'm going to be married."

He almost tripped over a hardened rut. "Married?"

"Aye. Martin Frye asked me." She sighed. "Did you think I would wait forever, John? I'm four and twenty."

He was annoyed. That impetuous, sly boy always wanted something to which he wasn't entitled. Now he had Alice.

"You're not angry, are you?" she asked softly, finally looking at him. When he didn't answer, she added, "I know you're not in love with me, John. You never were, not the way I wanted." Another sigh drifted by, a fragile, wispy evaporation of air on this crisp autumn day. "I suppose we might have married and been happy enough in our way, but I wanted something more, something special, something I couldn't live without."

He bit down on his tongue, looking away from her, afraid she might read in his face those thoughts now flooding through the barrier.

"And I know you want the same," she added.

They walked on, silent. A stiff wind caught the fringe of her shawl, ruffling it frantically.

"Why did you let her go, John?" she asked, plaintive as a little bird at his shoulder.

"I didn't," he responded. His heart beat thickened, the two broken parts shadowing one another. "She left me."

It was almost six weeks since she'd left him and the wound was still raw. Nothing healed it, not his mother's calm words that tried to soothe, nor his own need to forget and move on. The day she left, when he came in from the fields and his mother told him, he went up to her room, as if he couldn't quite believe she'd gone, and found the pearl earrings she left for him. Both of them this time.

In the evenings, by the fire, he sometimes pretended to sleep, just so his mother wouldn't talk to him. Vince often sat by Lucy's old chair now, waiting for her to come in, ears pricking at every slight noise, every wail of wind or beat of rain on the windows. His mother, exclaiming no good could come of "sloping around all mournful," would sing songs with false merriment, her foot tapping as she worked at her sewing or wrote to her daughters.

Only once did she mention Lucy's name, recalling the pickles in that particular jar were ones she and Lucy made together. The very moment she said it, her expression hardened, she slammed the jar down on the table before him and talked of something else. John had no idea what she said next. Spreading the pickle on his pork pie, he choked it down, not tasting, not feeling.

* * * *

Nathaniel finally came home to Souls Dryft, ready to play the role of war hero, full of unlikely sea tales and a little too much ale. Finding Lucy gone, he accused his cousin of being careless and letting her go.

"I didn't," John replied stiffly, just as he'd done to Alice. "I didn't let her go. She left me."

Nathaniel ranted and raved. "I thought you'd at least manage to keep her safe here, idiot boy." Storming up and down by the hearth, stepping over Vince at the turn, he added crossly, "I didn't send her to you at once, because I knew what a little cork-head you were and she had her own problems to straighten out, but then I had to weigh anchor and there was no more time. So I sent her here, hoping the two of you together would sort it all out." Lifting his palms to press on the low roof-beams, he exhaled a rich, fulsome curse. "Love conquers all, they say. Let the two lost love birds find one another, I thought to myself. I even wondered if I'd been wrong to keep her away from you, but no, says I, he thinks to marry that Alice creature who has no backbone and will let him walk all over her. I'd best be sure he's got the idea out of his worm-holed noggin, before I send luscious little Lucy into the fray, or I'll be blamed for causing mischief, as usual!"

He only paused for breath when his aunt pushed a tankard of cider into his waiting hand and then they watched while he drained it in one swallow.

"I take it you don't know what you sent her back to?" he growled, wiping the back of one hand across his gray-peppered beard.

"A husband," John snapped curtly.

"Who beat her with his fist." Nathaniel held out his tankard for more cider and burped. "I doubt she told you. It took me all my charm to wring it out of her and we all know you have none o' that."

John couldn't swallow. His hands clenched into fists on his knees and Vince raised his head from the hearth stones, as if he heard some warning sound no human ear could detect.

"That's why I took her to Yarmouth to get away from him," his cousin added. "Someone had to look out for the poor girl. She wouldn't tell me what you'd done to her, and I had only my suspicions in that regard."

Now John felt his mother's eyes scorching holes in the side of his face, but this was no time for explanations. "He beat her?" he murmured, closing his eyes, seeing the white scar along her cheekbone.

"On the wedding night. She took flight and went looking for you at Mistress Comfort's. Apparently you and I got our days mixed up. I thought we were to meet there on Friday, so I was there looking for you. So was she." Another long, low burp rumbled out of Nathaniel's belly. "Found me instead and I took her under my wing."

John stood, fists hanging at his sides. "You should have told me."

"Why? You took off back home, merry as a lark. Weren't too bothered, it seemed."

"That," he said slowly, "is a lie. I looked for her all over Norwich."

Nathaniel leaned back, holding the tankard to his chest, his face a mask of repressed anger. "How was I to know that? You never bothered about any woman once you'd had her. And she was running from her husband, a world of troubles on her heels." He set his empty tankard on the mantle. "My first thought was to make certain she was safe. I didn't know what you felt about the girl. No point saving her from one fire, I thought, only to drop her into another. You were never one for deep attachments. For all I knew she was just another wench you went out of your way to avoid. So I wrote to your mother..."

John rounded on his mother. She faced him boldly. "I didn't know she was married, or that you'd known her. He only told me she was a young lady in need of shelter," she said.

"...and your mother told me to send her here, when I went away to sea. So I did."

The dog by the fire sprang to his feet, perhaps sensing his intervention might soon be needed.

"I never thought you'd let her..."

"I didn't," John roared, raging, "She left me!"

"Of all the stupid, bumble-brained...."

"If you'd have told me what she ran from, I might have..."

"Big-nosed, hot-headed, infantile..."

"But oh no, I suppose you wanted her for yourself all that time!"

"Enough, the both of you." His mother bravely stepped between them, hands pressed flat to each puffed chest. "What's done is done. No sense crying over spilt milk. Instead of fighting, we must put our heads together and think what can be done now. Good Lord! Why is it that a man's only solution is to fight?"

"She left me, mother," John turned away. "She deceived me about who and what she was. Now what am I supposed to do? Run after the woman and snatch her away, like one of our bride-stealing Sydney ancestors?"

Silence was brief but weighty.

When he spun back around, mother and cousin were both eyeing him with arch deliberation.

* * * *

Lucy sat in her chamber, looking out on the cheerless street. Frost tipped the window ledge and that morning she'd had to break a thin layer of ice over the water in her wash basin. She didn't bother lighting a fire in her room, there was no point. She welcomed the cruel, frigid cold. Perhaps, eventually she would be numb and stop feeling altogether.

The walls of the house were quiet, so different to John's farm. There was no humming, no shouting, and no sounds of animals, except for the occasional whinny of a horse below in her father's stable. The weather was too bleak today and no one passed in the street outside. There was no sign of life. It was as if she were dead, held here in purgatory, until they all decided what to do with her.

According to the maid, her father was below in his library, deep in discussion with Lord Winton again. They could not, it seemed, reach any decision to satisfy them both. Lord Winton didn't want her back again, didn't want, as he said, "damaged goods," but he refused to relinquish her dowry. Her father, on the other hand, was insistent that Lord Winton return everything, or else agree to take his bride back to Norwich and forget the entire incident ever happened. Fearing no other man would take her now, he saw Winton as his daughter's last chance for respectability. Sir Oliver Collyer was a notoriously hard negotiator. He hadn't become such a successful businessman without reason. And Lord Winton was just a stubborn, mean-tempered, greedy old man. They were at an impasse.

Lucy assured her father the marriage was unconsummated and therefore could be annulled, but naturally he believed Lord Winton's word over hers and, to save his own pride, her spiteful husband insisted she lied. She wasn't sure whether he truly remembered what happened in any case, since the crack she gave him across the back of the head with the bed-warmer apparently rendered him unconscious for some time, resulting in a sizeable bump and a memory of the evening's events that was foggy at best.

Until one of the two men backed down, she was kept here, in her old room, under guard and in disgrace. Neither her stepmother nor her stepsister were allowed to visit. She had no letters, no communication with the outside world, apart from her maid bringing meals on a tray and the occasional tidbit of news. It wasn't very much different to other punishments in youth, when she was exiled to her chamber and told not to think of coming down again until she was ready to show due repentance. And due repentance usually meant until she was ready to admit she was a rotten, wicked girl, and then stoically accept the harsh sting of the cane across her hand.

She picked idly at the wood around the window frame, where similar marks measured years of frustration, boredom and captivity. As a child she'd stood at this window for hours, watching the world go by without her in it.

There was a brisk rap at the door and she jumped, thinking it was her father come to pronounce sentence. If he had his way, she would go back to Norwich with her husband, he could wash his hands of her, and the shameful event could be covered up. Knowing her father, she feared he would win.

But it was not her father.

"Lance! Are you allowed to see me?"

He looked askance. "Of course I am!" Closing the door behind him, he took barely three steps across the room and she flew into his embrace, the side of her cold cheek pressed to his velvet doublet.

"Oh Lance, thank you for fetching me before they found me." She'd had long hours to consider her brother's gallantry and thoughtfulness in riding ahead to find her before her father and husband did.

"If not for Mortimer Oakham sending me a letter, I might not have got to you first, Lucy. It was lucky he recognized you."

"And fortunate he didn't write to father instead of you."

"Yes. He's not such a bad sort, although he'd like to be."

Lance assumed his old friend wrote to him out of concern for his sister, but Lucy suspected Oakham's main interest was in removing her from John Carver's arms. If he couldn't have her, he didn't want his competitor claiming victory. That was the way men were.

"Many times did I get that man out of scrapes," Lance explained, "so he owed me one. In fact, he owes me several."

"He won't tell father where you found me?"

"I've sworn him to secrecy." He looked over her head. "You need a fire, Lucy. It's damned cold in here. My teeth are chattering."

She walked to the bed and sat, dropping like a stone. "I'd rather be cold," she muttered peevishly. "The fires of Hell will get me soon enough."

Hunkered down by the fireplace, Lance muttered, "This kindling is damp. I'll have the maid bring up some dry from downstairs."

"Leave the damn fire, Lance. I couldn't care less." It felt good to say 'damn' so she said it now as much as possible, in addition to other curse words she'd never used or heard before.

He flung a frown over his shoulder. "Stop being a desperate daisy. It won't do anyone any good if you get ill, will it? Least of all your blessed farmer."

"What about him? What does he matter? I'll never see him again."

"Precisely," her brother replied curtly. "So what good will getting sick do, since he won't know and no one else cares?" He stopped, straightened up and sighed. "Except me, of course." Walking to her window he stood with his hands behind his back, gazing out at the dull day. "What exactly happened with you and your farmer?"

What was the point in lying now? "Everything you can imagine."

Her brother shook his head, muttering under his breath, still staring out into the street.

"It wasn't all his fault," she added. "I know you'll say women aren't supposed to have those desires, but I did. At least I had the opportunity once before I die."

"Oh? It was only once then?" He swiveled halfway round to look at her, a wry twist to his lips.

Despite the chill room, her cheeks were warm.

"Hmmm?" He raised an eyebrow.

"It was a few times."

"I have to give it to you, Luce, you really did get your vengeance on father. Isn't that why you did it?"

She grabbed the bolster from her bed and threw it at him, but he caught it, his reflexes too sharp. "No it is not!" she cried. "I did it for love, something you'll never know because you think it might somehow make you less of a man!"

"Hush, little sister! Don't raise your claws to me, I'm only here to help." Now he was back to his usual patronizing self, knowing how to get her temper up.

"Help? How exactly?"

He carried the bolster back to her bed. "I'm going out tonight. Some wretched masked banquet the Countess of Swafford is holding for All Hallow's Eve. Father wants me to go."

"Aha!" Now it was her turn to mock. "He finally has the match within striking distance of his arrow. You and the savage buttock-biter, Lady Catherine Mallory, eldest daughter of the Earl and Countess of Swafford..."

"Quite. As much as it pains me to attend, I am in the Earl's employ and..." replacing the bolster, he tidied her bed with his long, restless hands "...I'm also trying to keep father in a partially civilized temper for your good, little sister."

"Well, don't bother on my account." She hugged the sturdy wooden post at the corner of her bed, watching him straighten the embroidered coverlet until it might possibly meet with his strict approval. "I'll face my punishment," she added gloomily. "After all, I did cause all this. I don't suppose anything you can do is going to appease my father's temper now." She blew out a deep breath of unhappiness. "No, you've done enough to help me. Save yourself, Lance. Get out while you can and don't let him plan your future."

He laughed at her. "I was going to ask whether you wanted to come with me to the banquet. You'd like a little entertainment, surely."

She was so surprised, it was lucky she had her arms around the bed post to keep her upright. "What about father? He'll never agree to let me out."

Lance walked around the bed and tweaked her freckled nose. "If I insist I won't go without you, he'll have to agree won't he?"

Her brother, of course, had one very important advantage: he was their father's only son and heir. He was a fine, faultless young man of impeccable standards and their father's greatest hope for future grand alliances. There was Anne, but she would not keep the Collyer name once she married, so Lance was their father's golden apple. Above anything, Sir Oliver wanted Lance to pay suit to the Earl's daughter.

"If he wants me at the banquet tonight, it'll have to be on my terms, with my sister at my side."

She thought then of John, all those miles away, and her heart ached. "I can't go out, Lance. I'd rather stay here." She swallowed her tears, knowing her brother would not know what to do if she cried. It would embarrass them both.

"But you must come out, Luce. You can't stay in this cold room all alone. It's not healthy to mourn so."

Mourn? Yes. That was what she did. She mourned for her love, her broken heart. "I wouldn't be very good company, Lance."

With a small sound of frustration he swirled away, his cape billowing out like great black wings, his boots creaking rapidly across the floorboards. Then he came back to her, just as swiftly, scratching his closely trimmed head the entire time. "Look, you must come. You must. I won't hear another word of refusal."

The idea of stepping out in public, facing the whispers and pointing fingers, made her sick to her stomach. In fact, she just might retch up her guts there and then, as she had done that morning. "I don't want to go," she murmured. "Besides, I've no costume to wear."

Slowly he smiled. "As it happens, Anne was planning to attend, but finding herself out of sorts this evening has retired to bed already. Her gown will surely fit you." Possessing considerable familiarity with the female form, he stepped back to run a critical eye over his sister. "It might be a little big and an inch or two long, but we'll manage."

Still she hesitated.

"What good will it do to pine away here for your farmer?" Lance exclaimed impatiently. He, of course, had no idea about love, didn't want anything to do with it or with the messes entailed.

But he was right, she realized sorrowfully. She would never see John again. Somehow life, and all its absurdities, would go on. Besides, for all she knew, he could have married Alice by now and forgotten the woman he once loved in a last mad, indulgent, roguish moment.

She couldn't blame him for forgetting her now.

Chapter 21

"How many times must I tell you to stand still and stop fidgeting?" the Countess demanded, hands on her waist, as she walked around her younger brother and oversaw the last-minute fitting of a new doublet in rich, darkest blue taffeta. The ungrateful object of her curt reminder had already made several sour remarks concerning this "fancy" set of clothes she'd ordered for him, but Lady Madolyn Mallory, Countess of Swafford, paid no attention to his sauce. "We're going to make the most of your good looks tonight, John. For once you'll stop hiding them."

He ground his teeth, refusing to look in the long glass before him. "I only came here to find Lucy. I don't need all this...damned fuss."

Ignoring his complaints, his sister congratulated the tailor on his excellent and speedy work. The little man bowed to them both and left the chamber, a fat purse of coin in his hands.

"I'll pay you back," John muttered sternly, pulling on his new lace cuffs.

"Nonsense." His sister reached up to ruffle his hair, annoying him further. "This is my gift to you. You so seldom bother to visit me..."

"I have a farm to run."

"...When I do have the pleasure of seeing my darling brother, I like to spoil him." She beamed that infamous smile which could and had dazzled the hardest heart. "Indulge me, John. What else could I do for my lovelorn brother?"

His sister thought it all very romantic. Nothing pleased her more, she said, than to see her little brother completely besotted, after so many years of artful avoidance when it came to affairs of the heart.

"What if she doesn't want me?" he grumbled, brushing the front of his new doublet with uncertain, unsteady fingers.

"For pity's sake, why wouldn't she? She'd be mad not to."

He'd like to agree, but Lucy had never hesitated to point out all his faults. She was no meek maid, easily impressed. His inherent Carver self-confidence was humbled by her. "What can I offer her? I'm just a simple farmer. I can't ask her to leave her pampered life behind and run off to a life of sin with me."

"Isn't that exactly what she did before?"

He glared at his sister and she blinked her blue eyes, laughing at him.

"I very much doubt she regrets it," she added. "When you meet her father, and Lord Winton, you'll understand!"

"Oh, I've met Winton," he grunted, frowning at his reflection in the mirror. His innards turned to ice, his fists clenched. Beat a woman, would he? Well, then the old cretin would soon find out what it was like to be on the receiving end for once.

"Now John," his sister warned, "you promised to behave. Be civil at the banquet tonight. Be gentlemanly, chivalrous."

His face grim, he snapped, "Don't worry, I won't embarrass you."

She threw up her hands. "You know what I mean. No fighting. No bloodshed."

He sulked. "Well, I'm not going to dance."

"You like dancing."

"Simple, country dances," he blustered, striding to the nearest chair and falling into it with all the elegance of a bull with a grudge to bear. "When it doesn't matter if you get the steps wrong, because everyone's drunk anyway and you have an excuse to grab the woman round the waist and hold her close." He waved a hand loosely. "All these dainty court dances are not for me. Stately traipsing up and down. I haven't the patience."

"Dancing is not simply an excuse to put your hands all over a woman."

He raised his eyelashes, one corner of his lip quirking. "That's what you think. Men know better."

His sister was still reprimanding him for this comment when the chamber door swung open and a small, dark-haired cannon ball rushed in. "Uncle John! No one told me you were here. I only just heard!" the projectile shouted accusingly and crashed, full speed, into his chest, just as he got hastily to his feet.

"Catherine! When will you learn to enter a room with ladylike dignity? Go back out at once, get dressed, knock on the door politely, wait for my word, enter with a curtsey and greet your uncle in the proper way. I am quite hoarse from telling you how it is done."

"Then save your breath, mother," the girl replied, still hugging John tightly. "And save me the earache."

"Catherine Elizabeth Mallory, you will not speak to me that way! And put your uncle down at once."

John looked down at his niece, amazed by how much she'd grown since the last time he saw her. She was certainly no more a scrawny child. Good Lord! It seemed like only yesterday when he, a boy of eleven, struggling to hold his sister's mewling, bad-tempered newborn in his arms, was suddenly struck with the idea of whistling and she ceased her wailing, much to everyone's intense relief, opened a pair of bright blue eyes and gazed up at him in wonder. From then on, they'd had a special bond. He couldn't help being fonder of her than he was of any other niece. Now here she was, all grown up and quite a beauty.

"I hear your father means to get you safely married off," he teased, pulling her curly hair. "I pity the man. Who is he?"

"No one," she declared with an unladylike snort to make her mother wince. "He hasn't found anyone yet brave or stupid enough to take me on. Not that it stops him trying."

"My daughter celebrates the fact most folk begin to call her a shrew," the Countess explained. "She currently finds it amusing, but I daresay it won't tickle her ribs quite as much when she is thirty and still unwed."

"Mother, I'm nineteen!"

"And sending your father steadily grayer as each day passes."

The girl turned her face up to his and pouted. "See, Uncle John? They can't wait to be rid of me."

He laughed. "Well, whoever the man is, he'd better treat you very well indeed, or he'll have me to answer to."

"Don't worry," she replied, glowering at her mother. "When I marry it will be for love and no other reason. And I don't just mean my love, he'll have to love me at least as much as I love him. And he'll love me for all my faults. Little things won't bother him and he won't mind if I ride astride instead of side-saddle. And he won't care how I wear my hair, or how loosely I lace my corset. And he won't care if other people do call me a shrew."

"That's an awful lot of 'ands,' young lady," her mother exclaimed, cutting them ruthlessly short. "Go and get dressed. For Heaven's sake, your hair is wet! Why did you wash your hair tonight, of all nights? You can't go out in winter with wet hair."

But Catherine's hair was already drying and curling as it did so, shooting out in all directions like the vapor of celebratory fireworks. "Mother," she pronounced solemnly, "you're becoming the most dreadful old scold."

"And you'll be a daughter with two very red slapped cheeks if you don't go and get your lovely new gown on."

"Oh, I'm not wearing that gown. I decided. Besides, I have other things to do before I go to the banquet tonight."

As the discussion quickly descended into an argument, John retired to the safe distance of his chair. Amused to watch his sister do battle with her own image, he made a mental note to write to his mother. She would be glad to know her most troublesome daughter now received a little dose of her own bitter medicine. More than a little in fact.

Into this fray came the Earl of Swafford just a few minutes after it began and probably in time to prevent a black eye for at least one of the ladies. Scooping his daughter to the door by one hand around the collar of her shift, he sent her to get dressed without a single word uttered. The door closed again, he now calmly greeted his brother-in-law.

"My niece has gained some width, but not lost her high spirits," John commented dryly.

"Some wenches," the Earl replied with a grim smile at his wife, "are sent to try us."

John couldn't agree more.

* * * *

As soon as they entered the grand hall of the Mallory's London house, Lucy caught a glimpse of Bess Percy, a notorious strumpet and one of her brother's most persistent hunters. Bess carried a mask up to her face, but lowered it enough to flutter her long golden lashes at Lance, being sure he saw her there.

Lance smiled and his eyes narrowed, but he pretended not to notice the large bosom, heaving in his direction. In fact he pretended so hard it was obvious. Now Lucy knew why her brother agreed to attend this banquet and suffer several hours of being sociable.

"Did you come here for Bess Percy?" she demanded pertly, lifting her own mask to give him the full benefit of her fierce glare. "I thought you had higher standards. Is there a man in London she hasn't ridden?"

Lance didn't bother hiding it. "Sometimes a man needs a good gallop to keep his parts in working order. It doesn't mean anything. It's just an exercise, the type one gives one's horse to keep the muscles from seizing up."

Disgusted, she shook her head so violently a few strands of hair burst free from her net and tickled her neck.

"Good old Bess is perfect for that very reason," he continued, escorting his sister forward. "It's never complicated with Bess and she never expects anything more."

Lucy decided not to lecture him any further. After all, who was she to question his morals or the deficient virtue of Bess Percy?

They were late arriving and the dancing was already underway. She stood a while, enjoying the music, comparing the rich brocades and guessing, with her brother, which couples had just argued before they came, which were in love and which kept secrets. It was an old game they'd shared for years, making up stories about folk they watched, sometimes creating conversations between the dancers, making one another laugh.

But her laughter died when she looked across the black-and-white tiled floor and saw a man she knew. Something about him caught her eye and held it. Perhaps it was the way he raised his hands to illustrate a point he made in his conversation. Then she saw his profile - the strong jaw and proud nose of his Norman ancestors. Her heart stumbled to a brief halt. Beside her, Lance chatted away, oblivious. No one else looked at the man in the blue doublet. No one pointed, or said he didn't belong there.

Perhaps it wasn't him.

Her heart began to beat again, but slowly.

She wondered if her eyes played cruel tricks. Every night she thought of John before she went to sleep, hoping to dream of him. It never worked. Her nights were restless, often entirely sleepless.

Good God, the man looked very like him.

If it weren't him, it must be a double standing there, chatting easily with the Earl of Swafford.

Confused, when Lance asked her to dance, she went with him, her hand limp in his.

* * * *

A flare of bronze first sparked in the corner of his eye and he turned to watch, forgetting his conversation. She walked down the dance in her mask, her hair up in a caul, her shoulders very stiff, spine straight. There might have been no one else present, for he saw only her. It felt as if his heart was burning. She looked smaller somehow. Perhaps it was the ornate gown, which almost seemed to wear her, instead of the other way about. He'd never seen her like this, Lucy in her natural habitat, surrounded by finery, gleaming with jewels, a feathered fan fluttering in her small fingers.

Then he focused on the man at her side. Tall. Handsome. Certainly not Winton.

"There is Lucasta Collyer Winton," his brother-in-law confirmed. "My wife tells me you have some business to discuss with the lady."

"Yes," was the curt reply. He watched his lover turn and walk back down the dance. "I suppose my sister didn't tell you what that business is?"

"Indeed, she did not. I'm generally the last to know anything."

John rubbed one hand across his mouth. "I mean to take that lady home with me. She'll have other ideas, I expect."

His brother-in-law squinted. "The lady has a husband."

"I'm aware of the fact."

"I see." Sadly acquainted with the bull-headed determination running a broad streak through the Carver family, the Earl had nothing more to say. He knew what little point there was in arguing.

"Who is that fellow dancing with her?" John demanded. "He's looking smug now, but he won't be soon when he has none of those fine teeth left in his mouth."

"That gentleman with whom she dances, is her brother, Lancelot Collyer."

John cleared his throat, took a breath. "Oh." He flexed his fingers, stretching them out until the knuckles clicked. Her brother.

"A very fine young man in my employ. Perhaps you'd care for an introduction?"

He wondered if her brother would try standing in his way and if so, how best he might be handled. Just then, she looked over at him. Despite the mask, her saw her eyes flicker, that lush green gold spark betraying her emotions. "Later," he snapped to his brother-in-law. "I've other business first."

* * * *

"Ah, the Earl signals," Lance whispered as the dance finished. "Duty calls."

Hurriedly she backed away toward the punch bowl, suggesting she would wait for him there. Under no circumstances could she cross those tiles and stand near the man in the blue doublet, whoever he was. "I expect the Earl wants to know when you plan to marry his daughter, Lady Catherine," she teased, her voice deceptively light.

Lance looked around the hall, remembering that particular horror. "Hmmm. I don't see the savage here. Hopefully she won't come tonight. She should be at court and with the Queen in mourning for Leicester she won't be able to leave."

Regarding her brother thoughtfully, she fluttered her fan. Men could be so incredibly blind and stubborn. "How do you know she's not here,

Lance? I doubt you'd know her if you saw her. How many years has it been?"

He scowled deeply, calculating. "Three or four. Or five. But I'd know that savage anywhere."

"I hope that's true Lance." She sighed. "For your sake."

"Meaning?"

"Lady Catherine Mallory just might take you by surprise." Stranger things had happened, she mused to herself. A person simply never knew what lay in store.

"Ha!" He laughed at that idea, so sure of himself and his infallibility.

"You'd better go to the Earl before Bess gets her claws in," she muttered, sighting Bess Percy's bosomy figure prowling nearby, seeking out her prey.

Lance kissed her hand and left her at the punch bowl, striding over to greet the Earl. She daren't look. Her brother was about to meet the man with whom she'd just spent one gloriously wicked summer in the country.

If that was John Carver over there and not a very, very clever imposter instead.

Oh Lord! Why was he there?

He must have found some sly way to enter the banquet uninvited.

Suddenly he looked over his wide shoulder and their eyes met through their masks. His gaze was heated, rigorous, knowing, as if he felt that volatile fluttering inside her. He smiled very slightly, raised his mask with one hand and winked very imprudently, leaving her in no doubt.

It was no imposter. John Carver observed her across that crowded hall with a provocative, covetous admiration, so compelling she could not tear her own gaze away. Even if fire broke out she wouldn't have run. His steadfast, pervasive scrutiny rocked her spine. She tasted him in her throat. She heard him groan as his damp lips played over her nipples and they actually peaked under her gown, taut and hard.

And now, rather than wait to be introduced to her brother, he came toward her through the crowd, pushing people aside ruthlessly until he reached her, bowed his head and offered his hand.

His clothes were very fine, his hair was brushed. He might almost have been another man, if not for those eyes, so blue and deeply searching, the breadth of his shoulders and the rough skin of his hands. As if he feared she might escape, he gripped her fingers and led her into the dance, a sweeping lavolta. She couldn't have told anyone whether he danced well, or even if she did. They moved through the motions together, but her mind focused on the touch of his hands, the energy thrumming through his fingers. At one point, with his hands on her waist, he lifted her high enough to cause a few gasps from the watching crowd, but since she was already flying, exuberant and giddy, it didn't matter to her. He might have thrown her in the air completely. As long as he was there to catch her, she wouldn't protest. Each graze of his fingertips quickened her pulse. His eyes never left her lips, riveted there, predatory.

Dimly, along the border of the dance, she saw the blur of faces watching them, lips whispering, fans drifting. John's forefinger stroked her palm and she looked up into his masked face. He must stop devouring her with his eyes, touching her like this in a banquet hall full of people, it was positively indecent. Surely everyone saw it. Was he mad? He smiled again, licentious and with a certain peremptory insolence.

No, he was not mad, just a rogue of the worst order. She supposed he was there to cause her trouble because of what she'd done to him. Now he wanted his vengeance.

The dancers spun, the men lifting their partners again amid many squealing, excited, but ultimately demure cries, and when John lifted her likewise, it was again too high and for too long. He put his head back to look up at her, his fingers spread wide around her slender waist, staking his claim. The other women were all down, their feet on the ground again, but Lucy was still suspended, sliding down his body, permitted, by his strong, merciless grip, to go no faster.

"Put me down," she choked out, her own small hands nervously fluttering against his flexing shoulders.

When he neither obeyed nor answered, she repeated her demand, agitated and pettish.

"I told you before," he said quietly, "I'm not accustomed to uppity wenches making all the decisions."

"Put me down, or so help me God..."

"What'll you do? Scream at me again? Throw your shoe at me again? Tell me you can't love me, drive me wild with that damnably irresistible, flagrantly wanton, deliciously insatiable little body and then leave me again?"

At last her toes met tile. The moment she felt that reassurance she flew into action, stamping him hard on the foot until he released her. Somehow she made it through the crowd and found her way to the punch bowl.

Her stomach made odd twists and flips. The supper she'd eaten earlier threatened to make a sudden reappearance. She glanced back at the dancers but couldn't see the audacious, salty-mouthed rogue. Turning away, she grabbed a cup of punch from the servant and drank it down swiftly.

"Lucy, my dear. Lucy Collyer! I'm so glad you came. Your brother wasn't sure you'd come. I told him he absolutely must persuade you." The Countess of Swafford glided toward her with a smile that gleamed as brightly as the priceless ruby gemstones, cut in the shape of pomegranate seeds, dangling from her ears. "He feared you were not well, but I am thankful you decided to join us."

Lucy curtseyed, her gaze lowered demurely. "I would not miss it, my lady. How could I resist a masked banquet with dancing?"

"And that is exactly what I told your brother." The Countess signaled to the servant for a cup of punch. "Sadly the Queen does not attend. She's in mourning for her beloved Robin, Earl of Leicester." The two women stood together a while, watching the dancers, and then the Countess said, "You recently enjoyed a stay in the county of Norfolk, Lucy?"

"Yes." No doubt the entire city of London was abuzz with rumors about Lord Winton's runaway bride.

"I was born and raised in Norfolk, you know. I have family there still. A mother and my young brother."

"I did not know, my lady." She hesitated. "Norfolk is a beautiful county."

"You liked it there? I'm very glad. Do you plan to return?"

"Oh…oh no. I don't suppose I'll go there again." She passed her cup back to the servant for more punch. "I am thirsty this evening," she muttered. "It's very hot in here." She was, in fact, extremely dizzy and, as the last word left her mouth, she stumbled against the table, gripping the tapestry cloth. It was possible, she thought drearily, that she'd contracted the sweat, a deadly disease capable, once symptoms set in, of vanquishing previously healthy folk in a matter of days. There were no reports of the sweat in the area, yet she supposed it had to start somewhere. Why not with her?

"My dear Lucy! You're very white indeed. Perhaps you should take some air on the terrace. I see you're overheated and it's not good for the blood. Our lawns lead down to the river. On a starry night there is a pretty view with willows and shrubs. Pity there are no stars or moon tonight, but we have rush torches lit around the house." The chattering Countess was already steering her out onto the terrace and Lucy couldn't get a word in edgeways. "You sit there, see the little stone bench? I'll tell your brother where you are. Now sit there, my dear, and be still. Don't move! Not a finger."

Not daring to do otherwise, she sat on the stone bench and stared at the ink black moonless sky. She barely felt the cold. Her stomach still churned, a strange heat lurking there as it had done for some time, since she'd left Norfolk.

Hearing steps on the terrace, she thought it was Lance come to find her, but when she looked over her shoulder she saw John, torchlight stroking the side of his face, casting his strong figure in precious metal.

Even when she closed her eyes and opened them again, he was still there.

"John Carver," she gasped out, trembling. "Why are you here? What can you mean by this? Have you any idea how much danger you court by coming here?" Her thoughts refused to link themselves in any sensible order. Instead, high ideals of what she ought to say and do mingled like tangled ribbons around a maypole. Ruthless, giddy passions, juxtaposed with plain, trivial matters that tried to work their way through and save her in the name of practical good sense.

He passed her seat, striding to the stone balustrade where trails of ivy rattled crisply. There, he peered down on the black lawn for a moment. "It's a long way down, longer than I thought. But it's the only way." He held out his hand. "Let's jump together."

"Ridiculous!" She clenched her fan so tightly, she heard one of the struts snap. "I can't go anywhere with you."

He dropped his hand and leaned back against the balustrade, arms folded high. "It's cold out here."

"I'm not cold. I'm too hot. That's why I came out here. The cold air doesn't bother me."

"You look pale."

"Good. Please go back inside." She opened her broken fan, but her fumbling fingers dropped it and in the blink of an eye he sprang forward, crouched down and rescued it from the flagstone.

Still on one knee, he ripped off his mask and looked into her eyes. "Marry me."

Voice high and fraught, she exclaimed, "I'm already married." Those were the words she should have said weeks ago, months ago, and saved them both this heartache.

"That doesn't count," he replied airily. "I'll dispose of the blackguard and you'll come home with me."

To him it was simple: he wanted and therefore, being John Sydney Carver, he thought he should have. For Lucy, who'd never even known what she truly wanted until she met him, there were too many complications, insurmountable hills to climb. He could not come here, into her world, and try to change it. Her world was cynical and cold. Courtesy was according to custom and love stood aside for duty, ambition and financial gain. It was a world where one fell in and out of favor in the space of a few days, where one's friends were abundant in fine weather, scarce in bad. In this world she survived by hardening her heart and presenting an urbane, facile appearance, her inner desires suppressed.

He was out of place in that ugly world and yet he was there, too forthright and plain-spoken, too enchanting, too ruggedly handsome in the rippling, blustery flame of the rush torches. So the best she could do was say, rather weakly, "If my father and Lord Winton discover you here with me...John, you could be killed. At the very least you'll be sued, ruined."

She tried to retrieve her fan, but he kept it. Their fingers touched. "You don't think I can defend myself, Lucy?"

She groaned at his typical male chest-thumping. "I don't want it to be necessary. I never meant to cause you any harm. That's the last thing I want."

He bowed his head, thinking for a while. "And what's the first thing you want?" he asked quietly.

It welled up in her, burst out over her lips. "If I said it was you, John, what good would it do? In a perfect world, I'd want you." She bit back her tears, angry at them. "But this world is far from perfect. Just like you and me."

Chapter 22

John got off his knee and sat with her on the bench. He would have put his arm around her, but she slid away to the end of that small, cold, hard bench.

"How is your mother?" she asked politely, as if this was any other, civilized discussion between two acquaintances.

"She's well, but suffering the aches and pains of winter." He paused. "Alice has been a vast help to her this season."

Her lips parted, but it took a moment for any sound to come out. "Oh?"

"Yes. She just married Martin Frye, by the way. In case you're interested. Don't suppose you are, though."

Her shoulders relaxed and she flipped open her fan, fluttering it under her chin, ignoring the broken strut. "I'm very happy for her. She's a very...pleasant young woman."

When he snorted with laughter, she tossed a haughty glare over her fan. "How is Vince?"

"Missing you. Stupid beast got too attached." Then he added flippantly, "He always does fixate on any old stray glove or bone he digs up."

She ignored the comment. "And my little Pip?" Flutter, flutter, flappity, flutter went the lame feathers of her fan, wielded as if the sun was beating down on her face and it wasn't a biting cold night at the very end of October.

"Pip?" He feigned confusion.

"My piglet!"

"Oh him?" He sighed, leaning forward to rest his forearms on his stocky thighs. "He's bacon."

The fan snapped shut, eyes filled with plump, glossy tears. "John!"

Abruptly he laughed. "Not really, you little fool. Your pampered pet is fat and happy. Certainly no more a piglet."

Her alarm shattered, transforming to piquant anger before he could blink an eye. "How could you! I don't know whether to believe you."

He slid closer, heart hammering away in his chest. "Best come back to Souls Dryft and make certain then."

"Get away from me," she cried, "heartless murderer of innocent pigs!"

Defending himself from her insults yet again, he asked her where she thought bacon and pork came from before it landed on her plate, to which she replied that she didn't ever have to think of it, until she went to live with him. Now she swore never to let another bite pass her lips.

He tried to recapture her hand, but she moved it constantly, opening and closing her fan, fidgeting with her hair, deliberately denying him the chance.

Of course he knew she'd be difficult, contrary. She always was, from the very beginning. He reached into that fine new doublet. "I bought you something."

"I....I don't want..."

He unrolled a small remnant of taffeta and there, in his cupped palm, lay her pearl earrings. "I promised myself I'd put them on you, the next time I saw you."

Rather than look at the earrings or at him, she stared up at the vast expanse of moonless sky. The sight of her in that mask, her profile lit by the flickering, dodging flames of the rush torches, reminded him of their first encounter and other thoughts, heated and sensual, quickly followed. "But I'll have you naked first," he whispered huskily. "And then I'll make love to you while you're wearing them, like I did before." Oh, that made her look at him. "When I took your maidenhead." Her green eyes widened under that mask, her lips parted for a damp breath, a ghostly cloud around her mouth.

"Don't say things like that. You mustn't. Someone might hear."

He rolled the earrings up again, tucking them back inside his doublet, smiling at the image in his mind. His blood quickened, a familiar sensation already aching in his lower regions, heavy and demanding. "Tonight, leave your window open for me."

"You're mad...utterly insane!"

"Possibly," he agreed, grinning. She was too beautiful in the amber torchlight, and he might just take her there on the terrace if she continued looking at him with her eyes flaring, lips pursed and proud little chin raised in defiance.

She pretended to be so brave, but inside, under that mask, she was a frightened girl who needed him. As much as he needed her.

"I love you so much, I might die from it," he said. "Then won't you feel guilty?"

He saw the flutter of a nervous pulse in her slender throat. It was too much to resist, but when he slid after her along the bench, she stood hastily, hurrying toward the doors.

After her like an arrow, he trapped her against the ivy-clad wall. "Don't run away from me," he breathed, holding her there, his lips on hers, his words whispered into her mouth. "For once, Lucy, don't run away. Haven't you run enough? Face up to it. Face what you've done."

His urgent kiss smothered her indignant cry of protest and very soon she melted against the wall. Her hands, once raised to push him away, now gripped his doublet, pulling him closer. He leaned into her body, wishing they had no barrier of clothing, hating her farthingale for keeping him at any distance. He wanted her back home again in simple, soft clothes, not full of decoration that scratched and discouraged touching.

"Let me love you," he breathed into her ear, while she trembled. "Let me love you as you deserve to be loved. Isn't that what you chose me for on that first night? You knew, even then, that I was the right man for you."

She made a small, halting sound and he felt the final moment of shaking uncertainty, before she gave in. Bolder now, she kissed him and he knew at last the solace he'd longed for. There were no more secrets. He would make up for all those years of unhappiness she'd spent without him, and she could stop running away from her life.

Music from the banquet slowly intruded on his thoughts. Remembering where they were, he stepped back, watching her smooth out her gown. Patience, he chided himself. If he stayed longer he might lose that precious commodity. The touch of her lips had resulted in the usual, almost-instantaneous effect on the single-minded barbarian in his breeches, and if he didn't get inside quickly, it would soon be past the point of no return. And he was trying to be chivalrous, as he'd promised his sister and his mother.

Without another word, he slid back through the doors into the banquet.

Well, she knew now where he stood and what he wanted. He'd nailed his colors to the mast. The next move was hers.

* * * *

She waited several minutes, recovering from that shattering kiss. What a fool she'd been, yet again, to imagine she might forget him eventually, at least enough to go on with her life without him in it. She'd actually expected, somehow, to function while he was elsewhere in the world, away from her, out of her hands.

But it was hopeless. She was a soul in bondage to him and there was no reasoning with this love.

John's mother had said to her once, "We shall never be younger than we are today." The truth of it surrounded her, lifted her up out of the abyss. Every moment counted, every breath, every word. She would never waste another and wouldn't let him either.

Lance found her by the ivy, contemplating her latest predicament: whether her impetuous lover seriously planned to scale her father's wall and enter her bedchamber that night. And whether she seriously meant to leave her window open for him.

"There you are, Luce. What are you doing out here in the cold?" He took her back inside through the doors where a blast of heat hit her immediately, making her wish she'd stayed outside. The candles seemed too bright, they scorched her eyelids. "Luce, I just have to nip out to the stables a moment. I'll be back in a blink. You'll be all right without me, won't you?"

Her upright brother was evidently in haste for an assignation with Bess Percy who now, she looked quickly around the hall to be sure, was nowhere to be seen. What a coincidence!

"Don't be gone too long," she replied, frowning. "I'm tired and not feeling well. I'd like to go home soon."

"Look, there's the Countess, she wanted a word with you…"

She looked as he pointed and there was John Carver talking to the Earl again, this time with the Countess at his side, too. What was he doing? What lies had he told to get himself invited to the banquet?

"What's the matter?" Lance eventually noticed her feet dragging. "I'll only be a short while. I thought you liked the Countess."

"Who…who is that man with her?"

"What man?"

"Dark hair. Blue doublet."

"Oh, that's her brother from Norfolk. The Earl just introduced me. Name of John Carver." Lance kept his face quite innocent, but his lips twitched and there was a slight flutter of his dark lashes, so unusually long for a man and always remarked upon, much to his irritation. "Don't you know him? I rather thought you did. Quite well."

She didn't reply. The walls and the dancers began to spin around her too rapidly. So this is why her brother brought her here. Were they all in on it? Her father certainly wouldn't know.

"Seems like a nice enough fellow," Lance continued. "Owns quite a few acres in the country and does very well for himself, I understand. Livestock, grain, fruit. Don't worry, he's not going to bite." This said, he hurried away once again into the crowd, leaving her keeling slowly, first to the right and then to the left. Lance didn't look back, in too much hurry to get his "exercise" with bosomy Bess.

She might have recovered her footing, if one of the dancers had not accidentally knocked into her farthingale. As she tilted a third time, her knees buckled. Eyes rolling up into her head, she rocked backwards, falling through the air for what seemed to her at least a day. Lights danced under her lashes, but they were eventually extinguished by her heavy sigh and then she felt cool tile under her and it all went beautifully, deeply, richly, black.

* * * *

John carried her limp form out to the litter.

"Where did Lancelot go?" the Countess worried. "He was with her earlier."

"It doesn't matter. We'll take her home and leave a message for her brother." He wasn't going to wait for Lance to be found. It was nearly midnight, it was frigid cold and the woman he adored was ill. Gently lowering his sweet bundle to the seat of the litter, he took charge of everything, suggesting he and the Countess ride home with her, while the Earl stayed to inform Lance, once he was found, of his sister's illness.

After a brief hesitation, the Countess agreed. "I suppose my husband should stay. He's still so angry at Catherine for avoiding the ball. He says that when she finally shows her face, it'll be the last time she goes anywhere or does anything without a guard at her side." Wringing her hands, she fretted for her troublesome daughter, knowing her husband's wrath and Catherine's fiery temper. Together, she said, they could cause a windstorm on a breezeless day. "He can find Lancelot and let him know we've taken dear Lucy home. That will give him something to do and take his mind off Catherine for a while."

He didn't answer, preoccupied in fussing over his charge, making certain she was warmly tucked up in fleece and fur blankets.

"John," the Countess urged, leaning down to touch his knuckles with her gloved hand, "Don't do anything rash if Winton is there. For her sake as much as yours."

He nodded, too worried about Lucy's health to have any other concern just then.

* * * *

The gentle sway of the horse-drawn litter rocked her like a cradle and in her fragile state, the soft, thick, warm fur he'd tucked around her was calming as a lover's caress. She heard their voices, soft, quick mutterings slithering over and around her, but she kept her eyes closed.

Brother to the Countess of Swafford.

It wouldn't occur to him to tell her would it? He'd talked of his sister before, of her good marriage and all her children, but never explained who she married. Titles meant nothing to him. He judged people by what they did, not what they called themselves or how well they dressed. He'd loved her even when he thought her a whore and he wanted no material things from her, or her father. For that last reason alone he was different to almost any other man she'd known before she met him.

Her eyelids fluttered slightly apart. In the corner of her half-closed eye, she saw his boot, his hand, his knee, the mane of his horse twitching. It felt safe to have him there.

When they arrived at the gates of her father's house, she sat up, insisting on walking inside herself. The last thing she needed now was her father and Lord Winton seeing her in John's arms. The pull was so strong between them surely other people must feel it, too, if they saw them together.

So she swore she was recovered, laughing over the incident as if it was nothing, as if the punch was strong and she tripped over her own silly feet.

"The hem of my gown is too long," she explained to the Countess. "It was meant for my sister, you see, and she's taller."

Her father was still up with his books. When he saw Lucy return without her brother, he leapt up from his chair, ripping the spectacles from his nose. But then he saw the Countess and his countenance completely changed, like day from night.

"Your ladyship! What an honor to have you in my humble home! Please do come in and sit by my fire. You must be frozen, traveling the streets on such a wretched cold evening."

He was all hospitality for his noble guest, ringing the bell for the servants and drawing up the best chair to his blazing fire, offering wine and cake, anything she might desire.

"We brought your daughter home, Sir Oliver," the Countess explained. "She took a turn for the worse at the banquet tonight."

As usual he had nothing to say to Lucy. He had dismissed her already, the moment he saw her grander company, and now he blinked his somber brown eyes and smiled without even looking at his daughter. Lucy had no doubt he was already plotting how best to use the Countess of Swafford's impromptu visit to his advantage.

"I'm afraid your son, Lancelot,

was not immediately to be found, so my brother decided we should bring her safely home." The Countess spoke louder, as if he might be hard of hearing, which would explain why he made no comment about his daughter falling ill. "This is my brother, John Sydney Carver, of Norfolk." She gestured to the silent man behind her, making him step forward into the candlelight. "John, this is Lucy's father, Sir Oliver Collyer."

Lucy watched this introduction with slightly hysterical amusement. Fingers pressed to her chilled lips, she imagined John's kiss there again, as it was three quarters of an hour ago and when he slyly looked over at her and her fingers slid away, it was as if she'd blown him a kiss. Quite by mistake of course.

She sneezed.

Following John's gaze, her father finally remembered her presence. "Lucasta, go up to bed," he snapped impatiently. "You've troubled the Countess quite enough, bringing her out in this weather in the small hours. We don't want you making her ladyship sick, do we?" Before he finished addressing her, he turned back to his guests and, with arms outspread, urged them toward his roaring hearth.

Head aching and heavy, Lucy let the maid take her off to bed. She longed to stay and hear what they talked of, but she also feared giving herself away, getting John in trouble. The way he looked at her was enough to bring steam out of her ears and if other people didn't see it, they must be blind.

Well, most of the time her father was blind when it came to her.

The maid had lit a fire in her room and spread her nightshift on the chairs before it. The bed was warmed with a pan of coals and a plate of bread and milk with raisins, an old childhood favorite when she was sick, waited on the bedside table. Lance apparently ordered it for her late supper, something to tempt her appetite and cheer her spirits. Now, for the first time since she was carried out of the banquet, she wondered where Lance had got to. Before he'd left her to follow round-heeled Bess Percy, he'd promised not to be very long. She worried for him. He thought he could defend himself against wanton, determined wenches, but sooner or later one of them would get her hooks into him, probably when he was least suspecting it.

"Did you have a pleasant evening, ma'am?" Ruth asked as she helped her change for bed.

"Better than expected."

"I'm glad, ma'am," the maid answered with real feeling. "You've been so sad of late."

Lucy took her hand and squeezed it lightly. "Do you remember the man I told you of, the one I met at Mistress Comfort's in Norwich?"

The maid nodded. "I do remember."

"Well, that's him." She had to say it, she realized. Swept up in the desperate gladness of seeing him again, she wished the whole world could know. They couldn't of course. "The man below. The brother of the Countess. He's the one."

The maid's eyes slowly widened, her lips making little put-put sounds.

"Don't tell."

"Of course not, miss!" the maid exclaimed, outraged anyone might doubt her discretion, or her loyalty.

Lucy took a deep breath. "Leave the window open, before you go."

"But it's cold out miss."

"I like the fresh air."

Her maid, having known her for fifteen years, didn't believe that innocently bland face, but she left the window open, following her orders without further question.

Lucy sat up in bed, hugging the bolster, thinking how strange it was that her lover was below, talking to her unsuspecting father. A few hours ago she would never have thought it possible, but there was her pompous father, welcoming John Carver into his home, groveling and simpering, so anxious to make a good impression on the Countess he sent his disappointment of a daughter out of sight.

Ha! If only he knew…

She chuckled, imagining his amazement should he ever learn the truth. He would probably explode in a puff of gray smoke.

* * * *

They stayed half an hour, his sister carrying the conversation in her usual tireless fashion. Occasionally Sir Oliver asked John a question, but both men did more thinking than talking. John was busy taking in his surroundings, the home of the woman he loved, and dwelling on thoughts far from innocent.

As they left, while his sister busied Sir Oliver with a discussion about a portrait above the stairs, he slid the maid a few coins and asked her one question.

"Do you love your mistress?"

"Yes, sir."

"And so do I." He smiled, remembering how his sister accused him of having a smile "irresistible" to all women. "All you need do is give me a number."

"A number, sir?"

"From left to right," he whispered, "which one is her window?"

Chapter 23

She woke with a start to see him clambering over the ledge, breathing hard and cursing softly into the still night. A low fire smoldered in the hearth, but all her candles were out. Not that she needed any light to know who it was, of course. Who else but this rogue would barge his way into her chamber, as if he had a right to be there?

"What on earth are you doing?" she hissed, knowing the redundancy of her question, even as she asked it. Why else did she leave her window open?

He panted, bent over, hands on his knees. "I need my swine-herd back, don't I?"

Pulse racing with gladness, she watched him strip off his clothes--he wasted no time--and then he leapt onto her bed, pulling the heavy damask drapes around them to keep out the draft.

"What did you say to my father?"

"Very little. My sister did much of the talking." In the dark of the curtained bed, they had to feel their way to one another. "She's good at it. Nothing stops her once she gets started." With his hands around her face, he kissed her.

"Your lips are cold!"

"Hmmm. Warm them for me." He nuzzled the side of her neck, pulling her into his arms.

"You shouldn't be here," she whined pointlessly.

"I left you behind once before, in Norwich. Never again."

She still couldn't quite believe he'd scaled the walls of her father's house to enter her bedchamber in the middle of the night and under her father's nose, not to mention her husband's. But what else might be expected of such a man, once a rogue, responsible for all manner of mayhem?

"I was worried tonight," he whispered. "Are you all right now?"

"It was too crowded and hot at the banquet." And she felt better now he was with her. John Carver naked was a potent miracle elixir, guaranteed to chase away every ague, from the worst of dull-day doldrums to the deadliest of apoplexies, but she didn't tell him so, in case it went to his already conceited head. Of course, John Carver naked was also, quite possibly, the cause for her recent worrying symptoms. She ran her hands over his broad shoulders, down his rippled chest and lean flanks, the darkness adding a new layer of sensual pleasure.

His arousal was already prominent when he said, "Your father should send for a physician." She was momentarily confused, her mind and fingers absorbed in the exploration of his beautifully-made physique.

"Why? Are you injured?" It felt quite healthy and functioning to her.

"For you, woman." When he laughed, the vibrations pulsed all the way to the head of his organ as she brushed her fingers playfully over it.

Oh yes, she'd fainted. Already she'd almost forgotten with so much to distract her, so much pleasurable anticipation and abject desire thudding through her body.

"It was naught." She sighed impatiently, her fingers stroking down his length to the warm heaviness of his sac, cradling it, feeling it tighten under her caress. Fainting? Who cared about that now, for heaven's sake? It wasn't the first time she'd felt faint in the last few days, but that was something else she thought it best not to tell him.

Her distant, casual dismissal of the incident at the banquet apparently reassured John that she was feeling better. "It's lucky I have no title," he chuckled, helping her nightshift over her head. "Otherwise I believe your father might have tried to throw his youngest daughter at me."

"Oh, you'd like Anne. She's pretty and submissive and causes no trouble whatsoever." She slid her arms around his neck. "She'll make some lucky gentleman a perfect wife."

"Good thing I'm a humble yeoman farmer then and he wouldn't dream of having me for a son-in-law."

"And Anne doesn't like dirt, I fear, so she'd never survive life with you."

"Can't see a damned thing in here," he muttered gruffly.

Ah yes, he liked to see, she remembered.

He drew back the curtains again to let in some of the soft glow from her fire and she lay very still while he surveyed her, his eyes caressing her naked body, until every pore, every tiny hair felt his worship. One firm hand swept her from hip to bosom, where he paused to stroke and hold her, his sun-browned skin so dark against her ivory breast. She shivered slightly for she was tender there, more so than usual. "I think your summer in the country put some of that much needed meat on your bones, Lucy. Finally. I told you a man likes something he can hold onto."

"Must you be quite so frank, plowman?"

"I speak my mind, swine-herd."

"Yes, indeed you do, but not every thought needs to be spoken aloud."

He lay beside her, propped up on one forearm. "Is your sister Anne more beautiful than you?" he asked, deliberately chancing his luck, as he liked to do.

She frowned. "I suppose you're bored with me already."

"Don't sulk, my sweet," he chuckled. "I'm quite certain there is no one to compare in all England."

Still she frowned.

"In all the world," he added for good measure, one hand to his heart. "At least the parts I've seen. I suppose there might be someone somewhere..."

"John Carver, you are my gall and wormwood."

He laughed louder, until she slapped a hand over his mouth, reminding him of the danger.

"Your mother may be afraid to use that ladle around your thick, cross-grained head, but I'm not."

Pulling her hand away from his mouth, he nodded, eyes shining, and whispered, "That's why I love you."

She wavered, startled as ever by his bravery and candor. "Where are my earrings, then?"

Grinning, he rolled her in the coverlet, swept her into his arms and carried her to the hearth. "First we need more light. We'll do this my way tonight, madam."

She watched, amused, as he hurried around the room, like a little boy enjoying his game, collecting candles, lighting them in the fire and setting them around her chamber, adjusting them carefully until she was bathed, to his satisfaction, in a warm, mellow blush of gold. Then he recovered the doublet he'd tossed to the floor and brought over his little taffeta parcel.

"Give me your ears, swine-herd."

"Head swine-herd," she corrected, kneeling on the coverlet, holding her hair back.

He slid the earrings carefully back where they belonged. "There. Perfect," he muttered throatily. "Just like the first night."

"But without the mask," she pointed out, "or the fleas."

He laughed and she anxiously put a finger to his lips, reminding him again of another difference in their circumstances this time. "And without my father and my husband down the hall."

* * * *

At the mention of her husband, John felt that anger seethe and curdle in his gut again. As if sensing the sudden jolt in his mood, she lay back, holding out her arms, eager and smiling. For a long moment he merely enjoyed the view, letting his anger settle again, other emotions mounting in its place.

Lifting her foot, he kissed her toes, while she stifled her giggles and purred, writhing like a playful kitten, her hands trying to reach for his erection again, greedy, lusty little hussy. Her breath came in quick, impatient, shallow gasps already. He saw the rapid rise and fall of her breasts, the firelight gently gilding those delectable mouthfuls and the sweet cherries at their peak, temptingly ripe. But he made her wait, holding her foot to his shoulder, running his other hand slowly over her belly and between her thighs. She lifted her bottom, while he cupped her sex and felt the dampness of her desire. His cock pulsed hard, answering the signal he felt against his palm and his fingers.

"John," she gasped, pleading softly.

When they had made love at Mistress Comfort's, all those months ago, she hadn't known his name, didn't want to know it. Now he made her whimper it, over and over, while he stroked her, sliding his fingers slowly in and out, his eyes pinned to her face, wanting to see her expression as he drove her to the edge and held her there. Tonight there was no mask for her to hide behind.

Lissome and goose-down soft, she arched, reaching in vain for him again, pouting, complaining she needed more of him inside her.

Withdrawing his fingers, he let her watch as he licked them, his eyes holding hers. Then he brought his hand, likewise her sultry, smoky gaze, down to his cock.

Her lips parted. Her pink tongue swept the plump lower curve of her mouth and then the upper.

More of him? If that was what she wanted, he would oblige. He would fill her, impale her so deeply...

He touched the swollen head of his member and felt the herald of a flood soon to burst. Capturing that plump bead of clear fluid on his fingertip, he leaned over her and offered it to those waiting lips. She took his finger like a hungry little bird and sucked it clean, long lashes fluttering briefly shut, before swinging wide open again, brazen challenge in the heated depths of her eyes.

Knowing he couldn't make her, or himself, wait any longer, he lifted her foot higher, sliding her ankle over his shoulder until she was lifted to meet him. He arched forward, guiding the proud, throbbing crest of his manhood to her threshold. And held himself there, probing her quivering, dewy flesh, inspecting her, as if to be sure she could accommodate his size. He enjoyed the play-acting, reliving that night in May when the stars of good fortune were on his side.

"John," she groaned again. "Please!"

Aha! She finally remembered.

He smiled, wolfish, lifted her second knee to his right shoulder and then drove himself into her. The penetration was ruthless, complete, earth shattering.

Pity they were not at Mistress Comfort's tonight, for there he could've freely cried out his pleasure. Instead he bit down on it, transferring his energy to other muscles, pounding into his lover, her position making every rampageous, plunging thrust so deep there was no place left for her to hide her secrets.

His beautiful, incredible swine-herd was already falling, it seemed, joyfully flinging herself over the precipice to which his teasing carried her. This first time tonight would be over too quickly. But they had all night. All night. He didn't have to persuade her to stay this time.

And when he felt the surge begin, he plunged, head thrown back, spending rapidly, gushing into her.

* * * *

It was growing light out when she heard the commotion and lifted her head from his shoulder, bleary-eyed, wondering if they were soon to be discovered. But the sounds came not from outside her chamber door, they came from below.

Still wrapped together in the coverlet, lying by the ashes of last night's fire, they listened to the distant rumble of voices, one of which was raised louder than the others.

He sat up, rubbing his head. "That sounds like my brother-in-law."

"The Earl of Swafford? What's he doing here?" She yawned. "It can't be."

But John was convinced he recognized that voice. He reached for his shirt and she wound her arms and legs around him, the side of her face to his back.

"Don't go yet," she purred, clinging tight. "Stay."

She spread her fingers over his broad muscles.

"Won't your maid come soon?" he asked.

"Not yet." She wriggled, clasping her legs tight around him, covering his back with kisses. "Stay! I command it."

"You're such a little madam," he admonished sternly, turning his face so that she kissed the bristles of his cheek. "I can't stay here playing stud to you all day. Some of us have things to do." Twisting further, he kissed her on her small chin. "My lady swine-herd."

"What things?" she protested. Not wanting him to leave her, even for half an hour, she couldn't imagine what would be so important that it took him away from her arms today. "You're my lover and you should do as I say, otherwise I shall be very upset and moody. You wouldn't want that, would you?"

"Heaven forbid," he chuckled dryly.

"Exactly. Your job is to keep me in fine humor."

He stroked her leg where it curved over his hip. "And to service you at least once a day."

"At the very least." She gave his torso another glad squeeze.

"But this morning I have matters to sort out with your father. And," he paused, "Winton."

The coverlet fell from her shoulders and she felt the cold in that chamber. "But there's nothing..."

"We can't go on this way, sneaking about. I want you free of Winton." He drew a deep breath and she loosened her hold, afraid her desperate clinging might suffocate him. "I will get that cretin out of your life so we can be together as man and wife."

Her newly tended heart flowered, blossoming at his words. She didn't mind it so much, after all, when he took charge. Cheek pressed to his back again, she finally allowed herself to say it.

"I love you."

Suddenly he pitched to his right and then tilted back. She hadn't the strength to hold him up and was, in the next moment, crushed under his weight.

"John!" She panicked, pushing at him, trying to extract her body from beneath his great sprawling, rangy form. His eyes were shut, his lips parted.

She'd killed him! Worn him out with her lusty demands. Oh dear Lord, he was dead.

"You see," she gasped, helpless. "This is what happens! I have no luck, none! I bring death and destruction wherever I go!"

Only when she slapped at his cheeks with increasing vigor did he finally let his eyelashes flutter open and she saw the glint of mischief, just before his lips burst into their familiar sportive grin. "Well, I never thought I'd hear you say it." Grabbing her around the waist, he wrestled her over onto her back, while she cursed and pummeled his shoulders. "The shock of it nearly did me in."

"You rotten, thoughtless…"

He kissed her hard, his legs pinning hers, his hands in her hair, anchoring her face. Thus all protests died away and she melded to his body with all the wanton wickedness of a truly irretrievable hussy. His hussy.

A sudden light scratch at the door preceded her maid's gentle inquiry, "Are you awake, Miss?

John reluctantly raised his head. "I thought you said…"

"She's not usually this early," Lucy replied with a brisk whisper, alert to the fact that something must definitely be going on below stairs. Hurriedly pushing him to his feet, gathering his scattered clothing, she called out to her maid, "What is it, Ruth?"

"Your father wants you, Miss."

Anxious, feeling sick again now she was upright, Lucy quickly forced her lover behind the tapestry screen, mouthing at him to get dressed. "Just a moment, Ruth." With him safely out of sight, she made a quick survey of the chamber, then dragged the coverlet back to the bed. Pulling on her shift, she ran finally to the door and unbolted it.

"What is it? What's happened?"

The maid sidled in, small eyes observing the profusion of re-arranged candles, some of their wicks still weeping bluish smoke. "I'm to get you dressed, ma'am, as quickly as possible. It's Master Lancelot."

"Lance?" That was the last thing on her mind just then. She expected herself to be the one in trouble, not her brother.

"He's to be married, ma'am."

"Married?"

"Yes, ma'am. Immediately. The Earl of Swafford insists upon it."

So it was his voice below. John was right. She glanced nervously at her dressing screen. "I don't understand. Lance to be married?"

"After last night." The maid lowered her voice to a hushed, scandalized whisper. "After what happened at the banquet."

Lucy drew closer, heart pounding in her chest.

"Master Lancelot," the maid whispered, "were caught with Lady Catherine Mallory, doing something he oughtn't."

"What?" Her brother would go out of his way to avoid the Earl's eldest daughter, the "savage," as he called her.

"You know, miss." The maid nudged her. "He were caught drinking from the young lady's cup...if you get my drift."

"But how? Why?" It made no sense.

"The Earl, her father, walked in on them, in the stables, in the dark. Apparently they mistook one another for someone else."

Her hands flew to her face, inappropriate laughter threatening to fly out over her tongue. Poor Lance. Now she understood.

"Young Lady Catherine protests she won't marry Master Lance no matter what her father says, and your brother's no happier about it, but your father is..."

"Happy as a horse in clover," she muttered, imagining his glee at this mistake landing him such a prize for a daughter-in-law. In the corner of her chamber, that tapestry dressing screen rocked back and forth, little curses audible. The maid looked over at it, eyes steadily growing wider.

"I can dress myself today, Ruth," she said hastily. "Go below and tell my father I'll be down presently."

The maid hesitated, lips curving into a knowing smile.

"Go on," she repeated haughtily.

Finally the maid obeyed, shooting the screen one last glance.

As she bolted her door again, he came out of hiding, tucking his shirt into his trunk hose. "Sounds like your father will have more on his mind this morning than your shenanigans. What the devil was your brother up to with my little niece? She's only nineteen, you know!"

"For once my brother's in greater trouble than I am," she said tersely. "You can help me dress." Flustered, head still spinning with the news of her brother's downfall, she added, "If you please."

"A novelty!" His eyes sparked. "Usually I'm undressing you. I'm not sure I can do it in reverse. Seems to go against the grain, against what's natural."

But he put himself to the new task more than adequately, and with only a few distractions and delays.

Chapter 24

Descending the stairs, she immediately saw her brother sprawled in a chair by the fire, looking rumpled and decidedly untidy for a man who generally prided himself on a pristine appearance. His face held the pallor of sour milk, but there was something of a bemused twinkle in his dark eyes, as if he still didn't quite know what just happened to him.

Poor fool. She'd had a feeling he was going to be surprised when he finally tripped over Catherine Mallory again.

Their father stood with his back to the fire while the Earl of Swafford, seated opposite Lance, laid out the marriage terms and details. The Earl expected no obstacle and would get none. Except, it seemed, from his own daughter, if what the maid said was true. Lady Catherine was widely known as a shrew and her feelings for Lance were no warmer than his for her, so it was more than likely she would dig in her heels over this marriage.

As for Lance, much as he might abhor the idea, he would never go against the Earl, his employer. Nor would he fail his strict sense of gentlemanly duty. A man of honor, if a mistake was made, no matter how heinous, he would pay recompense.

No one noticed her until she walked up to Lance and offered her congratulations. Without moving his head, he turned his eyes to where she stood and they narrowed enough to let her know he heard. He just couldn't bring himself to speak.

She patted his clenched hand and smiled, hoping to reassure him, just as he'd tried for her once, on the eve of her marriage.

"Lucasta," her father announced loudly, "your brother's wedding takes place tomorrow at Blackfriars. You will attend with your husband."

"No she won't," came a voice behind her. "She's not going anywhere with Winton ever again." A tall figure emerged from the shadows, the bright flare of a sword gleaming in his hand.

He must have broken into her father's library and taken that sword from the wall, she realized. Barely ten minutes ago, she'd watched John descend to the yard from her window and he'd waved to her jauntily, giving no clue of what he meant to do about their dilemma.

The rogue, it seemed, was back and very evident this morning.

Boldly he walked up to the group by the great hearth, greeted his startled brother-in-law with a nod and said to Lance, "I trust you know my niece is only nineteen."

"Yes. I am all too well aware," Lance replied, long fingers clawing at his shortly-cropped hair. Equally terse, he added, "Do you know my sister's a married woman?"

"She won't be much longer."

Sir Oliver opened his lips to protest and immediately became closely acquainted with the sharp end of his own sword.

"John," the Earl stepped forward bravely, one hand up, conciliatory. "Put the sword down. We can discuss this calmly."

But only Lucy's hand on his arm finally made John lower that sword. Even then he kept it poised, ready to attack on the slightest provocation.

"As you see, Sir Oliver," said the Earl, "my brother-in-law has come on a matter of business. Perhaps we should deal with that before we proceed with our other arrangements? It looks as though he's in some haste to resolve his issue."

Lucy watched her father's face. There was not the slightest change in his cold countenance. He stared at John Carver, his eyelids lowering slowly and then lifting again no faster. "What do you want, young man?"

There was no hesitation. John, naturally, came straight to the point. "Your daughter."

"My daughter is a married…"

"It was never consummated, father. I told you that."

Sir Oliver tipped his head back, regarding Lucy as if she was no more than a squashed cabbage leaf under his feet. She wondered if he even heard her.

"Haven't you endured enough scandal, man," the Earl exclaimed gruffly. "Your daughter clearly wants out of the match. Would you make her suffer any longer? For what cause? To save your own pride?"

In the midst of this tense scene, surely the most pivotal in her life's play, Lucy found herself pondering the oddities of men, of fathers in particular. Here stood the Earl of Swafford, admonishing her father for making her marry against her will, when that was precisely what he did to his own daughter in planning her hasty marriage to Lance. No one, however, would dare quibble with the Earl.

John reached for her hand and held it. Nothing else mattered. He was the finest, handsomest rogue that ever lived and he had come to fetch her. He wouldn't leave again without her and she wouldn't let him.

"I want your daughter, Sir Oliver," he said with the lethal steadiness of a very sharp, very precisely wielded knife. "I'm here to fight for her.

I'll shed blood if I must."

"That's all you want?" her father scoffed. "You came after my daughter with no thought for monetary compensation?"

John laughed, the sound ringing out loud and harsh. "She is all I want from you."

From his chair by the fire, Lance grumbled, "You'd better take care of her."

"And you take care of my niece," John rounded on her brother. "I'd better not hear of you playing around with other women. I know how you fine, rich, bored folk find your entertainment away from home."

"John, this is not the time," the Earl groaned. "It's too late for all that. If you saw what I did last night, you'd agree the marriage must take place, the sooner the better. I've always known that girl would cause me a burst spleen sooner or later. She's as much to blame as he is."

Lucy felt her father's familiar, stark disapproval focusing on the pearls hanging from her ears. "I see you found your missing earrings, daughter."

She was surprised he'd ever paid enough attention to notice them missing before this, or that he even knew she possessed such a pair of earrings. Everyone fell silent, looking at her, everyone but John, who kept a wary eye on her father, sword still raised at the ready.

"I assume this reckless fellow is the one who put the glow back in your cheeks, Lucasta, just as he put the pearls back in your ears. Yet it took him this long to come for you after the night you shared in May."

John's brows raised, eyes quizzical. Lucy's pulse slowed.

"No, she didn't tell me," he continued crisply. "I am not a stupid man, John Sydney Carver, whatever my daughter thinks of me; I can work things out for myself." And his thin lips bent in a motion that might have been a smile, or a snarl. "I had no idea when I met you last night, but now I see you here, just as her pearl earrings miraculously reappear, I can only conclude you are the man she went to in May, when she lost them."

Lucy tried to breathe. Thankfully her earlier nausea had faded. John's firm hand around hers helped enormously.

"I knew she'd left the house that night in Norwich, but I let her have her moment," her father said, somber as a parson presiding over a funeral. "She will come under the hammer now, I thought. Let her get it out of her, once and for all, and then she can do her duty." He paused, gazing up at the beams of his grand, arched ceiling, "I sensed Lord Winton's previous attempts to beget an heir with young brides had failed due to his own incapability. Four brides, all   unable to provide him with a son?" He shrugged. "Apparently it never occurred to Winton that his own seed might be at fault. Therefore, I thought my daughter's one night of misbehavior may actually be of use to us, that if Winton had no good seed left, she might still bear the fruit that so far failed to bloom in all his other wives. My daughter, I thought, will bear Winton an heir, one way or another."

Knowing her father well enough already, she was not shocked to hear this. Instead she accepted what he was, as she always did. His disease, ruthless ambition, was incurable. John was astounded, however. She felt it in his grip, saw it in the subtle widening of his eyes. She was ashamed for her father, not that he'd ever know or understand it. He didn't see how other families protected one another, loved one another without conditions, without thinking first what they could do for him.

At some point during his speech, Lord Winton came downstairs, hearing the early morning ruckus and eager to stick his nose in, but not understanding the first thing about any of it.

"Carver?" he exploded, eyes popping, "Why are you here?" His brows swayed, crusted tongue moving over his sharply pointed teeth. "Is this about those fleeces?"

"Fleeces?" John croaked sarcastically. "Aye, it's about the damned fleeces, Winton, and what you owe me."

"I told you, the quality was poor…I don't owe you a penny more."

John swore loudly, brutally. "You imbecile. Do you think I care now?"

Still Winton didn't understand and Lance mischievously piped up from his chair. "Looks as if he's taken what you owed him, Winton, plus interest."

A log fell from the fire, a few sparks bristling in the chill morning air.

John spoke again, clear and certain. "I love your daughter, Sir Oliver, and she's in love with me. So we have two choices: wait for old Winton to drop dead, or slice him through with this sword where he stands. I'm inclined to the latter for the sake of expediency." His strong fingers, knitted with hers, squeezed gently.

Lucy watched wisps of white hair spinning around her husband's head, saw his eyes scrambling from side to side. "It was you! You stole my bride away, Carver." The penny, it seemed, was slow to drop. Livid, he shook a gnarled finger, first at John and then at Lucy. "I will have satisfaction for this outrage! I'll see you hanged for this kidnapping."

His wandering finger was almost sliced off and only then did he see the sword in John's hand, impossible to miss now, the point of it pressed against his chest, in the rough vicinity of the withered organ he called a heart.

"No one stole me away," Lucy exclaimed hotly. "I went to him. I made my choice. Sue me if you must, not that I have a penny to lose."

"You've been cuckolded," Lance commented wryly from his lounging pose by the fire. "May as well give up and go home, Winton."

When the old man made a slight move toward Lucy, John lunged, the sword blade suddenly flush with Winton's sallow cheek.

If not for the Earl's swift intervention, that ugly, wizened head would have been separated from its neck with one strike. With one calming hand on John's arm, the Earl directed his words at Winton. "Your marriage is no more. It will be annulled. I'll see to it myself." He glanced over at her father. "There will be no further debate on who keeps what and so forth. Will there?" He raised his voice and repeated, "Will there?"

Lucy also looked at her father, holding her breath. He surely wouldn't want to anger his son's future father-in-law, or jeopardize the marriage shortly to take place, the great coup he'd longed for all these years.

Yes, she knew her father.

"Winton may keep the dowry," he spat, "but this John Carver needn't expect anything from me."

"I don't want anything from you," John scoffed.

"Except my daughter," her father pointed out, sneering.

"I am not your daughter, sir," Lucy said, surprising even herself. "I have not been your daughter for many years, only an object, an unwieldy piece of furniture unsuited to your house, a burden to be rid of. John Carver is my true husband, with or without your blessing."

There was barely a flicker of movement across his countenance, but Winton opened his sour lips to curse at her and she felt John's arm move, heard the quick inhale as he prepared to strike.

"No," she said quietly. "I'll deal with this."

Today she was ten feet tall. She walked up to Winton and swung, slapping him hard across the mouth, releasing all her anger, hurt and fear in that gesture. The monster haunting her all these months was vanquished. He was just a short, gnarled, ill-tempered old man, and he would never harm her again.

There was a stunned silence. Returning to John's side, she took his sword-free hand again. "Can we leave now?" She was smiling, her spirits so ebullient she couldn't quite get them under control.

Winton would have argued still, but the Earl cautioned him with one stern rebuke. "The best lesson a man can learn is when to concede defeat. It surprises me a man can live as long as you and not learn that fact. Sir Oliver has agreed you can keep the dowry, I'm sure a little extra in my daughter Catherine's bridal purse when she marries Lance will compensate him for that loss, but Lucy is henceforth free of your bonds." The Earl's eyes darkened another shade. He drew himself up to full height and added menacingly, "I am the Earl of Swafford and this is how it will be."

No one argued.

Hands behind his back, swiveling on his heels, he whispered to Lucy, "Welcome to the family and, as my father-in-law once said to me, good luck, you'll need it." A satirical spark in his eyes, the Earl looked around at the faces staring back at him and said, "There, that's two marriages sorted in the space of half an hour. My wife will be proud of me." Last of all, he took the sword from John's hand. "Now get out of here, both of you, before anyone changes their mind."

John looked at her, hope, love and pride, shining in those blue eyes that looked right into her soul. She nodded, smiling, her smooth hand wrapped tight in his roughened fingers.

And so they did as the Earl commanded, running away together into the fine new morning.

Chapter 25

1594

Lucy paused, one hand to her high rounded belly. Ouch. The baby was certainly making herself felt today. She'd already decided it was a girl and John was content with the idea. He could wait for a son. Another girl, he said, might not be so bad, as long as she was prepared to work for her keep. He had no space in his life for a purely decorative woman.

Or so he said.

The three-year-old, copper-headed bundle riding his shoulders as he strode across the yard was still too small to carry a bucket without spilling the contents all over herself. In many ways she was indeed purely decorative, but the notorious rogue disregarded his rules in her case. Fearless as her father, she bounced on that high perch, chattering nonsensically, clinging on by his ears, sometimes switching her hold to his chin, and in the process poking him in the eye or up the nose.

He didn't seem to mind. Whistling, he opened the gate and walked out into the lane. They both looked back at her. She waved, capturing the kisses they blew, as they did every day: one for her, one for the baby.

Lucy swallowed a deep breath of sweet, chalky lavender that blew around the house from the herb garden. Well, she couldn't sit here all day with her feet up like a fine lady, for pity's sake. Work to do.

Through the open window, she heard her mother-in-law teaching a truculent, argumentative, five-year-old how to bake bread and suspected there would be more flour on her eldest daughter's face and hair than there would be left on the table.

With a heave, she rose up from the bench by the door and, stepping down into the cool house, she looked back just once over her shoulder at the sun-bathed yard she'd seen in her dreams, long before she ever came there. It never ceased to amaze her that she'd been right, down to the smallest detail.

Heaven was just exactly the way she dreamed it.

As for John Sydney Carver, however reformed he claimed to be these days, she was very lucky indeed that he was once a rogue. They had them in heaven, too, it seemed.

About Jayne Fresina

I hope you enjoyed the ride with Maddie and Griff as much as I have. These characters will always have a special place in my heart, as they were some of the very first that ever slipped out of my pen. And yes, in those days, I scribbled everything by hand before I typed it up! Maddie's story has changed over the years, but those friends who read the first incarnation will recognize her and Griff immediately. Even with everything changing around them, they've remained the same. They are, possibly, two of the most stubborn characters I've ever met, although Maddie's little brother, John Sydney Carver, can give her a run for her money -- as you will see in *Once A Rogue*, the next book in this series. As for Maddie's daughter, Cate -- well, perhaps the less said about her the better. I'll let you read for yourself in *The Savage and the Stiff Upper Lip*. Suffice to say, Will Shakespeare had to get his inspiration for *The Taming of the Shrew* somewhere, didn't he? I'd love to hear what you think of Maddie's story, so please contact me through my website at www.jaynefresina.com. Thank you!

Jayne's Website:
www.jaynefresina.com
Reader eMail:
jaynefresina@gmail.com

WHERE REALITY AND FANTASY COLLIDE

Discover the convenience of Ebooks
Just click, buy and download - it's that easy!

From PDF to ePub, Lyrical offers
the latest formats in digital reading.

YOUR NEW FAVORITE AUTHOR
IS ONLY A CLICK AWAY!

LYRICAL PRESS INCORPORATED
WWW.LYRICALPRESS.COM

Shop securely at www.onceuponabookstore.com